A clandestine kiss . . .

Lady Ariel eased the tired horse into a gentle walk around to the stables. There was no one in sight, not even a face at a window. Jordan didn't know where everyone was, but he decided to take advantage of it. He turned to face the brave young woman at his side, reached out his hand to touch her chin lightly before placing a gentle kiss on her tempting lips. They more than tempted him. He would have liked nothing better than to explore the matter more deeply when he reminded himself where they were.

"Oh," she whispered, drawing back to stare into his eyes, somewhat bewildered—yet he sensed an awakened awareness of him as a man. No words poured forth, the kiss apparently rendering her speechless. . . .

A Perilous Engagement

Emily Hendrickson

A SIGNET BOOK

SIGNET
Published by New American Library, a division of
Penguin Putnam Inc., 375 Hudson Street,
New York, New York 10014, U.S.A.
Penguin Books Ltd, 27 Wrights Lane,
London W8 5TZ, England
Penguin Books Australia Ltd, Ringwood,
Victoria, Australia
Penguin Books Canada Ltd, 10 Alcorn Avenue,
Toronto, Ontario, Canada M4V 3B2
Penguin Books (N.Z.) Ltd, 182–190 Wairau Road,
Auckland 10, New Zealand

Penguin Books Ltd, Registered Offices:
Harmondsworth, Middlesex, England

First published by Signet, an imprint of New American Library,
a division of Penguin Putnam Inc.

First Printing, July 2000
10 9 8 7 6 5 4 3 2 1

Copyright © Doris Emily Hendrickson, 2000

All rights reserved

Chapter One

It was a fair wind, Jordan, Lord Harcourt, decided as it tugged at his hat. A good wind, an omen of what was to come—he hoped.

"Smells nice," Percy said above the rush of air and the clop of the horses on the stony avenue that led to the hall.

"Fruit trees," the newly acceded ninth Baron Harcourt replied with a great deal of satisfaction. On the left of the road a field of hops grew, gloriously green and luxuriant. To the right of the road an orchard, well tended and crowned with a cloud of pink and white, bloomed with promise of an abundant crop of apples.

"In any event, this looks auspicious. I mean to say, how bad can the house be if the crops are in such good heart?" Harcourt declared, feeling that he must be correct.

"Bound to be," Percy answered with a nod that did not disturb his perfectly set hat in the least.

The team slowed in response to the command from the baron as they rounded a beautifully tended lane to see the house. The baron gave a dismayed groan.

"Well," Percy said hesitantly, "perhaps it just needs a speck of paint to perk it up a bit?"

"Percy, it needs more than that. The windows need a good wash, indeed, the paint needs more than a speck, and heaven knows what we shall find when we go inside. I was told my grandmother lived quietly the years before her death. Apparently she did not wish to be disturbed in any way. Cousin Ivor, the late baron, was not around long enough to make any improvements after he inherited from her." The barony was an ancient one that permitted a daughter to inherit and hold the title for a male heir. Jordan's grandmother had held the title, passing it to Ivor at her death, who had been baron for only a short time. And now the title had come to Jordan. He jumped down from the curricle to study his newly acquired home in Kent.

He stood still, absorbing the sight before him. His dark hair under his hat had been slightly ruffled during the drive from the last posting inn, and his tall, lean form revealed an athletic nature. Accounted a handsome man, at the moment he appeared somewhat frustrated with what he viewed.

The Elizabethan manor house rambled in a haphazard fashion, quite as though the builder kept changing his mind about where he wanted it to go. The brick needed a bit of tending, but it was not beyond repair. The roof appeared to be acceptable. As for the window trim—it desperately required paint. Jordan was not one to allow exposed wood to turn a bleached gray. No, he wanted sharp black for paint; and those windows definitely needed a sparkle to bring the house to life.

Jordan turned when he saw a fellow come around the corner, giving the newly arrived pair a curious eye. Neatly garbed, he looked to be an estate worker of some sort. "Good day, sir. Help ye, can I?"

"I am Harcourt. Your name?" Jordan queried, taking note of the wary expression on the fellow's weathered face.

"Peachum, my lord." The man nodded with respect.

"Take my team and carriage around to the stables if you would." Jordan spoke pleasantly, but in a manner guaranteed to bring instant obedience.

Once that matter was settled, Jordan pulled a great brass key from a pocket and opened the front door. It had been years since his last visit; he'd forgotten the place was so old, yet there was a charm, a certain beauty to it. Or there would be once it was cleaned.

"Never thought to see you inherit a title and a blooming estate," Percy murmured as he gazed about the entry hall, taking note of the fine, if dusty, suit of armor that stood in one corner. High on the walls several racks of antlers were swagged with delicate cobwebs. A tall floor clock ticked away the minutes, showing the hour had turned two. It was the only indication that the house was—or had been—inhabited. At least someone was around the house to wind the thing! Jordan mused.

"Nor did I. I never expected Cousin Ivor would be killed," Jordan replied absently, stroking the wood paneling and taking note that there was no sign of worms or beetles or anything else dire—at least in this room.

"Killed?" Percy said with mild alarm.

"An accident. Somewhere on the estate, I believe." Jordan wondered if there was a servant to be found and where they would sleep that night, considering the condition of the interior. He was sure the solicitor had told him of a housekeeper. Dust was thick; everything had a neglected look about it. Whoever the woman was, she was not given to polishing wood.

The two men peered into several rooms on the ground floor, taking note of Holland covers shrouding the furniture. At least some attempt had been made to preserve items. They then sauntered up the stairs to the first floor to find more dust. That is, until they reached what must have been his grandmother's suite.

"I believe we may be able to stay here after all," Jordan murmured to his good friend.

"Smells like lemon," Percy observed quietly. "Polished to a turn. Nothing shabby about these rooms."

The sound of footsteps bustling along the hallway brought both men around to look at the door with curiosity.

"This ought to be interesting." Jordan glanced at Percy, a wry smile on his lips.

Percy frowned at his friend's levity and then scowled at the matronly woman who hurried into the room, quite out of breath and looking rather vexed.

"Oh, I am sorry, your lordship. I was in the laundry. Peachum came to tell me as how you had arrived. Should have pulled the bell. I am Mrs. Longwood, housekeeper to the late baron and your late grandmother before that. The solicitor wrote as how you'd come down from London as soon as you were gazetted. I'd have had more polish applied, but with none to help me, 'tis all I can do to keep these rooms in order." She bobbed a curtsy, then awaited orders she obviously expected.

If there was a hint of ill usage in her words, there was nothing in her face to confirm it.

With another glance at Percy, Jordan politely said, "Hire as many maids as you need to make the house habitable. I intend to make this my home. Is Peachum the only man in the stables? Or does *he* have help?"

"Oh, Peachum has his son to help him, but I fancy he could use another pair of hands, especially if you have more horses?" She gave him a calculating look, as though she wondered what changes would be made to the household.

"There is a baggage cart on the way with Barton, my valet, and Simnel, my chef from London. I'll discuss the matter of additional help with Peachum later. Mr. Ponsonby and I want a meal. Also, we will be staying here. If you might ready a room for him by this evening? I shall occupy my grandmother's suite. Barton and Simnel will need rooms, as well as Mr. Ponsonby's valet when he arrives."

"All will be as right as a trivet, my lord. At what time do you wish dinner?" The plump housekeeper, her apron crisp with starch, paused by the door, appearing anxious to take her leave.

"We are accustomed to London hours. Six will be fine. My chef ought to be here in time to prepare our meal." Jordan was polite, but as with his meeting with Peachum there was little doubt he expected total obedience.

When Mrs. Longwood had left them to the creaking peace of the house, Jordan strolled over to the window to gaze out at the countryside. "Nice view from up here."

"Wonder what happened to your cousin?" Percy mused, raising his brows as he stared out of the window, seeming intent upon the same view.

"Grandmother's solicitor didn't seem to have any details. He was anything but loquacious." Jordan frowned, recalling his frustration at the solicitor's evasiveness.

"Perhaps he met with an accident while out riding? Happens often, I suspect," Percy said, speculation clear in his voice.

"Possibly, although he was reputed to be a bruising rider. Perhaps Mrs. Longwood would know something?"

After a casual check of the bedroom and the dressing room, the two men left the pleasant and well-furnished sitting room.

"Furniture ain't old," Percy commented as they clattered down the stairs. "Leastways, it looks to be Sheraton or Hepplewhite, maybe Chippendale," he observed as they wandered into what appeared to be a drawing room of sorts on the ground floor.

"Odd that the old girl would refurbish the house, then neglect to keep it up," Jordan replied as he pulled off the Holland cover from the damask-covered sofa. "Amazing—the blue isn't faded in the least, and it seems fairly new."

Percy pulled the covers off two side chairs and shook his head in surprise as a pair of Sheraton's finest designs came to view, the blue damask glowing in the soft light from the shaded windows. "Perhaps she wished it nice for your cousin?"

"Well, it eliminates the need for redecorating right off—at least this room. We shall see in what condition the rest of the house is later on. I will have Mrs. Longwood ready this room as soon as she has your bedroom prepared."

"Glad I came down with you. Wouldn't have missed seeing your new digs for anything." Percy craned his neck to study the design on the ceiling. Strap-work tipped with gilt was delightfully complicated and festooned with delicate cobwebs to enhance the plasterwork. He shook his head, exchanging an amused glance with Jordan.

The two men left the house, intent on the stables just as the baggage wagon approached on the neatly graveled avenue to the house. Cotman, the coachman, had the reins and gave Jordan a pained look as though the ride south from London had been a severe trial.

Barton greeted his master, then darted a sour glance at Simnel. The chef bore the righteous mien of one who has been much put upon.

"Difficult trip?" Jordan hazarded.

"Dire, milord," the valet responded darkly. "With this prophet of doom and gloom along, it could hardly be jolly."

"Well, take heart, things are not so bad."

"The kitchen, milord?" Simnel said lugubriously.

"Take a look for yourself. I have not yet inspected that part of the house. You know that whatever you wish for that area will be purchased."

"Don't know why you put up with him," Percy said quietly as the baggage wagon with the grouchy pair trundled in the direction of the stables. The two gentlemen slowly followed on foot, looking about them as they walked.

"Yes, you do. He is a first-rate chef. If I am to be settled in the country, I intend at least to eat well."

"So—you do plan to remain here." Percy shook his head in bemusement as he sauntered at Jordan's side, following the baggage wagon to the stables.

"I do. I've an estate to run. Besides, London is not the same anymore."

"True," Percy agreed. "A chap inherits a title and a fortune, and all the matrimony-bent mamas haunt you. Not a moment of peace, if I know rightly."

"All the pretty young things who ignored me before now smile and nod. It was most illuminating." Jordan slanted a wry smile; his dark eyes gleamed with humor. He had never been one to have a high opinion of his own merits, but a vast fortune and a title had altered everything.

"Disgusting is more like it," Percy grumbled.

"You may not have a title, but you are pretty well to grass, my friend." Jordan gave his good friend a thump on the back. "I've no doubt you are just as sought."

Percy didn't reply as they had rounded the back of the sprawling house to see the stable block, all brick and sprucely neat. "Well, well, this is more the thing," Percy said after a low whistle.

"Appears to be a good housing above the stables." Jordan pointed out the neat row of windows to Percy, then strolled inside to carefully inspect the layout and the stalls. "Amazing, the very latest in stable design. Look at the stalls—all solid brick with provision for names above. It would seem my grandmother anticipated Ivor would want a large stable."

"Will you?" Percy wondered aloud.

"Just my carriage horses and any others needed. Kent is hardly hunting country from what I have seen so far."

"True," Percy agreed.

The dinner hour approaching, the two men went into the house once more, reluctant to face the gloomy interior, but hoping to have a decent meal placed before them. They entered the dining room, now polished and ready.

The food betrayed the unmistakable influence of Simnel. Percy took a sip of the savory-smelling soup and sighed with pleasure. "It would seem Simnel is in control."

"Indeed," Jordan agreed, intent upon consuming his soup and one of the warm rolls set before them by a rather flustered maid.

"I see Mrs. Longwood has lost no time in enlarging the staff," Jordan said once the girl was gone.

"Hope we get a pigeon pie. Simnel has a way with pigeon pie that no one else can match," Percy said as he stared at the bottom of his empty soup bowl.

Alas, there was none, but instead fricasseed mushrooms, sautéed spiced chicken, beans in a sauce only Simnel knew how to create, and assorted other dishes to tempt men who were hungry. When all this was removed, a plum cake Simnel had brought with him was set before them with a vanilla sauce the chef liked to offer.

"I believe we shall do quite well in the country if this is a sample of our fare," Percy said once his plate was left without a crumb to grace it.

"I shall never understand how it is that you can eat so much and never gain an ounce," Jordan said with a shake of his head.

"My mother insists I worry it off," Percy replied complacently, a twinkle lurking in his eyes.

"Bah. Come, let us see if there is a fire in the drawing room and discuss what is to be done on the morrow."

As he had requested, the room had been hastily tidied, although not all cobwebs were banished. It seemed a pleasant room, one in which visitors could be entertained with pleasure.

"Well, let us discuss plans for the coming week."

*   *   *

The next morning, following the excellent breakfast bearing all the marks of food prepared by Simnel, Jordan received a report from the chef regarding the state of the kitchen.

"Your esteemed grandmother saw to it that the kitchen was in fair shape, milord," the chef announced pompously. "It needs but a few touches to make it excellent."

Jordan read the list proffered by his chef and sighed with relief that not only was it short, but it contained no major items. "These are all acceptable. I shall write to London at once."

Percy eyed the list, observing, "He has even noted where the things can be bought. I say, you've a most efficient man!"

"He would not remain with me otherwise." Jordan rose from the table to explore the other rooms on the ground level of the house. The days ahead portended much work, promising and fulfilling, nonetheless. They would spend hours and days prowling about the old house, poking into corners and peering into rooms Jordan had not seen in the past.

"Ah, a billiards room—that's new. Let's have a game later." They walked on to the next door. "Here's the library with but a modest selection of books. I shall want it useable as soon as possible, then add my own collection to the shelves." He paused at the door to the next room, glancing at Percy. "This looks to be a small sitting room—most likely for the lady of the house?"

Percy nodded agreement. "Most likely."

It was then agreed to abandon the inspection for that day and enjoy an evening testing the billiards setup.

Several days passed in assessment, observing the clean-up of the house, and the commencement of the painting, but mostly settling into the house, making it feel like home. Books were unpacked, and items from London placed about until Jordan gave a satisfied look about him.

"I believe we ought to pay a visit on the neighbors, Percy," Jordan stated at luncheon. "Mrs. Longwood informed me the earl is away and only the women remain. Since it would not be fitting for them to come here, as might be customary, we shall go to them."

"The mountain to Mohammet, as it were," Percy murmured in reply while polishing off a tasty bit of rarebit.

"The Earl of Stafford has an old title—I checked it in the peerage, and 'tis one that his daughter stands to inherit since he has no son. Wife died some years ago, her sister looks after the girl."

"Might be interesting," Percy said, tossing aside his napkin as he rose from the table to join Jordan.

Within a brief time the curricle had been brought around, and the two gentlemen so recently from London ventured forth. The approach to the Stafford estate was heartening with well-tended land and buildings.

"It would appear the earl has a good steward in charge while he is away," Jordan observed.

Handing the reins to the groom, Jordan sprang from the carriage and strode up to the door. Percy followed, looking about with a curious gaze.

The door opened before the bellpull could be tugged, and the gentlemen entered with a wary look at the elderly butler.

"Lord Harcourt and Mr. Ponsonby to see Miss Maitland and Lady Ariel Brandon." Again, there was the note of authority that no servant could miss.

"One moment, my lord. I shall see if the ladies are receiving guests." The butler gestured to a bench in the entry hall, then left at once.

Jordan exchanged looks with Percy, but before either could comment, the servant returned. With a nod, he beckoned the two men to follow him. "They are happy to see their new neighbor."

"Word travels as fast in the country as in the city," Percy observed under his breath.

Jordan gave him a quick nod, then walked forward to greet his neighbors. "Miss Maitland, how pleasant to meet you. And this is Lady Ariel?" He turned from the plump, neatly garbed older woman to the young lady.

"Lord Harcourt, how nice." Dark, curling hair framed her face, and she was dressed in a simple blue muslin that could not disguise her nice figure. Jordan found himself being studied by a pair of very shrewd-seeming gray eyes set above a straight nose and a beautifully curved pair of lips. All this was set into an oval face of utterly enchanting loveliness. His guard immediately went up.

"How very pleasant to meet neighbors," he said. "May I present my friend, Mr. Percival Ponsonby?"

"Pleasure, ladies," Percy said with aplomb earned in countless London drawing rooms and balls.

The men settled onto a pair of chairs and listened politely as Miss Maitland began to acquaint them with the people who lived in the area and interesting events that were to come. After a hesitation, Miss Maitland, who had not permitted her niece to enter the conversation, said, "It is nice to know the grandson of a dear friend has settled in next door. I trust you *are* to be our neighbor?" Her long nose seemed to quiver with curiosity. Yet she seemed the typical companion and old maid—with a sweet smile, gentle manners, and kindly disposition.

Jordan excused her probing, imagining that country life brought little excitement. "It is my intention to remain in residence for some time to come, Miss Maitland. There is much to be done here. I must say, I am pleased with the excellent attention to the land and crops."

"That would be due to Mr. Shirley, your estate manager. From all I have heard, he is a fine man."

There was nothing amiss with her words, but Jordan sensed an implication. He frowned, casting a glance at Percy.

At last the niece spoke. "Do not mind my aunt, Lord Harcourt. I understand my father tried to hire Mr. Shirley away from your grandmother and he refused to leave, saying he was more needed there," Lady Ariel said in a soft, musical voice.

"In that event, I must express my appreciation to him when we meet," Jordan said with civility.

"Aye, I forgot, you'd not have met him, for he went to Tunbridge Wells to inspect some horses. He says he will not entrust this sort of errand to anyone else, as though Peachum would not do things right," Miss Maitland said with the air of one who was annoyed.

"You appear to know a great deal of what goes on at Harcourt Hall, Miss Maitland," Jordan said quietly, his voice stiff.

"This is the country, and gossip runs rampant here. 'Tis not so very different from London in that respect, I'll wager," the older lady said with a laugh. "Besides, Peachum's daughter works for us here at Stafford Court—or did until Mrs. Longwood lured her back."

Relaxing a trifle, Jordan was surprised to hear the door knocker sound, followed by a stately tread.

All four occupants of the drawing room turned to face the doorway as the butler paused at the opening to announce the latest caller. "Mr. Lytton, the rector."

Jordan rose, as did Percy. When the introductions were accomplished and the men seated, Jordan commented, "How pleasant to meet another of the community."

"Lord Harcourt, it is indeed a pleasure to welcome you to our humble village. Although not precisely humble, as we have the benefit of Lady Ariel and her dear aunt to grace our company. And now *you* join us. Indeed, we are most fortunate in our neighbors. And you have a guest. Dare I hope that you will be remaining with us for some weeks? You may be certain that everyone for miles around has looked forward to your coming, Lord Harcourt."

Speechless at this onslaught of words directed at him, Jordan merely raised his brows, daring to nod agreement.

In a voice that indicated her amusement, Lady Ariel said, "Lord Harcourt is determined to settle here for an indefinite period, Mr. Lytton. You will have to polish your best words for this coming Sunday with such esteemed parishioners in attendance at worship service."

Jordan gave her a wry glare unseen by Mr. Lytton.

"This is indeed a propitious event. I daresay you are ready to replace your cousin in all respects?" The rector, a tall, sparse man with his gray hair parted neatly in the center above his pale blue eyes, hawkish nose, and generous mouth—the better to contain his abundance of vocabulary, no doubt—turned to Jordan with eager expectation scarcely concealed.

Jordan frowned in puzzlement at the odd choice of words. He glanced at Lady Ariel, who seemed vexed with the rector, not that he couldn't sympathize. Miss Maitland seemed deeply annoyed.

Jordan ventured to say, "I shall do my best to conduct the affairs of the estate much as I feel my grandmother would have wished."

"Splendid! Splendid! I fancy it will not be long then that we learn of your betrothal to Lady Ariel?" The rector leaned back against the chair with the air of one who is supremely pleased with himself.

Thunderstruck, Jordan glanced at Percy, who appeared equally at sea.

"I fear I am unacquainted with any specification my grandmother left in regard to a marriage between the heir of Harcourt Hall and the lady of Stafford Court." He looked to Lady Ariel, who abruptly rose from her chair to cross to a window where she stared out at the garden, her hands clasped before her in obvious agitation.

Miss Maitland explained. "My niece was engaged to marry your cousin Ivor. There was nothing said to *me* in regard to transferring the betrothal to you, Lord Harcourt." She fastened a frosty glare on the rector that ought to have frozen him solid. "I would not pay the slightest regard to what Mr. Lytton says in this matter."

"But it is the custom hereabouts to marry the woman who was betrothed to a previous heir," the rector said righteously, and not a little indignant that his word would be questioned.

"*I* have not heard of such a custom," Miss Maitland said in a stiff manner, her back more rigid than ever.

Jordan ought to have been relieved. Why was it that he was piqued instead? He had been considered quite a catch in London. Of course, he was a mere baron, and Lady Ariel was the daughter of an earl. But it was irritating that cousin Ivor was deemed good enough and he wasn't.

At that propitious moment a maid entered the room with a large tray bearing tea and tiny cakes. Tea was served, with Jordan carrying a cup to Lady Ariel, who had remained by the window.

"Tea, Lady Ariel?" He held out the cup and saucer.

She turned to face him squarely, accepting his offer with a rueful smile and a candid look from her gray eyes. "I must apologize for such confusion on a first visit, my lord. Please believe me when I say I have no intention of holding you to that betrothal. I suspect our dear rector is a trifle over-eager to see me settled," she murmured, casting a wry glance at that gentleman.

"I must confess I am slightly confounded to be presented with a ready-made betrothal." He gave her a searching look while Percy engaged the rector and Miss Maitland in less dangerous conversation.

"It is not long since the previous Lord Harcourt was killed. He was an amiable gentleman. To think of another taking his place is not to be considered." She spoke loudly enough for all in the room to hear her. Then, softly, she added, "I do not wear black gloves, as Aunt Maitland said it would not be seemly since our engagement was of such short duration. I must do what is proper, you see." However, a faint frown settled on her brow, and she appeared concerned for more than manners.

"I fear I did not know my cousin all that well. He preferred to remain in the country near Cambridge, and I was much in London." Jordan avoided a direct reply to her remarks. Indeed, he scarcely knew what to say.

"You prefer Town, then?" She searched his face seemingly for a clue to his true feelings, not polite words.

"I have enjoyed my time in the city. Now, however, I intend to devote myself to restoring my house to what it ought to be. Perhaps I may call on you for advice should I have need?" he asked politely. All women loved to give advice, especially regarding furnishings. At least that was what he had observed.

"I doubt you will have need of any assistance from me, Lord Harcourt," Lady Ariel said, looking rather amused. "However, should you find yourself in a bind, I shall attempt to help. Your grandmother had the house redone a few years ago. Since she hoped for an alliance between Stafford and Harcourt, she begged my assistance. I selected styles, colors, and fabrics at her insistence. Should you wish to change things, I would likely be the last person to consult." She gave him an enigmatic smile.

"I shall bear that in mind, you may be sure," Jordan replied absently.

"There is some doubt concerning your cousin's death." Her whisper just reached him.

Here was a tangle! Jordan wondered precisely what had happened to Ivor. There were undercurrents in the room, and it would take time and tact to ferret out the whole of the story— but dig, he would. He merely smiled and escorted Lady Ariel to her former chair, where she serenely chatted with the rector as though nothing had been said about marriage to a stranger or a mysterious death.

Chapter Two

The callers left shortly after tea had been served. The two ladies walked to the terrace with Jordan, Percy, and the rector to where the carriages waited. Jordan offered his respects and farewells to Miss Maitland, then Lady Ariel. Percy nobly chatted with the rector about local coming events, of which there appeared to be few.

Miss Maitland was polite, but decidedly cool to Jordan. It reminded him of the days before he inherited.

It seemed to Jordan that Lady Ariel was sending him a silent message. To what purpose? he wondered. There was no mistaking that she tried to convey something with those eloquent gray eyes, however, and she did not flirt. She looked serious. It seemed to Jordan that the charming Lady Ariel wished to speak with him privately. He couldn't imagine why—unless she wished to explain something away from her aunt's hearing. But what?

While Miss Maitland turned to discuss with the rector the altar flowers for the coming Sunday service, Jordan took the opportunity to softly ask Lady Ariel if she would care to join him in an early morning ride on the morrow. She nodded agreement and quietly replied, "Nine? At the gate to Stafford?"

Jordan nodded his assent, then climbed into his curricle. The rector entered his gig as well after reminding the gentlemen that he looked forward to seeing them on Sunday.

Percy turned to his friend once the carriage had traveled some distance down the avenue. "Curious visit."

"This is the first time since I inherited the title that I felt as though I suffer a deficiency. Miss Maitland seemed to disapprove of me. And I believe she runs things at Stafford Court. Logical, I suppose," he mused.

"Lady Ariel's a charmer, though," Percy murmured.

As they approached the manor, they could see a ladder being raised so some of the upper windows might be cleaned.

"You going riding with Lady Ariel in the morning?" Percy asked with a sly smile.

"You heard? I trust Miss Maitland was too busy announcing her views on altar flowers to take notice. It appears Lady Ariel desires to speak with me in private."

"You are tempting the fates, my friend," Percy said, laughing at Jordan's expression of disdain.

"Come, I have more important things to do than ponder over a neighbor's problems—whatever they might be." He drove on ahead to the stables. He intended to confer with Peachum regarding their operation. Cotman would have his notions to consider as well. The older man was experienced in running a stable, and Jordan hoped the two would jog along well together.

"You're catering to them," Percy grumbled later as the two men purposefully strode back to the house after concluding arrangements.

"I have learned that happy, or at least satisfied, employees do their work more cheerfully. I get better results with fewer problems." Jordan glanced at his good friend, then added, "I have noticed that your man is not precisely ill-treated. You took care that he rode down here in style. He traveled with your groom in your curricle with some of your baggage, and I'll wager you did not instruct them to put up a second-rate inns."

"Have to coddle a good valet, dash it all. Do you have any notion how hard it is to get a really good man who knows the best blacking for boots and can tie a top-notch cravat?"

"Barton has been with me for so long I forget."

When they rounded the corner to the front of the house, Jordan was pleased to see the windows much improved.

"Evidently, Mrs. Longwood has found additional help," Jordan observed.

"My room was tolerably clean by last evening. At least, I have no quarrel with the conditions. I shall stay until you tell me it is time to move on," Percy announced with a grin. As an old friend, he knew to a tee when Jordan had had enough of company.

Following dinner, Jordan and Percy were seated in the library when Mrs. Longwood announced the arrival of the steward, Mr. Shirley.

The steward, a pleasant-looking man of medium height and coloring, his brown hair neatly cut, and his cravat of modest proportions, crossed the room to stand before Jordan. He bowed most correctly, then waited for Jordan to speak first.

"At last we meet," Jordan said pleasantly.

"I apologize for being absent when you arrived. When he wrote me, the solicitor was vague as to when you expected to be here. The matter in Tunbridge Wells was urgent. I wished to inspect a horse up for sale, as well as purchase needed supplies."

Jordan rose and stepped forward to extend his hand in greeting. "Well, you are here now. Come, join us in a glass of claret while you bring me up to date on matters. I am pleased with what I have seen of the land."

"But not the house, I'll wager," Mr. Shirley said with a wry expression as he pulled up a Windsor chair to join them. "Mrs. Longwood is not a bad housekeeper, but she would have it that only *you* must give her orders, not me." He glanced about the room, his eyes absorbing the lack of dust, the neatness of the books. "I gather she has found some maids. There are a few local women glad of work."

"They tend to disappear whenever I am around. If I weren't such an agreeable fellow, I'd say they think me a villain." There was a hint of query in his voice.

"Perhaps they mistake you for one like your cousin," the steward began, then fell silent with a guarded look at Jordan.

"Explain that, if you please. I did not know my cousin well at all. We rarely had met. I confess that I felt no great loss at his death. But I am curious."

Mr. Shirley took a deep breath and seemed to relax. "Well, he seemed a nice-enough chap as far as I could tell. But the maids did not remain when he came around. Mrs. Longwood had a devil of a time keeping staff once he settled in here. They came and went as if they were in a turnstile. When he died, Mrs. Longwood waited for you. She seemed to feel you might not wish to remain here."

Jordan exchanged a significant look with Percy. "And we are on trial? You may be sure neither Mr. Ponsonby nor I are given to seducing maids." He frowned, then continued, "What can you tell me of my cousin's death? The solicitor could tell me nothing. Mrs. Longwood would say no more than there had been an accident."

"He was out riding when it happened. Perhaps his horse was startled, and he took a tumble. His neck was broken, so his death was quick. No witness, as he was alone. I suppose it could have been a rabbit hole." Mr. Shirley didn't seem convinced of that possibility.

"You see to it that the pastures and areas for riding are kept stopped? There ought not be any holes." Jordan leaned forward to study the man he would be working very closely with in the coming weeks. He liked what he had seen to this point, but there was ground to cover yet.

"We catch the rabbits, and the fox seem to go elsewhere." He went on to explain his methods for ridding the land of unwanted animals.

Jordan listened with care, pleased with all he heard.

"Pardon me if I appear forward, but is it your intention to remain?" Mr. Shirley asked as he shifted in his chair prior to rising.

"Everyone seems curious about my intentions. Indeed, I intend to remain for an extended period. I find I quite like the country—and this house."

"Fine. There are books to examine, records I'd wish you to see." Mr. Shirley rose and had moved toward the door when Jordan spoke again.

"This seems a friendly neighborhood. We called upon our neighbors this morning. They seem agreeable people."

The steward halted, then turned to face Jordan.

"Miss Maitland and Lady Ariel Brandon at Stafford Court. The rector, Mr. Lytton, joined us. It was a brief call but enlightening."

"Miss Maitland would not like you, I'll wager; she discourages gentlemen callers," the steward said with not the slightest touch of a smile. "The rector likes everyone and is a worse gossip than an old maid."

"So Miss Maitland would disapprove of any interest in Lady Ariel? How was it she managed to become engaged to my cousin Ivor?" The thought that his cousin was preferred to him still rankled.

"I do not know, my lord." The man hesitated, then added, "There was some talk of compromise, but nothing came of it as he died so soon after the betrothal—but a week."

"I see," Jordan said with a thoughtful look at Percy. He turned his attention to the steward again as the man walked to the door. "I shall see you tomorrow."

"Indeed," the man replied politely.

"Shirley . . ." Percy mused aloud. "That's a very old family in Derbyshire. Any relation?"

"A younger son and far removed from the title, I fear," the gentleman replied with a grin. "My father wanted me to enter the church, but I prefer estate management. I cannot see myself as a vicar."

Thinking of the man they met earlier, Jordan could only nod in agreement. "Indeed. Well, I believe we shall get along famously. You have an apartment to your liking?"

Mr. Shirley looked startled, then smiled. "Yes. Your grandmother had a soft heart for me, I believe. I have rooms on the ground floor of the west wing. Quite commodious and comfortable."

"Very good. I look forward to meeting with you following my morning ride with Lady Ariel." Jordan waited to see what the reaction might be to his words. He was rewarded with a genuine start of surprise.

"Lord Harcourt, I . . ." He hesitated, then continued slowly, "I am not completely satisfied that your cousin's death was an accident. He might have been reckless, but he was a good horseman. Do take care when out riding."

"It appeared Lady Ariel wished to speak privately with me, and a morning ride seemed a good solution. Surely you do not think *she* had something to do with Ivor's death!" One to listen to advice when offered, he waited to see what the man he was coming to respect more and more had to say to the matter.

"No, I do not think she was in any way responsible. However, matters did not add up to my satisfaction. All I can say is to be on guard."

"I feel as though I have plunged into the middle of an intrigue," Jordan said with a smile that faded when he saw the serious mien on his steward.

"I shall say no more on the matter, my lord. May I suggest you keep your eyes and ears open and be a trifle wary of all who approach you for whatever reason?" The steward smiled as he added a final thought. "Unless you seek a wife, perhaps it would be well to let it be known you are not in the market for such. Sunday morning service is a good time. Miss Vipont is the premier gossip, who will happily spread news, thus sparing you intrusions."

He left them with more than a little to mull over.

"Well, well, fancy your steward being a Shirley," Percy murmured as he sought a chair by the sputtering fire.

Jordan walked over to stir the fire, then looked at Percy. "This has been quite a day. I cannot wait to see what tomorrow brings."

"I'd say we may want to do a bit of mousing about the area. I did not like to hear of the question regarding your cousin's death."

"True," Jordan replied absently. "From what little I knew of him and the few times we met, I cannot say I had any love for the man. Yet, I would not have wished him dead, killed by someone for an unknown reason."

"An angry father, perhaps?" Percy said, obviously thinking of the remark about the maids.

"That is possible. Come—let us try the billiards table. I shall need a clear mind when I meet Lady Ariel in the morning. What shall you do?"

"Now that Watson has come with the rest of my things and the curricle, I believe I will take a ride into the village and have a look about. Who knows what I might uncover."

Jordan took a deep breath, then said, "I know you mean to joke, but do have a care." His smile was strained.

"As to that, I should say the same for you—going off on a ride when your cousin died while enjoying the same."

They sauntered off to the billiards room together. Jordan selected a cue, then turned to his friend.

"You will have to beat me without my spotting you a single point," Jordan said with a forced laugh. He did not want to talk of death anymore this evening.

Miss Maitland shook out the embroidery upon which she had labored these past weeks and frowned at her niece. "I was not pleased that you should walk off by yourself to the window without a by-your-leave. Most impolite, my dear girl. Not the thing, you know."

"Yes, Aunt," Ariel replied softly. "But there is a rather fine view from that window. The gardens are very nice this time of year."

"Just so you pay no heed to the rector's words. Such nonsense I never heard in my life. Fancy him thinking that the new Lord Harcourt ought to marry you simply because his cousin had briefly been your betrothed. That man doesn't have the brains God gave a flea. Where did he come by such notions, I ask you!" She threaded a needle, then attacked the hapless embroidery as though it were the rector.

"I believe it was King Henry the Eighth who was an example of wedding his brother's promised bride, was it not? Did not his father arrange it?"

"Yes, and when he had no heir, he said it was God's punishment for marrying his brother's widow, although I do not believe they were actually wed."

"Betrothals were considered almost like marriage then. It was impossible to escape from one, once engaged," Ariel answered thoughtfully.

"Let that be a lesson to you, dear niece. Take care with whom you spend your time." Miss Maitland gave her niece a speculative look.

"And where do I ever go that you are not with me?" Ariel asked, a rueful smile on her lips.

"I do not go riding with you," Aunt reminded. "See to it that you have a groom with you when you go off on your wanderings. And do not leave Stafford grounds! You are a pretty girl, not to mention a great heiress."

"Indeed, I should not wish anything to happen to me," Ariel said with a pensive look at her aunt. Why she could not love the woman who had tended her so faithfully all the years since her mother's death she couldn't say. Her aunt was amiable, if a trifle reclusive.

Ariel rose from her chair and crossed to the window. She must be a dreadful girl, for she had not mourned when her betrothed was killed. An accident, they said, and she supposed it must have been, for Ivor had been a reckless rider, taking chances at every turn. The engagement had not been of her choosing.

"You ought to take up your embroidery, Ariel," Miss Maitland said presently.

It seemed like an order to Ariel, and she rebelled, however briefly. "My head aches. I believe I shall go for a walk in the garden. The house oppresses me."

"It would be better if you went to your room and had a cold vinegar compress on your forehead. I shall see to it at once." Miss Maitland put aside her embroidery, fully prepared to follow through on her words.

Closing her eyes, Ariel fought the urge to scream. "Thank you so much, dear Aunt. I believe if I could just sit quietly in the garden, listening to the birds, I would be fine in but a little while. Excuse me." Before her aunt could object, Ariel crossed the room at a swift pace, running down the stairs to the ground floor as though pursued. In a way, she was—pursued, that is. Every moment alone was treasured.

Finding a bench under a turkey oak, Ariel settled back against the rough bark to enjoy the sounds and scents of the garden. A fountain splashed in the center of the plots containing ordinary flowers and herbs, as well as interesting plants that her father had collected from all over the world.

She wished he would leave India and settle here again. Father likely found it difficult, but she missed him dreadfully. He did not get along well with his wife's sister, although he paid her well to look after her niece. If he came home, Aunt Maitland could go elsewhere. Goodness knew she must have a tidy sum tucked away in consols or a bank account. Ariel had checked the Stafford books to discover the amount her aunt re-

ceived, and it was most generous. Since she never spent a far-
thing of it, using household funds for her few purchases, it
stood to reason she saved it all.

A squirrel crept close, and Ariel wondered how it dared
come into the garden. Should old Turner see it, the animal
would never see another day.

"Shoo. Go away, you silly beast."

"Ariel, I cannot think the sun will be good for your head.
Come inside now," commanded her aunt from just inside the
terrace door.

With a sigh, Ariel obediently rose from her pleasant retreat
to return to the house. It was a lovely house, full of light and
charm. She had known just how to decorate Lady Harcourt's
home, for she had her own as a fine example.

"Coming, Aunt." Ariel looked forward to her morning ride
with Lord Harcourt. He was more handsome than his cousin
and appeared to have better manners as well. He hadn't surveyed her with a predatory eye, but rather seemed indifferent
to her charms. He also seemed sympathetic, and that had
prompted her to seek conversation with him.

Ariel joined her aunt and listened to her strictures on the
dangers of sunshine while thinking of the morrow and the
prospect of learning more of her new neighbor.

Jordan turned to watch the young woman who cantered
down the Stafford road to join him. He had been uncertain
whether or not to call this meeting off. Yet he had come, the
beseeching look from a pair of fine gray eyes overcoming his
reluctance to be involved with any lady.

"'Tis a glorious morning, is it not, my Lord Harcourt?" she
caroled out as she neared. Garbed in an flattering gray habit, a
neat small hat firmly in place, she was too attractive to be out
alone.

"No groom?" he admonished, feeling like her father, not a
pleasant sensation in the least.

"Oh, he trails behind me. He has known me forever and
knows I would never do anything amiss. Besides, he has had a
good report of you," she said shyly. "You are not like your
cousin, or so 'tis said."

"No, we are vastly different men. Or were, or whatever the comparison should be." He smiled at her, wondering what was on her mind.

She joined him, and he was aware of being sized up again, of her inspecting him from top to toe. "Well, do I pass?" he couldn't resist asking. Her gasp of indignation made him chuckle. "You were looking at me as though you anticipated adding me to your stables."

"Never that," she riposted. "I should never attempt to select a horse. I would end with a stable full of pretty steeds, all most likely with horrid faults."

"I rather doubt that, my lady. Indeed, I do."

"But I would select your beast, I think. He looks quite handsome."

They settled into a casual chat about horses until they reached the division between the Stafford property and the Harcourt estates. Here they halted again, with Lady Ariel giving Jordan a quizzical look.

"I had the strange feeling that you wanted to talk to me about something. Was I wrong?" Jordan asked at long last, while wondering why it was that he felt such accord with this young woman. Could it be because she practiced no womanly wiles? Her directness, the serious light in her eyes seemed proof that she differed from the London belles.

The smile that had enchanted him earlier disappeared as she became solemn. "Yes, you surmised rightly. I wanted to caution you to be on your guard. I did not know your cousin well, but I feel strongly that his death was planned. Although he took chances, he was a first-rate rider, and I believe it was no accident that he was thrown from his horse. Whoever wished him dead may feel the same about you. We do not know, do we?" She turned in her saddle to give him a most earnest look.

"You are the second to have fears on those grounds. But I doubt very much that I have an enemy in this area. For that matter, I have no enemies in London, either. I've been a rather dull chap, I fear. No outraged husbands chase me; no shopkeepers dog my footsteps. No, I am one of those rarities—a just and proper man." He spoke without boasting, instead feeling a little bit foolish to make such a statement. But he needed to reassure her. "I pay my bills and keep my distance from flirtatious wives."

"Perhaps you need a dog for protection. Unless you already have a dog?" she inquired, a delightful twinkle in her lovely eyes.

"Not in the city. Couldn't see a dog at the Albany—that is where I lived these past years since I left Oxford." Seeing her confusion, he added, "It is a nice arrangement of chambers for gentlemen. Sixty-nine of us live there in decent comfort, but I wouldn't like to keep a dog in the place. The country is the place for a dog."

They proceeded to ride on at that point. After a few minutes she queried, "You truly intend to remain here?" Her question was asked without even a coy smile, much less the usual artifice and batting of eyelashes.

"For the foreseeable future. There is much to do here." This was another query on his intentions. Perhaps he ought to make an announcement?

"I suspect you want to know what happened to your predecessor as well. Am I not right? I know I should want to find out all I could."

He chose not to answer that remark.

When they came in sight of the groom, Jordan saluted the man to let him know he was observed and that Jordan now turned her ladyship over to his care.

"I expect I shall see you at services on Sunday."

He answered her politely, "Indeed, how could I miss a sermon from the estimable Mr. Lytton?"

"I hope you paid not the slightest attention to the nonsense he spouted whilst taking tea with us yesterday?" She had turned again to face him, pausing.

She spoke casually, yet Jordan wondered if there wasn't a message in those words as well. "I have no interest in a wife at the moment. Perhaps in a few years when I am more settled?"

She laughed at him then. "Lucky you. You are allowed to choose a wife while I must take what I am given. You have no cause to complain, sirrah!"

Jordan watched her ride toward her home, a jaunty set to her shoulders. Was it a pose? Did he hear a wistful note in her voice when she pretended to chide him?

His return to the Hall was thoughtful, and he was relieved to see Mr. Shirley awaiting him as he rode into the stable yard. His own thoughts had not been pleasant. It would be good to listen to someone else for a time.

He turned his mount over to Peachum, then walked to the house with Mr. Shirley. When they reached the comfortable confines of the library, Mr. Shirley set down the neat stack of account books he had carried and turned to face Jordan.

"You had an agreeable ride this morning, my lord?"

Jordan studied his steward. "I did." After a pause, he continued with deliberation, "It seems that you are not alone in thinking there was something strange about my cousin's demise. Lady Ariel begged me take caution. She fears that whoever took Ivor's life might take mine as well. She failed to offer any motive, however."

There was a brief silence during which Mr. Shirley digested Jordan's words, then expressed agreement with her.

"She thinks I ought to get a dog," Jordan muttered as he gestured to a chair comfortably close to the desk. He lounged on his own chair, rubbing his chin while he considered the suggestion.

"Not a puppy, then, but a dog able to guard you well?" Shirley suggested.

"You realize all this talk is almost enough to send me back to London and my chambers at the Albany." Jordan plucked the topmost of the account books from the pile.

Mr. Shirley gave him a dismayed look, and Jordan grimaced. "I said almost. I'll remain, but it will be the dickens to feel as though I must look over my shoulder every other minute when I am out and about."

"You would not be compromised. It seems your cousin was not so finicky. As I mentioned before, rumor has it he compromised Lady Ariel into the engagement."

Jordan stiffened. He might feel comfortable with Mr. Shirley, but he had never liked gossiping. "That I know nothing about. The lady did not see fit to confide in me."

That ended the discussion, and they turned to the accounts

of the estate. Within thirty minutes Jordan came to realize he had a gifted steward, one he would be a fool to lose.

By the time Percy joined them to partake of a luncheon Simnel had conjured for their enjoyment, he'd had enough of accounts and books. "Why do we all not take a ride over the estate? Shirley can show me what he thinks needs improving, and I can agree."

Mr. Shirley looked abashed at this sign of confidence in his abilities. "It would be my pleasure, my lord."

"Harcourt. Call me Harcourt. I daresay you have as much right to it as anyone, considering your family."

"As you wish." Mr. Shirley tried not to smile and failed.

"Percy, how was your morning? I trust you had no one telling you that you had best mind your back lest someone do you in?" At his friend's amazed expression, Jordan explained what had occurred while on his ride, as well as what Mr. Shirley had revealed. He concluded with Lady Ariel's advice. "She thinks I ought to get a dog."

"A large brute with sharp teeth, a good sense of smell and keen hearing. He should be able to attack an intruder and know friend from foe," Percy said quite seriously.

"Oh, good heavens," Jordan said in disgust, tossing his napkin on the table, his pigeon pie forgotten. "If you keep on, I *shall* be inclined for the Albany!"

"But think of the challenge if you remain," Mr. Shirley murmured.

Jordan paused to give him a considering look. "I just hope it is not a dead end."

Chapter Three

"What is that?" Jordan asked, as Percy half carried, half dragged what had to be the ugliest dog in the world into the library.

"Purebred bloodhound, that's what. Peachum told me as how he knew a fellow who breeds them, and I was able to pick this one up for a song."

"What song did you sing? Something about wrinkles?" Jordan eyed the dog with misgivings. He suspected Percy had brought a surprise for him that he was not going to like in the least.

"He is the perfect dog for you! He will bark if someone comes near you, and be able to detect strangers, and if you get lost, he will find you in a trice." Percy placed the young dog on the wood floor of the library, then stood back to admire his purchase. The dog sat quietly, head cocked as though in question.

Percy looked so proud of himself that Jordan didn't have the heart to tell him that under no circumstances did he desire that ugly-looking mutt—purebred or not. The animal gazed up at Jordan with sad eyes, quite as though he knew just how unattractive he was and how Jordan didn't want him. It was too much. Jordan gave up without a battle.

"Very well, I'll give him a try." The dog, caramel brown with a black saddle, long floppy ears, droopy eyes, deep wrinkles in his face and a few elsewhere, walked to where Jordan stood, sniffed his boots and promptly sat down on his feet.

"He'll be fine once he gets to know you," Percy said eagerly.

Jordan looked down at the not-quite-full-grown dog and

sighed. "I believe he already does." The dog, deciding that he had found a master, settled on Jordan's beautifully shined boots and dropped his head to the floor.

"I found him a collar and lead so you can take him with you in the curricle whenever you go out." Percy produced straps of black leather, likely made at the local village saddlery shop.

Jordan extracted his feet from beneath the hound and walked over to stand by Percy. "Mere words cannot express my feelings adequately, old chap."

Percy blushed slightly red in his face and turned his attention to the bloodhound. "Think nothing of it. I thought you ought to have some sort of protection. What will you name it?"

Jordan looked at the sorry specimen of dog, thinking it should be called Ugly, or perhaps Homely. Then he glanced at Percy and said, "Well, what about Prince?"

Percy beamed approval. "Good name! I know you will get to like him, and he will be a fine companion for you."

Mr. Shirley coughed into the back of his hand and turned away from them, but not before Jordan saw him trying to suppress a laugh.

"And when I am not here, he can keep an eye on Mr. Shirley. Is that not right?" Jordan challenged.

This time the cough was genuine, sounding a bit strangled. "Indeed, my lord."

"And we can take him along with us when we go out on the pastures tomorrow. I feel certain he will find all manner of vermin—rabbits and the like?" Jordan added.

"No doubt of it, Harcourt," Mr. Shirley replied with a straight face that was most likely hard won.

The gentlemen settled down to discuss the day. Jordan kept an eye on the dog. He didn't quite trust the animal, yet it appeared to be trained. At least no puddle had appeared on the wood floor—other than that left by the dog's drooling.

When it came time to head for their rooms, Jordan said to Percy, "I suppose I get the privilege of walking him?"

Percy frowned. "I should think a footman might do. Although, I fancy it would be best were you to take him out. He needs to learn who is his master."

Jordan sighed. After putting on the collar and attaching the lead, he took the most unlikely Prince out to the side of the house and walked around while the dog inspected the area, nose to ground.

He ought not to be too hard on Percy, Jordan reflected. *The fellow meant well. And a dog would be good company. Didn't a man in the country always have a dog around?* Jordan studied the homely animal in the faint light from the house. *Maybe the dog would grow on him?*

When he returned after the successful outing with Prince, Jordan found Mr. Shirley waiting for him in the entry hall.

"Mr. Ponsonby went to his room. My lord . . . that is, Harcourt, will you truly keep this creature? I feel that you might be able to dispose of him without offending Ponsonby too much."

"No. Percy and I have been friends for too many years. I'd not hurt his feelings in any way for the world. The mutt stays." He glanced down to where the dog sat, tongue lolling, eyes sadly surveying his new owner. "But do you think I need keep him with me at night?"

"I understand hounds are given to howling when unhappy," Mr. Shirley said hesitantly.

"That's all I would need, is it not?" Jordan mused, then with a slight tug at the lead, marched to the stairs. "I leave you to a peaceful night of sound sleep, Mr. Shirley. I only hope I can claim the same."

When Mr. Shirley entered the breakfast room come morning, he found his employer there before him, Prince sprawled quietly on his feet beneath the table.

"He appears to take to you," the steward said.

"At least to my feet," Jordan said, trying not to sound grumpy. "He slept across them all night as well. I fancy he will be good on a cold night."

"Well, I must say that I think it is a fine thing you do, and who knows it may turn out well?"

Jordan gave him a jaundiced look and wondered what the life span of a bloodhound might be. The thought of eighty pounds of dog draped across his feet every night was daunting. Prince could add another ten, twenty pounds by the time he was full grown. "I believe I shall see about some sort of basket for him to sleep in—he gets a trifle heavy after a time. And he needs a bath," he concluded with a grimace.

"Seems sensible," Mr. Shirley agreed.

"How did it go?" Percy queried as he charged into the breakfast room with the look of a man who had the benefit of a sound, uninterrupted sleep without the advantage of a hound weighing down his feet.

"Different," was Jordan's laconic reply. He'd not make Percy feel guilty about a disturbed sleep. But some sort of bed for the dog was definitely needed. Either that, or there would be howling in the stables.

"What do you wish to inspect today?" Mr. Shirley asked with a guarded look at the dog. "And will the dog really go with you?"

"Among other things I should like to see the pasture where my cousin was killed. And yes, I think the hound will go with us. Either he keeps up, or he will have to stay behind."

Percy and Mr. Shirley exchanged looks, but said nothing.

The three men set out after a hearty breakfast, the dog loping along near Jordan, keeping a respectful distance from Fire King, Jordan's mount.

"Prince shows some sense, at least. That horse of yours would not tolerate a dog too close," Percy declared.

Jordan nodded his agreement, less interested in what the hound was doing and more concerned with the field they now entered. He turned to Mr. Shirley. "Where?"

"At the far end. This field abuts the Stafford estate at the upper part and drains into the creek down here." He pointed to the burbling creek that wound its way through the lower edge of the pasture.

"And the creek goes on into the Stafford land?" Jordan wanted to know. Brush concealed the lower creek from view.

"Right you are. Now, over there is where your cousin was found." Mr. Shirley pointed to a nearby area of meadow. "His horse returned to the stables, which alerted Peachum that something was amiss. He and his son rode out to discover what had happened and found your cousin, the former Lord Harcourt."

"With a broken neck," Jordan stated, feeling uncomfortable at the mere thought.

"Indeed," Mr. Shirley concurred grimly.

"But what startled his horse? Something must have caused him to react as he did, to rear up and unseat my cousin. And an expert rider like my cousin should have easily controlled his mount." Jordan looked about the meadow, then dismounted to prowl over the area, looking for a clue to the fatality. "No rabbit holes," he murmured.

Prince was nosing around as well, and Jordan nearly stumbled over the dog while examining the meadow. He put out his hand to brace himself against a sturdy oak so he wouldn't fall. About level with his eyes he spotted a gleam of metal. Wondering if it was what he suspected it might be, he turned to Mr. Shirley. "Have something sharp I can use to pry?"

Mr. Shirley dismounted, removing a slim knife from a leather pouch attached to his saddle before joining Jordan. "What is it?"

Jordan took the proffered knife to dig a lead ball from the tree. "Judging by the condition of the tree as well as this lead ball, I'd say entry was quite recent. I wonder why anyone would shoot at this tree?"

"Perhaps practicing?" Mr. Shirley hazarded, looking as convinced of this as Jordan.

"If it hadn't been for Prince, you would not have tripped," Percy reminded cleverly.

"Indeed," Jordan murmured, bending to bestow an absent pat on the dog. Jordan remounted and motioned the others to follow him.

They rode around the pasture, Jordan examining every bit of the land for anything unusual. "No rabbit holes," he observed again. He gave the others a significant look. He found nothing more, not that he had expected to find anything of import. But he hadn't thought to discover—with Prince's help—the lead ball, either.

At last, deciding he had tried the patience of the others long enough, the trio set off across the field in the direction of the house and stables. Prince loped along, staying close to Jordan, yet wary of Fire King.

"I believe we ought to pay another call on our neighbors this afternoon. What say you, Percy?" Jordan inquired casually.

"Fine with me. Lady Ariel is a dashed pretty girl, not that she would give me a second look with you around."

"And she had best not do that. Unless I miss my guess, her aunt has a higher title in mind for her darling girl. It must have annoyed her when Lady Ariel was forced into that betrothal with Ivor—even if it was of short duration." Jordan exchanged a look with Mr. Shirley, who nodded in reply.

"It would seem caution is wise in all things, my lord," the steward stated.

"Take the dog with you," Jordan said to Peachum when the groom took Fire King in hand. "And mind you, he is a good creature, so find him something to eat. I think it would be a good idea were he to be accustomed to the horses." If there was a note of hope in those words, Percy missed it. "Oh, and give him another bath. He's filthy."

"I told you he would be useful," Percy reminded his friend.

"I wonder if there is such a thing as a bed for dogs to be found around here?" Jordan said to Mr. Shirley.

"Perhaps. I shall investigate while you are gone calling this afternoon." He grinned when Jordan gave his feet a rueful glance before meeting his gaze.

"I would like to be able to walk without difficulty when I arise in the morning."

"Indeed, my lord. I understand." Mr. Shirley cleared his throat before heading off to his small office, where he kept the accounts and handled tradesmen.

"Good man," Jordan commented as he and Percy strode to the house. "Hope he remains."

"Why wouldn't he?" Percy demanded to know.

"He is a prime manager. Word gets out. Other people must know of him. Wouldn't be surprised if a few feelers were put out by someone wanting a fine estate overseer."

Percy craned his neck to see Mr. Shirley entering the office, a neat room in the ell that extended toward the stable block. "Well, seems to me that you two have hit it off just fine. No need to look elsewhere, I should think."

They had a light nuncheon, then once Barton had garbed his

master in clothes suitable for a visit to a future countess, set off for Stafford Court.

"Fine-looking estate," Percy commented as they slowly rode up the main avenue to the house. While not nearly as old as Harcourt Hall, it wasn't recent, either—perhaps fifty years old and built in an attractive Palladian style. Four pillars graced the front, above which sat an elegant pediment decorated by figures of some antique design.

The large oak door opened as they reined in before the entry.

The superior-looking butler stood with a disapproving mien while Lady Ariel drifted from the house, her smile welcoming. "How nice to have callers. Is it not a glorious day?"

Jordan handed over Fire King to the groom who had dashed up from the stables. Percy proffered the reins to his nag as well, and the two men walked up the several steps to the terrace.

"What a pleasant surprise. We will be pleased to have you take tea with us," Lady Ariel said, her cool gray eyes graciously welcoming.

Jordan nodded with equal politeness and walked with her into the house, Percy close behind.

Once in the drawing room, they found another guest, a young lady, as well as Ariel's aunt.

"Good afternoon," Miss Maitland said distantly.

"May I introduce Lord Harcourt and Mr. Ponsonby, Celia? Lord Harcourt is our new neighbor, and Mr. Percy Ponsonby is his guest. Gentlemen, my dearest friend, Miss Townsend."

"*Percy* Ponsonby?" Miss Townsend inquired with a hint of a smile.

"Yes, ma'am. Everyone in my family has names that begin with the letter P . . . to go with Ponsonby, you see. My eldest brother is Peter, then there is Pauline, followed by me, then Penelope, and last of all, Peregrine. Father is named Parnel and has often joked that the main reason he married my mother was her name—Philadelphia."

"Your mother is named Philadelphia?" Jordan asked in surprise. "I did not know that. Perhaps it helps explain a thing or two." What they might be he didn't spell out.

"I am delighted to meet you, Miss Townsend," Percy said politely, bowing low over her hand.

"Actually, my name is Patience, but mother said it is not very apt, so I go by my second name." Miss Townsend smiled nicely, revealing one enchanting dimple and long-lashed blue eyes that sparkled when she looked at Percy.

"No, really? How curious." Percy, succumbing to the inviting radiance, availed himself of the closest chair and proceeded to inquire after the Townsend family's health and what pastimes Miss Townsend favored.

Jordan sighed, knowing how single-minded his good friend could be when intent upon a task. He would be lost to the others until he had made extensive acquaintance with the charming young lady whose first name began with the fortuitous letter P.

"Miss Maitland, it is good of you to permit us to call again. I felt it only proper to become better acquainted with our neighbors. Our previous call was all too brief." His bow was all that was proper and appeared to please the older lady. Her cool mien seemed to melt a trifle.

"You may sit here and visit with me, young man." She motioned to the sofa upon which she perched.

Curious to see what had brought about the more agreeable manner, Jordan did as bid.

"How do you find things at Harcourt?" the lady inquired, glancing up from the knitting in her lap.

"Now that Mrs. Longwood has managed to hire sufficient maids, things are improving. I daresay that before long the house will be in as good condition as the land. I look forward to enjoying the house in years to come." Jordan watched as Miss Maitland's hands faltered on her knitting, then continued the row before she spoke again.

"I hear you are paying well. Several girls that once worked there before have returned." She gave Jordan an assessing look before she added, "Apparently you do not have the same attitudes as your late cousin?"

"We are of different branches of the family. It is not unusual for cousins to be vastly different, ma'am." Jordan wondered how many faults were to be laid at his cousin's and now his doorstep.

"So, you have been out looking over your land, I hear?" She glanced up from her knitting, her eyes searching.

For a woman who remained within the house for the better part of her time, she was well informed.

Jordan nodded. "I am pleased with Mr. Shirley. He is a fine administrator. I certainly hope that no one tries to lure him away from me."

"Pay him well and he will stay," she observed.

"We also heard you have a dog," Lady Ariel inserted, her eyes alive with curiosity.

"Word travels fast. Yes. Percy assures me it is a bloodhound. I suppose it is, for there are enough wrinkles to vouch for the dog being a worrier and he certainly is a hound."

"Bloodhounds worry?" Lady Ariel queried, looking quite at sea.

"No, I don't suppose so, they just give the appearance of being worried—or sad. In fact, he is the saddest-looking dog I have ever seen."

Lady Ariel chuckled, hiding her mouth behind her hand when her aunt looked askance. "I cannot wait to see him. What is his name?"

"Er"—Jordan glanced to where Percy sat entranced with Miss Townsend—"Prince."

When Lady Ariel thought that over, she smiled. "You tease?"

"I fear not." Jordan was about to explain when the butler entered the room.

Pausing by the door, he announced, "Sir Henry Banks."

Miss Maitland dropped her knitting, quite ignoring it when it slid to the floor as she rose to greet her visitor.

The older man was a trifle stout, possessed a neat head of gray hair cut in the Brutus style, and dressed in a dandyish fashion far too young in appearance to look well on him. Jordan disliked his orange-and-puce waistcoat. But he rose, as did Percy, out of respect. He then moved to a chair near Lady Ariel.

"Miss Maitland, I am indeed honored that you receive me

after all this time. It has been an age since we last met in London. Dear lady, you have little changed."

Miss Maitland tittered, then urged him to join her on the backless sofa of the latest design, where she listened in rapt attention to all he had to say.

The pair renewed an old acquaintanceship, ignoring the others in the room, which suited Jordan fine. He watched the fellow, thinking him overly earnest, there being a hint of falseness in his speech. He smiled too much. Jordan's ears perked up at the next bit of speech from the stout gentleman.

"Perhaps you know that my wife died last year. Now that I am out of mourning, I am renewing old friendships. You, dear lady, were one of the most charming I knew back then." He sighed, with a fond look at Miss Maitland.

If ever a chap poured the butter-boat, it was this fellow. Jordan mistrusted him even more—and his motives in seeking out a spinster lady.

Jordan exchanged a quizzical look with Lady Ariel.

At last Miss Maitland seemed to become aware of her lapse in manners as she gestured to the others in the room. "Permit me to introduce an old friend, Sir Henry Banks. This is Lord Harcourt and his friend, Mr. Ponsonby. The young lady is a friend of Ariel's, Miss Townsend." Miss Maitland's hands fluttered in the air before her as she bestowed a smile on her new guest.

Jordan thought Miss Maitland's introduction sadly lacking in propriety, placing him before a young lady. However, he knew that some people thought a title more important, and Miss Maitland seemed a trifle flustered, so perhaps that accounted for her lack of courtesy. He gave Miss Townsend a warm smile; Percy did as well.

"Have you noticed the view from our west window, Lord Harcourt?" Lady Ariel inquired politely after a few minutes of conversation. She turned to Sir Henry to add, "We have a pleasant view of Harcourt Hall from here. Come, I will show you," she said, returning her attention to Jordan.

She rose and Jordan followed, bemused at what he believed to be a ploy to get him alone. Maintaining a discreet separation, they walked to the indicated window to gaze off to the west.

"You found something in the field?" she asked quietly.

"Your aunt employs someone to spy on me, perhaps?" He stiffened. Was this a clue to whoever murdered his cousin?

"I enjoy viewing the countryside, and I confess I was watching you. I have a glass in my room. It is directly above and over one room from here, so while I cannot see your house very well, I can view that field. I thought you might be going out to investigate where your cousin was killed, and I was right. What did you find?"

Ariel studied the man at her side. *Was he angry because she had been watching him?* She was allowed to go out so rarely—what else could she do to know what was going on in the world? He looked fiercely serious. Ariel decided she had gone beyond the pale when he suddenly cleared his throat and smiled at her. She smiled back, relieved he was not truly angry. "Well?"

He succinctly explained what had been discovered. He gave her a significant look when he revealed the finding of the lead ball.

"Ahhh," she breathed. "I had a feeling that there was something odd. How did you happen to spy the ball? I have walked that area a number of times and have not seen it."

"Actually, I tripped over Prince and braced my hand on the tree. It was then the ball came to my notice."

Ariel chuckled, as she supposed he intended. She appreciated being given facts. So often men considered women unworthy of confidence. *He really was nice if somewhat dashing, not at all like Ivor.* She thought his well-cut coat of corbeau superfine and the biscuit breeches understated elegance. He needed no padding and wore his fine garments with an air of excellent breeding. She rarely saw a gentleman of his physique, particularly one so handsome.

"Is something amiss? I trust I have not upset you with the information?"

He looked so anxious Ariel hastily put him at ease. "No, nothing you said upset me. Something else came to mind. I should like to see that tree."

"Ariel, dear girl, ring for Cummins to serve us refreshments." To Sir Henry, Miss Maitland added, "I am so fortunate to have such a comfortable situation here. Dear Ariel is the best of nieces, and Stafford Court is all one might ask for a home."

Sir Henry dutifully looked about him and nodded. "I must confess it is quite up to snuff. The grounds and the outside of the house appear in splendid shape, no doubt due to your careful interest, ma'am."

Miss Maitland tittered again, a becoming pink tingeing her cheeks.

"Mercy," Ariel whispered to Lord Harcourt, "I have never seen dear Aunt in such a flurry."

Ariel did as instructed, then allowed Lord Harcourt to seat her, thinking how polished he was, how gentleman-like in his manners. *Why couldn't it have been someone like him who had sought her out rather than his cousin? Lord Harcourt indicated he had no desire to look for a wife. Why? He was personable, had a fine estate, and possessed enough money for two men.* That she had previously declared she also would never want to marry she quite forgot.

"Ariel, will you pour tea for us?" Miss Maitland cooed.

Giving her aunt a wary glance, Ariel performed her hostess duties correctly. If nothing more, she wished to show Sir Henry that Miss Maitland was a proper teacher.

Celia and Mr. Ponsonby had drawn their chairs close to the table where the tea tray had been placed so that Ariel was able to serve them easily. She rose to offer Sir Henry his tea, and as she bent over to hand him his cup was startled to see his gaze linger on the neckline of her gown. It was not high, but not so low as to cause reproach.

Puzzled, she retraced her steps, offering tea to Lord Harcourt last because he was next to her and she did not want to hint they should talk more about the lead ball and the tree.

"Do you wish sugar, Lord Harcourt?" she asked, adding softly, "or a ride in the morning?"

"Indeed, precisely what I wish," he replied, barely repressing a shudder as she poised a lump of sugar over his cup. It seemed to go in, but instead found its way to her cup.

"Thank you," Jordan said, heartfelt in his appreciation. He wasn't one much for sweets and liked his tea with only a dash of milk. When he observed the others resuming conversation, he lifted his cup to his mouth and softly said, "Nine?"

"Nine," Lady Ariel replied with equal caution.

They finished the tea and tiny cakes, which were most unlike Simnel's more elegant offerings. Then Jordan rose, reluctantly followed by Percy. Neither gentleman would ever overstay when paying an afternoon call.

"Miss Maitland, thank you for the charming visit and the excellent tea. It was a pleasure to meet you, Sir Henry." Jordan bowed politely, waiting for the other man to reply.

"Well, I daresay you will see me here and about. I am staying at the Rose and Crown in the village. Neat and clean and the food seems most agreeable. I intend to renew my acquaintance with my dear friend, Miss Maitland."

The room was so silent one could hear with clarity footsteps far down the hall beyond the room.

"How lovely," Lady Ariel exclaimed. "I feel certain that my aunt will be happy to visit with you."

Feeling that nothing he said could possibly top Sir Henry's announcement, Jordan bowed to Miss Maitland. Percy followed suit after murmuring something to Miss Townsend.

Lady Ariel walked with them to the door, taking the opportunity to repeat, "Nine, remember," in a soft voice.

"I will not forget, I assure you. The same place?"

She nodded silently.

The two men left the house, walking around toward the stable while looking about the grounds.

"Odd, that Cummins didn't order our horses brought around," Percy mused.

"He was nowhere to be seen when we decided to leave. Besides, I want to get a look at the stables. And I would like to know if everyone working here now was here when Ivor was killed."

"I say!" Percy cried, much struck. It totally distracted him from thoughts of the charming Miss Townsend.

Chapter Four

The only one around the stables was a sober chap who gave Jordan and Percy suspicious looks when they appeared at the doors to the main stable block. All was neat and proper from what Jordan could see in a brief look.

"Our horses?" Jordan said politely.

"Cummins sent no order for them. Sorry. I'll get them at once. Prime bits of blood and bone, they are."

"You have served the Earl of Stafford for many years?" Percy asked casually. "Never met the man, but Miss Maitland seems agreeable."

"As to that, Lady Ariel is the one who is agreeable around here. The earl is away from home. Likes to ride, she does, when the old dragon allows it."

"So you have been here a long time?" Jordan said with quiet persistence.

"Indeed, milord. I have a couple of lads working with me, but I'm the head groom. Weems at your service." He led forth Jordan's horse, then returned for Percy's.

"Do you have any trouble keeping the lads who help you?" Percy wanted to know.

"Had a chap take off not long after your cousin was kilt, milord," Weems said to Jordan. "Unsettled lad. Said as how he was going to go to London to seek his fortune."

"I see. A local lad? One of the parish boys?"

"Aye. He worked for the Townsends afore he came here. As I said, he was a restive sort."

Exchanging a look with Percy, Jordan thanked the groom for his services, and the pair left, cutting through the back of the land until they reached the high pasture on Harcourt land; where they cantered on to the Hall.

"Perhaps you would not mind too much if I asked you to pay a call on the Townsends, perhaps mouse about in the stables and see if you can learn anything about the lad who left there to go to Stafford?"

"No trouble at all, old man," Percy said with a wide grin. "Just say the word and I'm gone."

"I suspected as much. Perhaps tomorrow?"

"Wonder how the girls will fare with that popinjay caller, Sir Henry Banks?" Percy mused.

"Miss Maitland is the object of his desires, I feel certain. I wonder what is up his sleeve?" Jordan dismounted, handing the reins to Peachum.

"You are becoming suspicious of everyone, I think."

"Not everyone, just those who do things that are not logical. With all those from whom he might choose, why does Sir Henry decide to visit this particular spinster? I should very much like to know. We shall have to see what Lady Ariel and Miss Townsend learn, if anything."

Ariel rejoined Celia, choosing a chair some distance away from the sofa where her aunt sat conversing with Sir Henry. She gave the pair a thoughtful look, then turned to Celia, long her dearest friend and confidante.

"Perhaps this is a fortuitous happening. Sir Henry is staying in the village, and unless I am greatly wrong, he means to call on Aunt Maitland often. I believe that might be a very nice thing," Ariel reflected.

"I should think your aunt has been lonely here. Not that you are not the best of company, but she rarely sees anyone else, does she?" Celia also gazed thoughtfully at the animated pair deep into reminiscences.

"She was agreeable to our new neighbor, Lord Harcourt," Ariel reminded.

"I rather like his friend," Celia said shyly. "He may not have a title, but Aunt Susan informs me that he is quite wealthy. She told Mama." Cecil gave Ariel an impish grin. "Mama always listens when Aunt Susan tells her the latest from the London papers and what she has gleaned from the gossip she hears. My Aunt Susan goes everywhere and has a prodigious memory."

"How fortunate for you. I believe Mr. Ponsonby was quite taken with you."

"Never before have I been glad my first name is Patience!"

The girls stifled their amusement with difficulty. When they received an admonishing throat clearing from Miss Maitland, the two excused themselves to stroll in the gardens. Looking happy to see them go, Miss Maitland devoted her attention to her gentleman caller, her first in many, many years.

Once free of the house, Ariel led Celia away to the west and through the wooded path to the edge of the main garden. From there they could see the Harcourt pasturage in the distance.

"Is that where the previous Lord Harcourt died?" Celia asked in a hushed voice.

"Yes, it is. I watched earlier to see the new lord find a lead ball. It was embedded in an oak not far from where my late betrothed landed when he fell. I cannot call him Ivor as does Lord Harcourt. I wonder what *his* given name might be? I heard Mr. Ponsonby call him Jordan. I thought that was a river in the Bible."

"Well, according to Aunt Susan, Lord Harcourt was plain Mr. Jordan Robards before your Ivor died after his grandmother had gone aloft. Rumor has it that he lost his heart to the girl one of his cousins married."

"Who was this cousin?" Ariel asked, her curiosity growing by the moment.

"The Marquess of Torrington! I must say, Lord Harcourt does not look like he is wearing the willow. He acts quite normal in all respects. Perhaps Mr. Ponsonby would know?" Celia slanted a look at her dearest friend.

"I do not suppose we ought to inquire about something so personal," Ariel said hesitantly. She truly wanted to know. "If he is mourning the loss of a beautiful girl, he most certainly wouldn't take a second look at anyone else."

The girls turned about in time to see Sir Henry's rather dashing gig jogging along the avenue to the main road that ran to the village.

"Is that what they call a whiskey?" Celia whispered as though someone might hear her and disapprove of her query.

"I believe it is, although I'm no authority. You will have to ask Aunt Susan!" Ariel said with a mischievous grin.

Chuckling at this witticism, the girls returned to the house and entered to seek out Miss Maitland.

"Did you girls have a pleasant walk?" Aunt Maitland said when they found her in the entry.

"Indeed, ma'am. How nice that an old friend has come to call on you," Celia said.

"Will he be in the area very long?" Ariel wondered, thinking that Sir Henry was what Aunt Susan would call an old dandy.

"So he said. We must give an entertainment for him while he is here. Perhaps a musical evening? Or maybe cards would be better. There are not many who are musical, and I feel certain Ariel would not want to play for an hour!" Miss Maitland appeared to be in a quandary.

"We could have a dancing party. I feel certain that Papa would not mind were we to hire a few musicians to play for us. I should like that very much, I think." Ariel exchanged a significant glance with Celia.

Her wish was not to be discussed, for Miss Maitland gasped in dismay and stiffened as she looked out of the narrow window in the entry.

"Oh, dear. Here comes the rector. I fear we are . . . that is, we must welcome him, girls." A flustered Miss Maitland returned to the drawing room after a few words with Cummins, who had materialized from the rear of the house.

Resigned to a lecture on something or other, the two girls slowly made their way to the drawing room.

"I would rather it was anyone else," Celia whispered.

"He means well, however. Recall that the gossipy Miss Vipont is always made welcome," Ariel added as the rector was heard in the entry. He entered the room, bowing to Aunt Maitland, then to Ariel, and lastly to Celia.

"Ladies, what a splendid afternoon. Although this time of year it is rare not to have a lovely day. And I always say that even if it rains, it is a blessing from God sent to improve the crops. Cannot have apples and hops without the rain. I believe

I saw a stranger heading toward the village from this direction." He turned to Miss Maitland to continue, "He must have called in here, as who else around here would entertain a gentleman of his magnificence?" Such blatant fishing was not unusual with the rector. After all, if one did not seek the truth, it was likely that one might make errors in conversation. He never called his conversation gossip.

"Sir Henry Banks did call here not so long ago," Miss Maitland confessed with a hint of a smile. "He is staying in the village for a time, I believe. We were just saying that we must have a party while he is here. One so seldom has an excuse to entertain on a grand scale."

"Grand scale!" The rector seized upon these momentous words and smiled thinly. "I imagine there is no harm in an entertainment here at home, although I rather doubt one should consider doing any entertaining on a grand scale. True, it is not as though Lady Ariel is wearing black gloves, but still . . ." He made a sad face.

Ariel did not like the little look he darted her way. She had not wished to be engaged to the previous Lord Harcourt in the first place. There was no law that ordered one to wear mourning for a betrothed, especially one of such brief duration. She had not argued with Aunt when she decided that mourning wasn't necessary.

"No, indeed." Miss Maitland nodded with assurance. "I insisted that Lady Ariel did not require black gloves or any other paraphernalia of mourning. Surely you, of all people, would agree that an engagement lasting but a week is scarcely requiring the sort of mourning a wife might don?" She gave the rector a dismayed look that defied him to disagree. "Perhaps one of these days a suitor of whom we may all approve will happen along."

"I still say it would be most fitting if she were to marry the new Lord Harcourt," Mr. Lytton insisted. "That is the most proper thing for her to do. It would still any gossip that lingers."

"I was unaware that gossip was 'lingering' regarding my niece, Mr. Lytton," Miss Maitland said, her back rigid with annoyance.

Seemingly unaware he was causing displeasure, Mr. Lytton plunged on. "Why, it is talked about from one end of the parish to the other. The belief is that Lady Ariel will be on the shelf if she does not marry soon, and who better than Lord Harcourt, the heir to his cousin? It is deemed most appropriate by one and all."

Ariel looked on this pronouncement with barely concealed disdain. She turned to Celia, who gave her a look of commiseration.

Miss Maitland swelled to majestic proportions and said, "Well, I think it a lot of nonsense, and I wish you would explain to all those gossips that I have no intention of putting Lord Harcourt in such a position as you describe. It could only annoy him to hear it again, sir." She gave Mr. Lytton her haughtiest stare, then unbent to politely offer tea, which he eagerly accepted.

Ariel wondered who might be the "someone properly suitable" that she would be allowed to marry. *What a pity Papa did not come home from India.* Ariel had a feeling that he would not agree with Aunt Maitland's estimation of who a properly suitable gentleman would be. Not that Ariel had the slightest desire to marry Lord Harcourt. Not in the least!

When Mr. Lytton left Stafford Place, he headed immediately for Harcourt Hall. It was clear to any who might have been interested that Mr. Lytton had a new mission in life—to see Lady Ariel Brandon established as the new Lady Harcourt. As far as he could see, it was the only proper way out for everyone, and so he repeated to the various ladies of the parish time and again.

Surprisingly, Lord Harcourt and Mr. Shirley were in the library rather than out on the estate. Mr. Ponsonby lurked in the corner, but Mr. Lytton ignored him.

"Good day, gentlemen. I trust I find you in good heart?" Mr. Lytton took a step back as he noticed an incredibly ugly dog that had wandered out from behind the desk to growl at him.

"Do not mind Prince there," Lord Harcourt said to the caller. "He is a good dog . . . or will be eventually," he added in an aside to Mr. Shirley.

"Ah, yes, I am sure. What is it?" Mr. Lytton asked hesitantly.

"Purebred bloodhound," Mr. Ponsonby said gleefully. "Fine dog. Why, he can track anything."

Mr. Lytton ignored that gentleman to concentrate on his lordship. "I have just been to call at Stafford Court."

"Indeed? Won't you sit down, sir. Perhaps a glass of wine?" Lord Harcourt was not behind in his hospitality.

Conversation was general for a few minutes, and then Mr. Lytton sailed into his new favorite topic.

"Poor Lady Ariel," he began, going on to relate the gossip floating about and concluding with a flourish. "Traditions are most important in the country."

"I was unaware of any gossip, Mr. Lytton. And as to there being a custom such as you have described, I suspect it is somewhat new and infrequently applied. I feel certain that something else will come along to supplant the gossip you claim abounds. In my experience it usually does," his lordship said smoothly. "I do not see I am under obligation to assume a betrothal to a girl I scarcely know just to please the tattlemongers. For all we know, Lady Ariel has taken me into a dislike. Besides, do you not agree that two parties ought to know each other somewhat before entering into marriage?" Lord Harcourt added as an extra argument in his favor, "It would seem a sensible arrangement."

"Well, her aunt seems to think there will be someone who will come up to scratch shortly. I cannot fathom who it might be—unless dear Miss Maitland has a surprise in store for us at her coming entertainment. A gentleman has called on her. He is, I believe, too old for Lady Ariel—from what little I could see of him in his carriage as we passed. I saw him on his way to the Rose and Crown. He drove a new caned whiskey. Dashing little carriage for a man his age, I should think. Perhaps this man, this Sir Henry Banks, she called him, knows of a gentleman worthy of our Lady Ariel?"

Jordan paused in the act of offering Mr. Lytton a glass of canary. He finished his task, then turned to give Mr. Shirley a significant look, raising his brows in an eloquent bit of pantomime.

"Have you made your rounds for the week, Mr. Lytton?" Mr. Shirley inquired. "I trust we do not keep you from completing them?"

"Oh, I am in no hurry. No hurry, at all," the rector said, oblivious to the dismayed looks shared by the others in the room. "I wish to discuss this most pressing need with the one who can most appropriately satisfy it. It would indeed be a sad day were Lady Ariel to wed the wrong man!"

When the matter of a proper gentleman for Lady Ariel had been discussed from one end to the other, Mr. Lytton finally rose from his chair, setting his empty glass on the sofa table with obvious regret. "I do hope that your Christian sense of duty will prevail upon you to do the proper thing, Lord Harcourt."

With that final word of pronouncement, Mr. Lytton bid them farewell and left the house, clambering into his aged carriage with surprising agility. Percy watched as he encouraged his equally aged nag into something that resembled a trot.

"By dash it, he is humming a happy tune after all the misery he has put us through," Percy said, sounding quite as grumpy as they all felt at that moment. Prince gave a bark of seeming agreement to that pronouncement.

"We learned that Miss Maitland intends to give some manner of entertainment," Jordan said. "Do you know anything about Sir Henry Banks, Percy? Name rings a bell somewhere, but I can't think what."

"Nor for me, either. Dash it all, poor Lady Ariel, to have that rector lecturing her every day of the week," Percy said as he poured himself a glass of claret. "I understand he goes there often to pay his respects. Although, why that is necessary is beyond me. Should be enough if he sees them on a Sunday." Percy took an appreciative sip of his wine and turned back to look out of the window once more. If he was keeping watch to see if the Townsend carriage might be seen as it went back to the Townsend house, he said nothing to the others.

"What were the *exact* circumstances of the betrothal that has captured the thoughts of the parish, Shirley?" Jordan asked, pouring a glass of claret for the steward, then one for himself. It wasn't as though a fellow got dry while the rector was calling—the chap talked enough for two sets of teeth. Jordan felt in need of a restorative and expected his steward did as well.

"I do not precisely know the details other than your cousin was able to get Lady Ariel alone and they were found by none other than Mr. Lytton. He lost no time in telling Miss Maitland of the impropriety. Were he not a parson, one would think he relishes sinful behavior."

"It gives him something to sermonize about," Jordan said with a wry smile.

"Well, Miss Maitland was fit to be tied."

"And soon after, my cousin departed this earth. It stretches all belief that it was accidental."

"Got a point there," Percy agreed from across the room, indicating that while he might be watching out of the window, he was listening with both ears to what was being said. "Perhaps it is as you said before, an irate father seeking justice his own way."

Mr. Shirley eased back in his chair, looking thoughtful. "I believe Lady Ariel has a sad time of it with her aunt. The old lady is most solicitous of her niece, but does keep her rather cloistered. The girl possesses a fortune even before her father might die." At Jordan's start and Percy's whistle, Mr. Shirley went on, "You did not know? She presently has an income of at least ten thousand pounds a year. Once her father dies, she will be a countess in her own right and inherit Stafford Court and the fortune he has amassed. The man has an incredible talent for making money," Mr. Shirley concluded. "A regular nabob, I'm told."

"I sense a 'but' in there somewhere," Jordan said shortly.

"But I think she is unhappy, kept at Stafford Court with few friends. Celia Townsend and her sister Jane are the only ones permitted to associate with her. If the rector is correct when he says Miss Maitland intends to have some manner of entertainment, it will be a first since I have been in this area. You might say Miss Maitland is more than somewhat withdrawn."

"Lady Ariel seems no green girl!" Percy protested.

"Perhaps not in some ways, but she is an exceeding protected young woman, however. I pity her." Mr. Shirley picked up the ledger they had been studying before the rector arrived.

Jordan nodded agreement to resuming work on estate matters. His thoughts lingered on Lady Ariel—the princess in the wood-and-glass prison. All she needed was a tower to make her imprisonment complete. Miss Maitland seemed agreeable, but she exerted tight control over her niece. *While that was likely proper, the girl ought to get about more.* Frowning at the thought of the young woman so utterly under that old dragon's control, he had a hard time concentrating on the ledger before him. Something ought to be done for her, but what, he didn't know.

At Stafford Court Ariel paced back and forth near the window. She felt restless, wanting more than her narrow life offered. How would she ever find a husband if she never went anywhere or entertained?

"I have had quite enough of my own company. I should very much like to have a group to converse with on occasion. And something more to do!" Ariel gave her aunt a mutinous look. "Poor Celia must be bored to flinders with so little to do when here."

"We have company from time to time," her aunt insisted.

"The Townsends and the rector! I must say, Sir Henry is at least a new face. What do you fear from a few new guests, dear Aunt? I can scarcely be kidnapped from my own home!" Ariel found herself blinking back tears. She had not repined her cloistered existence before. The arrival of the new Lord Harcourt had awakened her to the lack of diversity in her life.

"But you must be protected my dear."

Ariel grimaced. "I believe I will order a billiards table. It will be a surprise for Papa when he comes home."

Miss Maitland turned an affronted look on her niece. "You do not need a billiards table! Why, it is a game for men. What has happened to you? You have always obeyed me in the past. And what makes you fancy your father will like such a thing?"

"If I learn how to master the game, he will like to play with me. And it will give me something to learn," Ariel concluded before marching off to find the steward. She intended to send off an order for the billiards table before Aunt could rescind it. With a feline smile of pleasure at besting her aunt, who undoubtedly meant well but suffocated her, Ariel explained what was wanted to Mr. Greenwood.

The steward looked slightly taken aback, but was not about to deny so sweetly requested an item, particularly if it was to be a surprise for his lordship. He agreed to expedite the order and said he thought he knew just the sort of table the earl would appreciate and would have it delivered at once.

Satisfied her wish would be swiftly carried out, Ariel slipped from the office wing and up to her room via the back stairs without encountering her aunt.

Once there, she went to the window that looked toward the Harcourt pasturage. *Why did her mind turn to him? True, he was handsome and somewhat dashing, and had polished manners.* She thought she had seen something deeper in him, however. He did not have his late cousin's shallowness. He seemed genuinely interested in those he met. He might associate with the best people and come from a fine family, but he exhibited concern for his friend's feelings. Witness how he had accepted that poor dog when she suspected he would never have selected such for himself. How she knew that to be true, she couldn't say, but of this she was convinced.

She did not desire pity from him . . . yet she was not certain what she did wish. Did she have time to find out? Something about the arrival of Sir Henry disturbed her. She was happy that Aunt Maitland had a gentleman friend, but he might influence her to select someone to marry Ariel. She felt uneasy. Things had changed.

Then Ariel sat down on the edge of her bed with a thump. What would happen to her should Aunt marry Sir Henry first? Surely, they would wish to live elsewhere? Perhaps a better companion might be found? Not that Aunt was dreadful. It was just that she thought Ariel needed to be kept on a pedestal. Ariel had tolerated it in the past. Now, she found it greatly hampering and extremely dull.

In the meanwhile, Sir Henry Banks found himself well set up in a pleasant room at the Rose and Crown. He wrote a letter and requested of his genial host that it be mailed. He sauntered about in the few shops the town boasted, asking polite ques-

tions about those who lived in the area and making small purchases, the sort that pleased the shopkeepers while enabling
him to pass the time of day with a good reason for lingering.

He appeared well satisfied with all he learned. In his room,
he rubbed his hands together with the air of one who has a
great deal to please him. He had plans, and it appeared he was
well on his way to securing the sort of future he felt he de-
served. Miss Maitland was the key, and she looked about to
fall into his arms like a ripe plum.

At nine the following morning, Ariel rode forth from the
stables, informing Weems that he might stay well to the rear as
she had a wish to be alone.

She rode in the direction of the main road, looking forward
to a sensible discussion with Lord Harcourt. She must convince him of the need for care as well as the necessity of digging deeper into the cause of his cousin's death. She brushed
off her jacket with the hope she looked her best—as best as
possible for one who had to depend on fashion illustrations
and a local mantua-maker. She was quite ready to meet his
lordship.

If he remembered they were to meet.

She need not have worried. Apparently he had looked for
her, joining her at once when she met the main road.

"Good morning," she said with a modest smile, admiring
the sight of him sitting astride his magnificent horse.

"Good morning to you. May I say you look most comely
this fine morning? Alone?"

"Weems is somewhere back there," she replied, giving a
vague wave in the general direction her groom ought to be.

"You have something you wish to discuss," Lord Harcourt
rightly guessed.

"For one, I am curious about Sir Henry Banks. Can you tell
me anything about him?" Ariel asked, suspecting this was not
quite proper, but wanting to learn regardless.

"Both Percy and I have been trying to place the fellow, and
it hasn't come to us as yet, but we have not given up. I know I
have seen him someplace in London. Where has yet to jog my
mind."

"Well," Ariel said dryly, "I do hope your mind gets jogged soon. I have the strangest feeling that he means to pay court to my aunt. There was something in his smile that was too pat if you know what I mean."

"Do not think you are foolish to ask such a question. I had the same reaction. In fact, I believe you have jogged my memory. As I recall, there was some talk about Lady Banks at the time of her death. It was sudden and unexpected. They had not been married long, and I recollect her family was not pleased with her alliance. However, Sir Henry is a most charming gentleman, one the ladies seem to appreciate."

"I do not," murmured Ariel.

The topic was dropped, but she continued to wonder what was in store for her. The entertainment her aunt promised could mean almost anything if it actually came to pass, considering how rare it was for them to entertain. Aunt said it was because the earl, Ariel's father, was away. Improper, Aunt said.

"Aunt intends to have a party, although I do not know when. I would like you to attend. Mr. Ponsonby as well. My friend Celia was most impressed by him. He seems a charming gentleman, and I do not think he is one to toy with a young woman's affections. Am I right?" Ariel turned her face to study the man who rode at her side. He was smiling, and she felt better, somehow.

"No, I daresay Miss Townsend may be the recipient of Percy's attention. I cannot say how it will proceed, but he is a fine man and a proper gentleman. You need have no fears on her account."

"Good," Ariel responded. They rode into the village in pleasant accord, Ariel finding her escort to be the nicest gentleman she had ever met. That Celia might find a husband would cap things off splendidly.

Chapter Five

Stafford was a pretty village. Half-timbered houses lined the main road through the center of the village, their freshly painted trim giving the feeling of prosperity. It was a charming place, with a very small market house in the center of the village green. A few chickens wandered about the area, dodging horses and people with accustomed facility. Along the street a blacksmith had a shop, its signboard remarkable for the exquisite ironwork used as supports. Beyond was a chair maker, his sign illustrating his craft with a simple Windsor chair. Further along a woman sat plaiting straw before a small house. It was a tranquil scene, and Jordan wished he might feel more at ease.

It would not have been proper for Ariel to join Lord Harcourt within the Rose and Crown for any reason other than a cloudburst, so they merely rode past the building, giving it a casual inspection. It looked neat and clean, the sort of inn that had lavender-scented sheets, a good mutton at dinner, and a fine cheese for afters.

"So you think Sir Henry is insincere?" Jordan wished to know. The gossip he recalled regarding the death of Lady Banks was too vague to be of help. Surely the man was nothing more than a lonely widower who desired the company of a pleasant woman. What was wrong with that? Many men wished to be married, seeking a wife when their previous one had gone aloft, perhaps quite soon. So why was he, and the others troubled?

"Indeed, I do wonder about his intentions," she replied, sounding uneasy.

Jordan looked about him as they rode into the heart of the village toward the green.

"Perhaps I am merely being silly to worry," Lady Ariel replied, unknowingly echoing his thoughts. "Oh, there is Miss Townsend about to go into the village shop. Her sister, Jane, is with her. I should like to speak with Celia for a moment, my lord." She gave Jordan a hesitant little smile as though she quite expected him to growl his displeasure.

More than willing to pause, Jordan obligingly reined in Fire King and dismounted, then assisted Lady Ariel from her mount, a docile little mare called Blossom.

Miss Townsend waited for them to one side of the door to the village shop. Jane studied Jordan with open curiosity. She said nothing, apparently shy but most observant.

From a quick look at the interior, Jordan surmised it was one of those establishments where one could buy almost anything needed from needles and thread to a packet of tea and a pound of cheese.

"I need some ribands for my blue sprigged muslin. Are you looking for anything in particular?" Miss Townsend inquired with a discreet glance at Jordan.

"I am," Jordan interposed. "I should like to find some manner of basket to use as a bed for my newly acquired dog."

"I have yet to see him," Lady Ariel said with a twinkle in her pretty gray eyes, "but he sounds like an amazing animal."

"Well, I can hardly say he is much to look at, but Percy bought him for me, and I shouldn't like to disappoint my good friend. Besides the dog . . . well, grows on one."

"How kind you are," Miss Townsend said. "I do not think there is a basket of that sort to be found here. But I know of a man who weaves baskets for those who wish one. If you like, I can give him your order. How big is the dog?"

"Big. And likely to grow bigger from the size of his paws. I have been told a bloodhound can weigh up to one hundred pounds, so that may give your basket maker some idea as to what I need."

Nodding her neatly bonneted head, Celia Townsend entered the store with Lady Ariel at her side, Jane behind. Jordan found a post not far away where he could hitch the horses, tossing a coin to a lad so he might keep an eye on them while Jordan joined the ladies.

As he entered the store, the clerk was measuring some riband for Miss Townsend while Lady Ariel examined a bolt of white cambric. Jane had found several items on her list and stood waiting her turn to be served. Jordan wandered about the shop and turned when the tinkle of a bell signified that another person had entered.

"Miss Vipont," Lady Ariel said politely to the greatest gossip around, "how pleasant to see you."

Iron gray curls peeped from beneath a remarkable crushed velvet bonnet. Her plump face beamed smiles on one and all, particularly Jordan.

"Do I have the pleasure of seeing the new Lord of the Hall?" she asked in the loud voice of one who does not hear very well.

"Harcourt, ma'am," Jordan instantly replied with a bow before Lady Ariel could introduce him. He anticipated her polite act would join him with Lady Ariel in the gossip's eyes, and that was something to avoid. "I am pleased to make the acquaintance of another of my new neighbors."

"Down from London. I trust we shall see you for a time?" She peered at him with inquisitive eyes, planting herself before him so it would be impossible to move around her. "And does Lady Harcourt join you?"

"I intend to make the Hall my home, but alas there is no Lady Harcourt. It will be some time before I will have the leisure to spend in looking for a wife."

"Really?" She smiled again, looking like a satisfied pigeon at a spill of grain. "Your cousin, the late Lord Harcourt, was not here long. You do not look like him."

"So I have been told. My late cousin and I are vastly different people, not that I do not admire his taste. Lady Ariel is all that is charming." Jordan bowed in Lady Ariel's direction, taking note that she blushed in a fetching manner.

"I shall have half an ell of this cambric, Mrs. Fitz," she said to the shopkeeper, turning away so Jordan could no longer catch sight of that pleasing blush. He had never thought of young misses as being so appealing, yet there was something about Lady Ariel that drew him. Perhaps it was the thought that she needed someone to champion her?

"Making new handkerchiefs, I'll wager," Miss Vipont opined. "Now, that is a fine task for a young lady." She turned her attention back to Jordan. "You approve of our village, your lordship?" she said, attacking Jordan unexpectedly.

"Er . . . very much. I daresay it is one of the more pleasant villages in this part of the world," Jordan replied, knowing full well that he had not the slightest idea if he was correct in his estimation.

"Think so myself," the spinster declared, seeming pleased. She selected a small bag of peppermints, which Jordan insisted upon paying for much to her confusion and delight.

When Lady Ariel, Miss Townsend, Jane Townsend, and Jordan left the well-stocked shop, he waited to see what they would say.

"Well, you have put the cat among the pigeons, for certain, my lord," Miss Townsend said, a smile lighting her eyes.

"Indeed," Lady Ariel added. "You have no time to look for a wife? You are busy, indeed."

"But you think that Lady Ariel is charming? Fie, sirrah," Miss Townsend teased. "What confusion you have created!"

"Mr. Shirley thought it a good idea to mention such a thing to Miss Vipont. I gather she a bit of a gossip?"

The young ladies exchanged a look, then smiled.

"Indeed, she is," Miss Townsend said. "She will be in a rare quandary as you gave her a bit of gossip to share, then compounded it by being excessively kind when you bought her peppermints, a favorite treat. I do believe that by nightfall there will be not a single woman, young or old, who will not be informed that you are not in want of a wife, but that you are terribly gallant. It is really too bad of you, not to be wife-hunting when there are so many hopeful ladies here about."

A frown crossed Lady Ariel's face, and she moved toward her horse, her neatly wrapped parcel in hand. "Perhaps we ought to return? I shall drive over later to visit with you, Celia," Lady Ariel said when she paused by her mount, taking her reins from where they had been looped.

Jordan promptly assisted Lady Ariel into her saddle, tossed another coin to the eager lad who had kept an eye on the horses, then mounted Fire King.

"I trust I shall see you both later," Jordan said to the Townsend girls. "Do let me know what you learn of the basket for Prince, please, Miss Townsend. At present the dog sleeps on top of my feet, and I assure you that he is a heavyweight and likely to grow more so quickly at the rate he eats."

Miss Townsend chuckled, promising to do what she might, then marched off in the direction of her home with her sister trailing behind.

Jordan and Lady Ariel rode silently for a time, passing the church, where they would attend services on the coming Sunday. He wondered what theme the rector would use to welcome the new baron to the community.

"You are fortunate that you have so agreeable a friend," Jordan said as they meandered from the village on the road that led to the Hall and Stafford Court.

"As do you," she responded quietly. "Did Mr. Shirley truly suggest you tell Miss Vipont that you are not in want of a wife?"

Jordan decided not to evade the topic as he might have wished. "Yes, he thought it might be wise."

"I see." She was silent for a time, then nodded. "I agree with him. It will keep the spinsters in great hopes and not tie you to anyone in particular."

"Am I to be the object of the matrimonial bazaar, Lady Ariel? Vexing, indeed." Jordan flashed her a grin, enjoying the smile she returned. She certainly was a fetching little thing, he mused. She rode well and handled her mare with a sensitive touch. She always spoke in a pleasant voice. Her concern for her aunt was commendable, especially since Miss Maitland had confined her niece so rigorously. But then, the responsibility of keeping an heiress from the charms of a fortune hunter might create problems he'd not considered before.

"Every unmarried man must be the object of such interest, unless he is an utter toad," she said. "I feel certain that Mr. Ponsonby will also attract attention."

"Actually, it would not be so bad a thing for Percy. He is well fixed financially, and I suspect he would be inclined to settle down if he could find the right woman—with a name that commences with the letter P, of course." He shared an amused look with his companion.

"Like Patience, perhaps? A pretty, not-so-patient prize, I assure you. She is the best of friends and has a delightful temperament. We have been close since infancy."

"Percy intended to ride over to the Townsends today, but I do not know when. We are not under the other's feet, if you know what I mean. He is always free to wander off where he might please, as am I. He is the sort of guest one likes—he can entertain himself."

"I wonder when Sir Henry means to call on my aunt again. For he will, I am certain of it," she said firmly, glancing back at Weems, who trailed behind them. Behind him the road led back to the village and the inn where Sir Henry stayed.

"I suppose so. I imagine his intentions are honorable. I cannot think Miss Maitland would countenance any other sort!"

Upon reaching the avenue that led into Harcourt Hall, Ariel at last spoke her mind. "There is something I must say. Please . . . do take great care for your safety. Your cousin died under odd circumstances from what little I know. I should not wish, well . . . that is, do take care," she concluded, blushing and feeling a trifle forward.

"I thank you for your concern, my lady," Lord Harcourt said, giving her a searching look before they parted.

Ariel rode slowly, musing over the past hour. When she approached the house, she observed Sir Henry's caned whiskey before the front, one of the grooms standing in attendance by it.

"Has he been here long?" she queried as she dismounted.

"Thirty minutes, perhaps."

"I see. Thank you," she said to Weems, who had followed directly after her to the village and back. Taking the trailing skirt of her habit in hand, she entered the house, ignoring Cummins when he poked his head out of his little room at the back of the hall. He disappeared, returning to polishing the silver, no doubt.

She walked softly up the stairs. At the top she paused, hating herself for her suspicions, yet wanting to know what was going on. If Sir Henry had remained here for half an hour, this was more than a polite call. She listened as Sir Henry spoke.

"My dear Miss Maitland, allow me to assure you that I know just the young man for your purpose. Oswald Dudley is heir to Viscount Stone and as complacent as you might desire. He is short of money, but stands to inherit some eventually. His problem is that the present viscount is hale and hearty and likely to live to a ripe old age."

"But he comes of a good family?" Miss Maitland inquired.

"None finer. The chap is pleasant, if a mite quiet. He is what you might call biddable. Needing money sometimes has that effect. He could be here at once, for he's staying close by."

"So, this compliant, mild man you think would do for our purpose? It would be a disaster were we to be wrong."

Ariel wondered at her aunt's insistence, as well as what this "purpose" was that required a man who was docile. *Biddable? That word was usually used to describe the type of woman who wouldn't say boo to a goose. Who would wish for such insipid character in a man?*

"Allow me to write him a letter inviting him to join me. If I offer to pay his shot, I would wager he would be here in a trice. Once you meet him you can decide if he isn't all I have promised."

"Yes, Sir Henry, I think you should write at once. I confess I am increasingly uneasy." The click of a cup on a saucer was heard as well as the rustle of Aunt's dress. She must be rising from the sofa where she liked to sit, Ariel realized.

A chair scraped over the floor, and someone, likely Sir Henry, could be heard moving. Thinking quickly, Ariel tiptoed partway down the stairs, then turned to walk up, making a bit of noise as she did.

"Ariel, is that you, dear?" Miss Maitland called.

"Indeed, Aunt. I found the cambric I wished so that now I can make those handkerchiefs for Papa."

"Such a good girl," Miss Maitland enthused, "always wishing to make something for the earl." She appeared at the door to the drawing room, Sir Henry immediately behind her. The pair did not look like conspirators.

"Good day, Sir Henry," Ariel said quietly, wondering what it was that this Oswald Dudley person was supposed to do. If only she dared ask—but that would reveal she had been eavesdropping.

"I shall see you later, Frederica," Sir Henry said as he bowed over her hand. With a polite nod to Ariel, he walked down the steps, looking quite at home.

"Frederica, Aunt? But you allow no one to call you that," Ariel said softly once Sir Henry was out of the house. She was highly curious about this turn of events. What prompted the sudden closeness of two people who had not seen each other for many years?

"Fancy his remembering my Christian name after all this time. He says it is a beautiful name, poetic."

Ariel stared at her aunt as she drifted past and on up to the next floor, no doubt seeking her room. She was behaving like a young girl enthralled with a beau.

Somewhat dazed, Ariel slowly followed. She had an odd feeling about all this. Something was afoot, and she could not think it was for her good. It certainly gave her something to mull over.

Jordan considered his conversation with Lady Ariel as he strolled into the portion of the house given over to estate management. He could recall not one thing reprehensible about Sir Henry. So why did he share Lady Ariel's uneasiness?

"A good day, Harcourt?" Mr. Shirley said pleasantly as Jordan joined him in the office.

"Indeed. I met the redoubtable Miss Vipont, and I think I've found a source for a dog bed." That Lady Ariel had urged him to be careful he omitted.

"Good." Not particularly interested in the sleeping habits of a dog or the local gossip, Mr. Shirley offered the figures for the hops production, and the men discussed the improvements to be made to the oast houses.

"There is a new screen that I feel would aide in drying the hops," Mr. Shirley said. "It would give excellent ventilation, yet keep the smaller hops from falling through."

"Excellent. If we have it brought in now, all should be ready by harvest," Jordan replied. But his mind was not really on the matter. Rather, his thoughts returned to Lady Ariel and her worry over Sir Henry. *Was* there something peculiar about his sudden appearance and his attentions to Miss Maitland? It seemed quite plausible.

True, the gentleman claimed a long-ago friendship with Miss Maitland. Jordan could not explain why he was so troubled. Perhaps he merely felt that Lady Ariel was somehow threatened; yet that must be preposterous. From all accounts the woman was devoted to her niece.

"It strikes me as rather odd that Miss Maitland has not taken her niece to London for a Season, Shirley," he mused, his straying thoughts becoming evident to the man before him. "If her father has ample funds, money shouldn't be a problem. So why not?"

"I have wondered the same," Mr. Shirley admitted. "The girl is amiable from all accounts. Perhaps the aunt is not comfortable in Society?"

"I should very much like to know." Jordan turned at the sound of footsteps to see his friend approaching.

Percy wandered into the room. He looked at Jordan and shook his head. "Went over to the Townsend place. Tried to mouse about for any information on that young fellow who worked at Stafford Court for a time. I'm afraid I learned nothing of use. He's an orphan. Took off for a better job at Stafford and left there to go to London. Itchy feet, they said. Sorry."

"Well, you cannot make up what isn't." He turned back to his steward to resume the discussion. "What is the situation in the brew house?"

"Ale is good," Percy volunteered. "Quite tasty as a matter of fact. No problem there."

Jordan asked Mr. Shirley directly, "Vats in good repair. Supplies at the ready?"

Talk fell to the making of quality ale and beer. Although the brew-master would take charge, it didn't hurt to make sure all was as it should be. Jordan put aside the disturbing thoughts regarding Lady Ariel to concentrate on his newly acquired estate. There was so much to learn, and time simply flew by.

*   *   *

Ariel joined her aunt—now restored to something more resembling her usual self—at the nuncheon table.

"I believe we should have a nice evening party, my dear. Hiring a few musicians is an excellent idea. When say you we should have this party?" Aunt Maitland asked.

"Perhaps three weeks? It would give me time to have a new gown made. I should think you might like one as well. You would look very nice in a pretty rose India muslin."

"Do you think so? Perhaps I shall. It has been some time since I indulged in such."

"High time you did, then. I believe I would like a blue dress—perhaps a touch of lace. Everyone has seen what few gowns I possess. I'd like something fashionable."

"Do not think to tempt the new neighbor. He has made it plain that he does not seek a wife," Miss Maitland cautioned with a concerned look.

"I do not wish to tempt anyone at the moment, dear Aunt. When the right man comes along, I shall know, I feel certain." Ariel smiled, but her thoughts turned to this Mr. Dudley Sir Henry was to invite. Did her aunt think Ariel wanted a meek creature for a mate?

"You will marry the man selected for you or not at all, dear child." The firmness in Miss Maitland's voice brought a chill to Ariel.

"Surely you would never seek to marry me to a man I could not like?" Ariel studied her aunt's face, thinking that while she looked as sweet as sugar, there was an underlying steel in her, and it might be foolish to try to thwart her will.

"We shall see, shall we not?" And with those ominous words the conversation ceased.

The following Sunday everyone in the village attended services, gratifying the rector no end.

Jordan invited Mr. Shirley to join him in the Harcourt pew along with Percy. "Seems sinful to have so much space to myself when the other pews are bound to be crowded."

Mr. Shirley looked unsure, but at length accepted. He seemed unaccustomed to such courteous treatment, which made Jordan all the more determined that the intelligent and pleasant gentleman should spend more time with people who were assuredly his equals—if not in rank, in heritage.

The service went much as custom. If there had been a craning of necks when the new Lord Harcourt entered, that was understandable. The sermon was quite fine, as one might expect. Mr. Lytton did himself proud. He included a reference to the new member of the community, somehow connecting Lord Harcourt to the prodigal son, although how he could baffled most who actually listened.

Following divine service, Jordan made his way to where Lady Ariel stood with her aunt and Sir Henry Banks. *Dash it all, the chap had all the appearance of a decent fellow, a jolly good sort.* It annoyed Jordan that he retained this instinct about Banks, cautioning him.

"Good day, Lord Harcourt," Miss Maitland said with perfect courtesy.

"Good weather for the fruit trees, I suspect," Sir Henry added with a glance at the sky, where a few clouds drifted but not threatened.

Lady Ariel turned to face Jordan. "I am to inform you that Miss Townsend was able to see the basket maker and that the basket will await you as soon as that man can make it. Perhaps in a week."

"No doubt she might have conveyed the message to Percy," Jordan said with seeming disinterest in Lady Ariel. He had caught the annoyed glint in Miss Maitland's eyes. "I see that even now he is chatting with her and her mother." He gestured politely to where his friend animatedly conversed with two nicely garbed ladies.

"We are to have a party three weeks hence, my lord," Miss Maitland announced. "We would be pleased if you could attend."

Jordan thought that if anyone sounded reluctant to invite him to a party it was Miss Maitland. It was the sort of invitation one usually did not accept. "I would be very pleased to attend. I look forward to meeting more of the gentry about here."

"Miss Maitland and I will be celebrating our engagement," Sir Henry inserted with a fond look at her.

Lady Ariel gasped, stiffening as though receiving a blow. She obviously had not heard this bit of news before. She paled, clasping her hands before her. "How lovely, dear Aunt. I feel certain Papa will be most happy for you. I shall write to him at once."

Jordan wondered why Miss Maitland looked less than delighted at this offer from her niece.

"There is no need, dear girl. I will inform the earl when next I write him. I daresay he will wish to make some arrangements."

For what? Jordan wondered. Of course—if Miss Maitland married, she would wish to live with her husband. That would necessitate a new companion for Lady Ariel—unless she married. That must be what was meant, arrangements for a new companion, something Lady Ariel could not do.

Ariel stared at her aunt and Sir Henry. Was this what they had been conferring about the day she had tiptoed up the staircase to overhear an urgent conversation? *Married?*

"It is very sudden," she murmured, voicing her thoughts.

"There is little purpose in waiting at our age," her aunt pointed out.

Miss Vipont, apparently sensing that something momentous had occurred, came marching over. "Dear Miss Maitland," she observed, "and I believe this is Sir Henry Banks. How nice. And you look well today, Lady Ariel."

Ariel wondered if an announcement would be made or if Miss Vipont would be allowed to guess. Since it was not her place to say a thing about the coming marriage, she remained silent, only giving Lord Harcourt a worried look.

Mr. Ponsonby and Celia joined them at this point to chat amiably about the weather and the forthcoming party at Stafford.

Miss Vipont stood her ground, something like a determined hound with the scent of a fox in his lair. "You are enjoying our little village?" she asked Sir Henry.

"Indeed. I hope to make it my home. I have sold my estate and have been traveling about, looking for a place to begin anew. And then I remembered Miss Maitland. We knew each other well years ago when in London. It is a pity how often we lose track of friends over the years. I am happy to renew this particular friendship." He smiled at the woman at his side with warmth.

Miss Vipont took note of his comments and soon was on her way. Likely she would speculate on this particular item for weeks to come.

So, Ariel thought, the engagement was not to be general knowledge. She cared not one way or the other. She had to write to her father as soon as may be, though. It wasn't that she did not trust her aunt; it was rather that she wished him to know her opinions on her future from her own hand.

"I can see something has upset you," Celia murmured when they managed to stroll along the grass before the church and away from the others.

"You may as well know. Aunt is going to marry Sir Henry. He just announced it."

Celia darted a glance at the happy couple. "Good gracious! I cannot believe that it could be arranged so quickly. He has been here such a brief time! You do not look overjoyed, I fear."

Ariel took note of the question in those words and replied at once. "He is looking for a place to live. You do not suppose he plans to live with us at Stafford Court, do you? Surely he would prefer to have a place of his own? I can't think what Father would say to that arrangement. I shall write to him at once."

"Do you mail your own letters? Or do you hand them to Cummins?" Her blue eyes were anxious.

"Indeed, I give them to him." At Celia's frown, Ariel said, "You do not think she might destroy my letter? I doubt it. Why would she? On the other hand, it would not hurt to be safe. I will write tonight, and when you come to visit me tomorrow I can give it to you to post for me. Agreeable?"

"Assuredly. I confess I have not warmed to your aunt, although I know she has been devoted to your care all these many years." Celia gave Ariel an apologetic smile. "I cannot forgive her for denying you a Season."

"Indeed, she has been like a second mother. But I imagine she is not to everyone's liking." She looked back at the group clustered before the church. "We have three weeks to plan this party. I wonder what will happen between now and then?"

Chapter Six

Mr. Shirley entered the breakfast room on Monday morning to find his employer sitting at the far end of the table, looking more than a little disgruntled. Draped across his feet sprawled Prince, who seemed angelically unaware of any wrongdoing—such as slobbering on a newly polished pair of Hoby's best boots.

"How went the night?" Mr. Shirley inquired with caution, valiantly trying not to laugh.

"He believes my feet are toys provided for his amusement. I can scarcely move at night, and he will attack, even when I think him sound asleep—as I would like to be. One cautious move and he pounces."

"Let us hope that Miss Townsend can persuade that basket weaver to speed up the process." Mr. Shirley selected his morning meal, then sat some distance away from Jordan, as though to avoid sharing the hound.

"I asked Mrs. Longwood regarding some manner of pillow for the dog, and she merely gave me a strange look, then walked off muttering to herself. If needs be, I shall remove one of the pillows from my bed to place in that basket. Might as well, Prince seems to appropriate whatever he wants regardless."

"Well, and how is our dog this morning?" Percy asked cheerfully as he entered the room. He strode to the sideboard to select his food, apparently oblivious to the displeased expression on his friend's face.

"If he is partly yours, I wish you would take him for a night. My feet get rather numb by morning," Jordan said, sounding quite as annoyed as he looked.

"No, do they? Tell him 'move' and mean it. He should obey. Bloodhounds are supposed to be very smart dogs." With plate in hand, Percy edged onto a chair, then poured his morning coffee with a steady hand.

"I am of the opinion that Prince hasn't heard about that yet," Jordan grumbled.

"Prince," Percy commanded, "come."

The dog's floppy ears seemed to perk up. At any rate, he rose from his station across Jordan's boots and went to sit by Percy's chair.

"Sit." Prince sat as nicely as one could wish and assumed a mien of doggy innocence.

"My, how clever of you. Percy, my lad, I give you the task of training this animal. You clearly have a superior talent with dogs. I have never seen anything to equal it!" Jordan said, hoping he didn't sound too extravagant in his praise.

"Indeed, Mr. Ponsonby, that is a rare skill. Not everyone has that special rapport with an animal. Incredible," Mr. Shirley added to cinch the deal.

"Well, I do have a way if I say so myself. Always train the dogs at home. You need to be firm, let them know you are in charge."

Jordan rubbed his nose so to conceal his grin. He exchanged a glance with Shirley, then took a deep breath. Perhaps Percy had something in his approach. Certainly he had Prince sitting at his feet—and not drooling on his boots, either.

"Bit of a shock yesterday, wasn't it," Percy commented as he attacked the eggs and slab of gammon on his plate. "Miss Maitland, that is."

"I have no idea what Miss Maitland plans to do, but I should think it would necessitate finding an appropriate companion until such time as Lady Ariel marries. There must be some kin available." Jordan turned to Shirley for confirmation. "Do you know of any relative or other person who might properly serve in that capacity?"

"No one ever comes to visit. Sir Henry is the first to make any impression, it seems. I realize that Miss Maitland is a spinster of some duration, but it seems odd to me that an engagement would be announced so rapidly. After all, she has not seen the gentleman for many years. And he is just widowed in the past year—scarcely out of mourning."

"Quite so," Jordan agreed.

"Suppose it will be made official at this party to come?" Percy asked between bites.

"I suppose so. But it will be a nine-day's wonder. Miss Maitland has created a sensation." Jordan rose from his chair, thankful to see that Prince remained by Percy's chair, looking at him for permission to go, which Percy ignored. With a hopeful glance at Shirley, Jordan murmured something about going to the stables and left.

Mr. Shirley followed.

Percy finished his meal, then gave the hound a tasty bite before commanding him to come with him. Prince obediently followed at Percy's heels, just as he ought. If the dog hoped for some of the tidbits of gammon cut up and now reposing in Percy's pocket, it was not too surprising.

Ariel greeted Celia Townsend with subdued pleasure when the two girls met in the entry of Stafford Court.

"I had hoped you would come this morning, dear Celia. I wish to seek your advice about a gown for the coming party. I thought it should be blue. What do you think?" Ariel glanced back to where her aunt watched from the doorway to the library.

Celia walked with Ariel to the stairs, then slowly mounted them, deep in thought. "I think a light blue would be nice, not dark. What sort of trim do you plan?"

Ariel continued speculating on the fabric, trim, and style of gown until they had reached her rooms. Once inside her suite, she closed the door behind them and leaned against it with a sigh of relief.

"I am so glad you are come. It has not been the easiest of mornings, let me tell you. Aunt talks of nothing but Sir Henry and his excellence." Ariel strolled across to her desk, where she extracted a neatly written letter from between the pages of a book.

"But?" Celia queried.

"But she says not a word about a new companion for me. I

have no desire to live with her and Sir Henry after they are married. I cannot like that man, no matter he is the Cream of Society." Ariel folded the letter she had managed to write to her father after her aunt believed her in bed and asleep. She made short work of melting the sealing wax, then used her personal seal on the blob of red wax.

"Aunt Susan says she has not heard of him, so he must be in very small Society, hardly the Cream," Celia said.

Ariel looked up at that. "How very interesting. I trust your aunt implicitly. She is very careful to verify facts and never is malicious. And she has never heard of Sir Henry Banks? Small circle, indeed."

"Precisely my thought," Celia said with satisfaction.

"Do you think he is hoaxing Aunt?" Ariel asked quietly. "Does he think she has a small fortune to gain? Although she must have a sizable amount set by."

"Anything is possible. He does appear genuinely fond of her, from what little one can note while in their company." Celia eased back on the window seat, leaning her head against the frame. "It is not considered seemly to display affection in public. One has to look for clues."

"What sort of clues?" Ariel prompted.

"Aunt Susan says it is the gentle smile, the caress on a hand when assisting one into a carriage or out. Little things," Celia explained.

"That is not very helpful. I have not seen him assist her in any way at all, much less touch her." Ariel hesitated a moment, then added, "There is something else."

"Do tell," Celia begged with the familiarity of one who had been a dear friend to Ariel since they both were in leading strings.

"When I returned to the house the other day, Sir Henry had been here over thirty minutes—which means it was a call of some importance or he would not have remained beyond fifteen." She sought Celia's eyes, and the other nodded in agreement at that opinion.

"I confess to unladylike curiosity; I tiptoed up the stairs to eavesdrop. They were discussing a 'purpose,' something they planned in the near future. It did not sound like their marriage, for they mentioned someone named Mr. Oswald Dudley. Apparently he is the heir to Viscount Stone. He's a meek sort of man, and in need of funds, although why that ought to matter to their purpose, I cannot say. However, Sir Henry was to write him immediately to invite him here at Sir Henry's expense."

"Here to Stafford Court?" Celia said, looking horrified.

"No, to the Rose and Crown in the village. But wherever he is to stay, he is part of their purpose. What do you think?"

Celia stared out of the window at the lovely gardens below for a time.

"Well?" prompted Ariel. "I have my ideas, but I should very much like to hear yours."

"Perhaps his purpose is to marry you, so your aunt will feel free to wed Sir Henry?"

"Amazing! That is just the conclusion I reached. Will you ask Aunt Susan if she has ever heard of this tediously tame gentleman? For Sir Henry said that Oswald would serve their purpose because he was such a docile creature, so undemanding."

"How curious. Think—if *you* are to marry the man, what difference would it make whether he was meek or not? You have never been one to dominate anyone!"

"Thank you. I try hard to be a lady as Aunt Maitland says I must. Do you know she permits Sir Henry to call her Frederica?" Ariel cast an expectant look at her friend.

"No! But she never allows anyone to call her that."

"Sir Henry told her it was a romantic name. She floated up the stairs just as if she were in a daze."

"This is serious," Celia decided. "We do not know precisely what Sir Henry intends, but I would wager he is up to something suspicious. They are behaving like young fools, as Aunt Susan would say."

"I do think you are fortunate to have so wise an aunt. Would that my aunt could be more like yours."

"Indeed." Celia appeared to gather her thoughts for a time, then said, "I believe we ought to inform Lord Harcourt of this latest development. Mr. Ponsonby as well. They both seem well acquainted with Londoners. Perhaps they may remember something of Mr. Oswald Dudley?"

"Excellent idea!" Ariel said with a nod. "Now—my dress, blue silk and simple design, with a lace edge at the neck and puffed sleeves with slashes in them to show a bit of white. What do you think?"

"I think it sounds splendid, and shall we take the gig to the village? I can slip in and mail your letter while you wait in the gig. Then perhaps we could think of some excuse to call at Harcourt Hall?"

"Never!" declared a scandalized Ariel. "That simply is not allowed. If Aunt heard we had been there by ourselves I would be in the suds for certain."

"I have it. Leave it to me," Celia said with an impish smile. "Come, why are you sitting there? Put on a pretty bonnet and your gloves. We have an errand."

Totally mystified, Ariel did as suggested and followed her best friend down the stairs to where Aunt Maitland sat behind Papa's desk in the library.

"Miss Maitland, we have a small dilemma and want to know what you think it best we do," Celia said modestly.

"Well, what is it?" Aunt asked impatiently.

"Lord Harcourt requested my help in finding a basket for the dog that Mr. Ponsonby gave him. I asked the basket weaver to make one, and it is already finished. He worked very hard to get it done quickly. Since Lord Harcourt does not know where the man lives, do you think it would be the polite thing were Ariel and I to bring it to him? I thought to put a dear little blue bow on the basket and would not want to hand it to just anyone to take."

"Yes, indeed," Miss Maitland said absently after the flow of words had ceased. "Just go and leave me in peace. I have the books to tend."

Not taking time to query why Aunt was going over the books when Mr. Greenwood had been entrusted with the care of the estate, Ariel hurried along the hall, pulling Celia behind her until they were safely out of the rear door and on their way to the stables.

"Whew," Celia whispered as they neared the stable block and took note of Weems watching them with a curious eye.

"I agree. Now to get away before she realizes that we are

about to be most improper," Ariel added before turning to the groom to request the small carriage.

Weems obediently hitched up the gig, not wasting a moment in speech. He appeared to sense the girls were in a hurry, for the gig was ready in record time.

"Thank you so much, Weems. We have an errand of great importance," Ariel said softly, although there was little likelihood Aunt could hear a word out here.

"Figured as much, seeing how you look." He assisted the ladies into the gig, then handed the reins to Ariel.

She competently guided the horse along the avenue out to the main road to the village.

"Well, we handled that rather well, I believe," Celia declared with relief once clear of Stafford.

They covered the road to the village quite rapidly, not meeting anyone on the way. Once by the inn where the post was collected, Celia stepped down from the gig to hurry in to hand the important letter for posting. Within minutes they were on their way to the basket weaver.

"He really has it ready?" Ariel asked doubtfully. "You didn't just make that up so we could have an excuse to go?"

"He has a reputation for being quick, and I will wager you anything you want that it is ready for someone as important as Lord Harcourt!"

And so it was. Celia coped with the large basket, tucking it against her skirts so it wouldn't bother Ariel while she drove. They paused long enough for Celia to buy a length of blue riband from Mrs. Fitz with the money Ariel had tucked in her reticule. Then they headed out of the village to Harcourt Hall.

"I wonder if he will be there?" Ariel said with a dismayed look at Celia.

"He will have to be. We must talk with him."

"Right," declared Ariel, wishing she felt a trifle more confident.

They tooled up the avenue, seeing nothing but burgeoning hops and falling apple blossoms. When they reached the house, they didn't pause in front, but continued around to the stable block.

Celia knew who Peachum was and waved at him when he came out of the stable to see who had arrived.

He rubbed his chin as he approached the gig, taking note of the placid mare that Weems had hitched to it. "Be you in the right place, ladies?" he queried, with a slight emphasis on the word ladies.

"We need to talk to Lord Harcourt. We are hoping he might help us. And"—Celia whisked out the basket to view—"I picked up the basket he ordered."

"He'll be right glad to see that, I reckon," Peachum said with what passed for a smile. "I'll let Mr. Shirley know, and he can fetch his lordship."

Ariel watched as Peachum disappeared into the ell that jutted out to one end of the old house. A newer wing, it yet had the look of the old, just better windows and nicer doors.

Mr. Shirley appeared for a moment, seeming to verify that the women were actually present. He disappeared, and within minutes Lord Harcourt came striding from the wing, a smile lighting his face making him more handsome than ever. Something within Ariel fluttered, and she wondered at the cause. Just the sight of him made her feel warm and quivery.

Behind him Mr. Ponsonby followed with Prince trotting along at his side.

"Miss Townsend, you really have the basket! Thank you very, very much!" He plucked it from her hands to examine and exclaim over the workmanship.

"Here is the bill, for I know it is highly improper for a lady to give such a present to a gentleman."

"It is?" Ariel whispered. "I thought it was only something truly expensive."

"That basket was ten shillings, I'll have you know," Celia whispered back.

Even to Ariel, ten shillings was not a small amount. To Celia it was vast, indeed.

"Ten shillings? Cheap at twice the price if it will keep that animal off my bed," Lord Harcourt exclaimed.

"Nonsense," Mr. Ponsonby said. "Put the basket down and we shall see."

Harcourt did as requested.

"Get in," Percy ordered quietly. Prince gave him a look of disgust, but got into the basket, looking around at it as though he would far rather chew it to bits and pieces. "Sit."

Prince sat.

Celia clapped her hands in admiration. "Well done, Mr. Ponsonby. Please show me some more of his tricks."

Peachum helped Celia from the gig, then took the reins so Ariel could also get down.

Lord Harcourt stepped forward to whisk Ariel from the gig, taking his time to place her on the cobbled stable yard. She looked up at him, unconsciously pleading while trying to ignore the most peculiar feelings. She had never felt like this before, and it had to be Lord Harcourt's effect on her. *Strangely wonderful!*

"We have a new problem. It was fortunate that the basket was ready. We had a good excuse to come over here."

"What has happened?" He took her arm in the most polite manner possible to escort her into the shade presented by an arbor over which roses were growing, their green buds just visible. The arbor led from the stable yard to the gardens, offering a pleasant transition as well as a welcome fragrance come June.

"It is someone named Mr. Oswald Dudley. I chanced to overhear a conversation between my aunt and Sir Henry regarding this man." She continued to explain what she had overheard and her concerns. "I have no idea what they plot, but I am most curious about Mr. Dudley."

Jordan looked down at the pretty miss whose troubled eyes betrayed how worried she was. He urged her to sit on the narrow bench within the arbor, then joined her.

"I do recognize the name. He is young, still in the process of acquiring his Town bronze, and given to gambling." At her look of alarm, he added, "Not heavily, but more than he should for someone who is not wealthy."

"Perhaps he plays against his expectations?"

"Possibly," Jordan replied while assimilating the information she had given him. "It would seem to me that your aunt may intend you to marry this stranger."

"That is what Celia and I decided. I hoped you might be able to tell me something of him."

"Percy," Jordan called. When his friend appeared, Jordan inquired, "Oswald Dudley?"

"Good grief, who wants to know about him? He's a beef-witted greenhorn, a regular cabbage-head. Not enough sense to come in out of the rain. Why?" Percy looked from Jordan to a rather pale Lady Ariel.

"It would appear Miss Maitland is in the process of arranging a betrothal not only for herself, but for Lady Ariel as well if what we suspect is correct. And to none other than Mr. Oswald Dudley."

Percy looked utterly thunderstruck. "But he has no money— until Viscount Stone goes aloft, that is. He has no wit, no graces."

"No charm?" Miss Townsend asked with a militant sparkle in her eyes.

"None whatsoever. Why, Prince has more charm than that man does. My apologies, Lady Ariel. It is just that I could never see a woman of your obvious intelligence married to that dolt."

"Why would she do this?" Jordan wondered aloud. "Surely Miss Maitland could do better than that? Lady Ariel is most pleasing, will have a title some day, and has ample funds. I find this most puzzling. Lady Ariel does not need to marry someone who has money and rank, but Dudley has neither, which is all the more perplexing."

"I agree," Percy inserted, looking intrigued.

"Has anything been mentioned about where your aunt and Sir Henry plan to reside after their wedding? I fancy if what we fear is true, Dudley would move in with you, for he has no home of his own that I know about," Jordan said, anger growing within him. It was not right, to join this lovely young woman with a person such as Dudley! *Unthinkable.* That Miss Maitland might approve an alliance with Dudley while she had objected to marriage with his cousin was above all things most curious.

Percy shook his head in obvious bewilderment. "Makes no sense at all."

"Well," said a very downcast Lady Ariel, "I expect Celia and I had best return. Thank you for the information, even if it was what I most feared to hear."

"Thanks to you for delivering the basket. I feel certain that Percy can train the dog to appreciate it." Jordan walked with Lady Ariel to where the gig waited. Peachum had estimated the call to a nicety, returning the horse and gig when wanted.

"Nothing has been said to me regarding Mr. Dudley. I gather I am to be surprised with his appearance."

Jordan gave her a wry smile. "You can surprise your aunt by being unconcerned about the man. But I think you shall not marry him."

"She said she is my guardian while Papa is in India. Perhaps she has the power to compel me to wed Mr. Dudley, even if I refuse. I have heard there are ways and means of accomplishing such things," Lady Ariel said with a conspiratorial look at her friend, Miss Townsend.

"You have been reading Minerva novels. You cannot be forced to marry a man against your will." Jordan stood at her side, studying her winsome face, wishing he could offer more reassurance.

"I shall take great comfort in that knowledge, even if I suspect that Aunt will try to get around that law."

"The rector won't help her," Percy said suddenly. "He believes you should marry Harcourt and is a pretty determined man from all I have seen. He'll stand your friend. Even were she to get a special license, where would she find a clergyman willing to perform a questionable wedding?"

Miss Townsend, Lady Ariel, and Jordan all stared at Percy as though he had just grown two heads.

"Well, I mean to say, that is, you heard him natter on about Harcourt as well as I did," Percy said, flustered and taking a step back from the others.

Jordan snapped his fingers as an idea struck him. "It just might work."

"What?" cried a rather alarmed Lady Ariel.

"If they suggest you should marry this Dudley fellow, you can blithely inform them that you are secretly engaged to me. The rector will support that, I'll wager." Jordan had the odd feeling that he had just made a major step over some invisible boundary and he was falling through space.

"You cannot mean that," Lady Ariel said, her hand flying to her throat in what appeared to be dismay.

Jordan had to smile. The first time in his life that he had mentioned marriage to a young woman and she took leave to doubt his sincerity. "I do." Those words as well had an ominous ring to them. He shrugged them away. *Just because they discussed such a thing didn't mean it would take place, did it?* He sought to reassure her.

"I am sorry if such a plan is displeasing to you, Lady Ariel. I had thought it could serve in the event you needed help." Jordan sobered, thinking he was ten kinds of fool.

"You mean it to be a ruse? A trick, perhaps?" Relief washed over her, a visible thing. She glanced at her friend, then nodded. "I shall bear that in mind, Lord Harcourt. It is more than generous of you to offer such extravagant help to this poor damsel—a knight in shining armor, indeed."

"Well, as to that, Mrs. Longwood has polished that armor in the entry hall, and if needs be, I believe I can don it."

Lady Ariel smiled, quite as he had hoped. She looked incredibly fetching, and not a little vulnerable. She needed a man to protect her. Where was her father when necessary? He hoped her letter reached him in time.

Jordan plucked her up, setting her in the gig with ease. She was nicely tall and slender as a wand, with a neat little waist. *Really, she was a pretty creature.*

"Well," she said breathlessly, "you have the basket now and can train your dog. We had best return before Aunt demands to know details. I fear I am not very good at prevaricating."

"It is nice to know that someone has that quality," Jordan said, then stepped back as she took the reins in her capable grasp while Percy assisted Miss Townsend.

"We can see you before long, I trust," Jordan suggested. "I can think of some excuse to pay a call, I feel certain. I am extremely curious to know what develops." Jordan bowed, then smiled into Lady Ariel's eyes, a knowing and, he hoped, kind smile.

"Good-bye," she said, still sounding breathless but smiling in return.

Ariel gave her knight one more glance, then guided the gig down the avenue to the main road. It took but a brief time to take Celia home. Without getting out, she bid her friend farewell for the moment, then headed for Stafford Court. What would she find when she entered the house?

The caned-back whiskey was just where she expected it to be—before the front entry.

The groom who had been expecting her return came running up to take the reins. Ariel thanked him with her usual courtesy, and then she stared at the house.

She loved this place so much. How could she endure to share it with a man such as described to her by her friends, for she considered both Lord Harcourt and Mr. Ponsonby friends now. *Unsupportable!* And precisely what did her aunt have in mind for Ariel's future?

The entry hall was empty of people; not even Cummins was around. Voices drifted down the stairs, however.

Leaving her bonnet on and carefully holding her skirt, Ariel walked up the steps, taking them slowly one by one. She dreaded this, whatever it was. She felt as though a black cloud hung over her, ready to pour rain.

She paused in the doorway to the drawing room. The large, comfortably furnished room had two fireplaces with sofas and chairs ranged before them. The pleasant room now held three people—Miss Maitland, Sir Henry Banks, and a younger gentleman who looked as though he would prefer to fade into the wallpaper.

"There you are!" Miss Maitland cried.

"Celia and I did explain about the basket, dear Aunt," Ariel reminded.

"So you did," Miss Maitland agreed in a mollifying manner with a hasty look at the shrinking figure across from where she was seated. "Well, come in, come in."

"I had thought to remove my bonnet and freshen up as we have callers."

"There is someone I would like you to meet. Now."

Knowing full well precisely who the stranger was, Ariel advanced into the room to halt by her aunt. She waited politely silent, watchful.

"Ariel, may I present Mr. Oswald Dudley. Mr. Dudley, this is my dear niece, Lady Ariel Brandon."

Mr. Dudley struggled to his feet to manage a rather untidy bow in Ariel's direction.

"Mr. Dudley is visiting the area and staying with Sir Henry. I have invited him to call as often as may be. I wish you to become better acquainted. He will be at the party."

Ariel nodded, then curtsied properly. "How do you do."

A good look at Mr. Dudley revealed that he was untidy, had nothing to say for himself, and certainly no manners to recommend him. And this was the man her fussy, doting aunt wanted her to marry? *Never!*

Chapter Seven

"How'ja do," Mr. Dudley mumbled and bowed again. At least, Ariel surmised it was a bow. He might have been just checking his boots, which were badly in need of polish.

She gathered her wits and replied, "This is an unexpected pleasure, sir. I trust Sir Henry will offer a selection of the delights to be found in this lovely part of Kent for you to enjoy. It is not called the garden of England for no reason, you know."

"I suggested that you might be the most proper person to introduce Mr. Dudley to our area, my dear," Aunt Maitland said, a hint of firmness in her voice once again.

"I would not think to do so on my own, but I am sure I can find a number of others to join us, dear Aunt. I am ever aware that you wish me to be proper at all times. And I would not wish to do anything to bring disgrace to Papa." Ariel gave her aunt a sweet smile, then turned to invite Mr. Dudley to see the gardens. There were always gardeners around at this time of day, something on which she counted. "These are considered to be rather fine, sir. I believe you will find few gardens of better quality."

Conversation was not one of Mr. Dudley's strong points, it seemed. He had little to say regarding the prospect of viewing the gardens. While it was still early in the year, fine weather had brought forth a lovely display of blooms. Undaunted by his lack of enthusiasm, Ariel began her tour with a favorite place.

"I like the topiary garden best," Ariel ventured to say. This garden was mentioned in the various guidebooks offered to those who liked to view stately homes and usually given high praise by those who inspected it. "It is one of Papa's favorites. He designed that peacock you see over there. He said it reminded him of the peacocks in India."

"Fine thing," Mr. Dudley muttered. At least, Ariel thought those were the words he said.

Discouraged at his disinterest in topiary, she pointed out a statue she admired in the near distance. "That is a figure of Spring. I think it rather clever that she is holding a pot of spring bulbs in bloom."

When no comment was forthcoming, Ariel turned to the fountain at the demi-lune, where a dainty statue of Diana the Huntress posed with her bow as water arched over her head, merrily splashing in the half-circle pool below.

"This is another favorite of mine. Do you have any particular interests, Mr. Dudley? Do you hunt, shoot, or play billiards?" she inquired with the vain hope he might say something she could interpret. It was a trifle difficult to discover a topic that engaged Mr. Dudley's attention when he spoke so rarely, and then in a manner puzzling to understand.

Eventually, defeated in her attempt to draw the insipid Mr. Dudley out, she gave up, suggesting they return to the house. This appeared to meet with Mr. Dudley's approval, for he turned at once and marched her briskly back to the steps that led to the terrace and the entrance to the ground-floor hall.

Cummins magically appeared from wherever it was he usually hid himself. "Your aunt is in the library, Lady Ariel. I believe it would be a good thing for you to find her."

Surprised at this loquaciousness on the part of the taciturn butler, Ariel nodded, then gently steered Mr. Dudley in the direction of the library. It was odd how much time her aunt spent in there of late. She silently approached the door, halting briefly to survey her aunt.

That couldn't be guilt on Aunt Maitland's face, but if not, what was it? Ariel wondered. Mr. Dudley was close on her heels, so Ariel perforce entered the room.

"We have now done the gardens," Ariel reported. "I shall send notes to several people I know. Perhaps Mr. Dudley will enjoy meeting them and seeing something of the area?" Ariel hoped that her aunt caught the intimation that Mr. Dudley had not enjoyed the tour of the gardens.

"Yes, well, I feel certain you will know what might appeal to a young person your age."

Sir Henry rose from a chair on the far side of the room, a book in hand, to survey the pair near the door. "Having a pleasant day, Oswald? Lovely country here. Good to leave the demands of London for a time, is it not?"

"Indeed," Mr. Dudley said with amazing clarity.

Astonished, Ariel could only wish that Sir Henry might be present whenever she was obliged to accompany his guest. It certainly would make conversation easier.

Excusing herself, she walked to the small desk near the windows, where she kept a supply of paper and goose quills. It didn't take her long to pen two notes begging for help. Saying nothing to her aunt, for after all, she had agreed to additional people and did not seem to care who was there, Ariel hastily found a footman and requested that he deliver the missives as quickly as possible.

Returning to the library, she whiled away an hour trying to converse with Mr. Dudley, inviting Sir Henry to voice his opinion when possible. As to her aunt, whatever occupied her attention at the vast desk to one end of the room was absorbing to say the least. She said nothing and paid not the slightest heed to the other three.

It was going to be a long day, Ariel thought. Indeed, the afternoon would drag with the speed of a snail unless she got help.

Jordan looked up when the maid brought in a crisp white paper with his name on the outside. He didn't recognize the handwriting, so unfolded the note at once.

"Percy? Come here. Our presence is wanted as soon as possible over at Stafford Court. Seems Oswald Dudley has arrived, and Lady Ariel has discovered it is next to impossible to entertain him. Miss Maitland has burdened Lady Ariel with the job, and she pleads for help. Do you think I shall need that suit of armor yet?"

"At least keep it polished," Percy replied with a chuckle. "What does she say?"

"In addition to wanting us over there, she would appreciate it if we might bring Miss Townsend and her sister, Jane. The more people around, the better."

"She's right, you know. If that Maitland woman and Sir Henry are trying to push a marriage on Lady Ariel, they won't like it if there always are people around."

Jordan set aside the papers dealing with his late cousin that he had been studying and rose, not too unhappy to leave the work behind for the moment. He hoped to find a clue why Ivor had died and had found nothing so far. "Get your hat and gloves, and let us be on our way."

"I agree," Percy replied, not at all displeased to see the pretty Miss Townsend again.

Jordan sent an order to Cotman, hoping his coachman would have speedy assistance.

Within a very short time the two men, seated in the landau that had been his late cousin's purchase, left Harcourt Hall in the direction of the village. Cotman, looking quite unruffled, drove the team with deft speed, understanding there was to be no dawdling.

The Townsend girls were neatly garbed and waiting for the gentlemen in the Townsend drawing room.

"You received a message from Lady Ariel as well?" Jordan began when Percy stepped forward to offer his arm to Miss Townsend.

"I daresay they have," Percy said, "for there is a paper just like the one you received, Harcourt. Shall we go at once? I sensed a hint of urgency in that note."

Jordan exchanged a look with Mrs. Townsend, said all that was proper, then offered his arm to Jane, and they all left for the landau.

"I think it is very strange that Miss Maitland has invited this stranger to Stafford Court—even to spend the days," Miss Townsend said with a puzzled frown. "It is not the least like her to want strangers about. I wonder what Lord Stafford would say to all this?"

"It will take an age for Lady Ariel's letter to reach her father," Jane added. "Poor girl might be married to Mr. Dudley by that time."

"Zounds!" Percy said in dismay.

"I believe it will have to be the armor, Percy," Jordan said slowly. "I cannot see any way out of this dilemma. If needs be, back me up in what I say, will you?"

"We all will do whatever is necessary to save Lady Ariel from a disastrous marriage. Unless, of course, she decided she quite likes the man," Miss Townsend said.

"Unlikely event," Jordan said as Cotman turned the carriage into the avenue leading to Stafford.

"This is such a beautiful estate, well managed, too," Miss Townsend said thoughtfully. "I could see why a man who was in need of funds would be happy to step in here."

That remark brought no answer. There was none, really. All wished to make an assessment of Mr. Dudley before offering further comment. They drew up before the house standing serenely in the afternoon sun.

Percy assisted the girls from the carriage.

"Cotman," Jordan said quietly, "when you take the carriage around to the stables, try to learn anything you can regarding Sir Henry or his guest, Mr. Dudley. I would deem it a great help."

"As you say, milord," the elderly coachman said with a touch of his hand to his hat in a salute before he drove away from the graveled area in front of the house.

Cummins opened the door, looking most pleased to see them. "Good day, my Lord Harcourt, ladies, Mr. Ponsonby. I believe Lady Ariel is yet in the library, as is Mr. Dudley."

Not by a flicker of an eyelash did Cummins reveal his estimate of the guest. It wasn't his place. However, the very fact he welcomed the quartet so warmly spoke volumes, or so whispered Jane to Lord Harcourt before her sister hushed her.

"Celia and Jane!" Lady Ariel exclaimed with warmth, swiftly crossing the room to meet them. She smiled at the two gentlemen and offered her hand in greeting. "Lord Harcourt, Mr. Ponsonby, how very good to see you all. I should like you to meet a visitor to Stafford, Mr. Oswald Dudley. Sir Henry you already know."

Mr. Dudley performed beautifully—that is, he mumbled something quite incoherent and neglected to bow.

"I believe we would all enjoy tea on the terrace," Ariel said. She drew them along, Mr. Dudley following rather reluctantly, to the entry and out the front door.

Once gathered in the sunny, sheltered terrace on the south side of the house, Jordan managed to draw Ariel aside. She gave him a questioning look as he casually pointed out a not-in-the-least-distinguished shrub.

He glanced behind them, then quietly said, "I believe a suit of armor will be necessary from what I have heard, if you understand what I mean by that?"

"You mean a pretend engagement?" Ariel whispered, turning a bit pale.

"The moment I saw Dudley again, I knew. Actually, he is not a bad sort otherwise. But he *is* a gamester; I'd not wager on your estate remaining intact were he to get his hands on it, or even part of it."

"Aunt has been closeted in the library for the past day or two, and I do not understand why—unless she is putting together a proposal to offer Mr. Dudley on my behalf. Can she make an agreement that would be legally binding? With Papa in India, is there no one to stop her from handing me to Dudley on a silver platter?" She cast Jordan a troubled look.

They both turned to survey the visitor, then resumed the examination of the undistinguished shrub.

"But what would she bargain? Once you marry, all your funds would go into his hands. Or do you have money in your own right as you will the title?"

"Trustees would handle that, but I do not know them, and who is to say they are any more trustworthy than my aunt?"

"Suit of armor, dear girl. That leaves the suit of armor. I've asked the others to support us should it prove necessary. Agreed?" Jordan gathered her hand in his, liking the softness, the fragility of it.

Ariel thought a bit, glancing at Mr. Dudley's insipid expression. Jordan could almost see her mind at work. "There is scarce any comparison between you. I agree."

"We shall entertain Dudley, take him about the area—you will have to guide us as to where we ought to go, for I know only slightly more than he would," he reminded her.

"Very well. We have an alliance. Oh, here comes Cummins with our tea. Let us now begin as we intend to go on in the coming days."

Jordan helped her to sit, then selected a chair close to hers, only to pull it even closer to her.

Mr. Dudley frowned.

Jordan smiled, then leaned over to avail himself of Lady Ariel's left hand. She could still pour tea if she wished. Her shocked expression was rather amusing before she schooled it into politeness. "Will you pour, Cummins?"

From her confusion when the butler had appeared with the tea tray, Jordan surmised that it was an unusual circumstance. Come to think on it, the butler had seemed to be out of sight the other times Jordan had called.

"You did not bring your dog, Lord Harcourt," Miss Townsend said, her eyes revealing inner mirth.

There followed a rather dull recital of the animal's accomplishments and other details guaranteed to irk the unwanted guest. While incorrect behavior, Jordan felt it helpful. The chap revealed his lack of manners by not joining the discussion at all.

Mr. Dudley looked bored.

"So, how long do you intend to rusticate in the village of Stafford?" Jordan asked the newcomer after the tea had been poured and Cummins had handed around the tiny biscuits Cook had made in anticipation of callers.

"Month, perhaps," Dudley replied.

Ariel looked startled at these clearly spoken words.

"A month? In Stafford? There is not a great deal to do hereabouts as a visitor."

Mr. Dudley looked about to answer that, then clamped his lips shut.

"Ariel and I have found much to do, haven't we?" Jordan inquired with a limpid look at the young woman sitting so cozily at his side.

A look of surprise flashed across her face before she smilingly agreed. "So true. I would not know what to do without Lord Harcourt."

"You said you would call me Jordan, my dear," he reminded, although there had been no such arrangement. He counted upon her being quick on the mark and she was.

"Jordan," she said with a blush.

Mr. Dudley frowned, an awesome scowl that said volumes even if he remained silent.

They finished the tea and biscuits, then straggled from the terrace to where the gardens might be viewed.

"Saw them," Mr. Dudley observed.

"Earlier Mr. Dudley and I walked through a part of the gardens—the topiary, and a bit of the others," Ariel explained. "It was not very long before you all arrived. I was happy to see you, Jordan." Ariel gave him a luminous smile that didn't appear the slightest bit forced. She accepted his arm, leaning on it while she gazed up into his face with the look of one who is utterly besotted.

Mr. Dudley abruptly excused himself and entered the house from a French door that led into the library.

They all looked to one another, utterly mystified.

"Well, what brought that on?" Celia Townsend demanded. "Surely he will not back down at the sign of a bit of competition? Although, I can see why he might. Lord Harcourt is formidable, indeed," she concluded with a delightful laugh that brought Percy's attention.

Ariel smothered a laugh, then Jane giggled, and even the gentlemen smiled.

"I fear it is likely more serious than we think. But it is always good to be able to laugh at peril," Jordan said, refusing to relinquish his clasp of the dainty hand that was so trustingly placed on his arm.

Oswald sidled into the library, then sought out Sir Henry. "Ahem." He waited politely until he had the baronet's attention. "Thought you said I'm to marry that girl, Lady Ariel."

"Well, and so you are. Cannot accomplish it in one afternoon, my lad." Sir Henry oozed sympathy and enthusiasm.

"Remember there is a fortune involved. A large fortune. And it comes with the lovely Lady Ariel."

"She's taken with Harcourt," Oswald mumbled. "Seen it for myself."

Sir Henry exchanged looks with Miss Maitland, who had listened from her chair behind the desk.

"What makes you say that, Dudley?" Sir Henry asked intently, sitting up a bit straighter.

"Said so. Just now. Do something." He tossed a look at Miss Maitland, then returned his disconcerting gaze on Sir Henry. "Soon. She's callin' him by his first name."

"I feel certain you must have misunderstood," Miss Maitland began in a soothing voice. It was the kind of tone one used to calm one of unsound mind.

"Hearing good. Know more than I say. Something's afoot." With that, Oswald stalked from the room, headed in the direction of the stables.

"Curious," Sir Henry mused aloud. "I thought you said she scarcely knew Harcourt. We cannot allow a repetition of the previous Harcourt affair."

"Indeed not. We must do something," she agreed, looking sweet and comfortably benevolent. "But what?"

"What are we going to do about that man? I confess he is most unsettling," Ariel said quietly to the group now assembled in the topiary garden. "This entire situation is disturbing in the extreme. I will not wed Mr. Dudley!" She wrapped her arms about her as though chilled.

Jordan gestured to the pleasant arrangement of curved stone seats where they could talk without being overheard. If anyone drew near, that person would be seen instantly. They all sank down on the cool stone in varying degrees of proximity. Jordan kept Ariel close to his side, hoping to offer her what comfort he could.

"I could not tell if he liked you or found you repulsive," Celia Townsend said, only half joking.

"Heaven knows. I could not tell," Ariel replied, refusing to take umbrage at the remark.

"We will have to walk carefully," Jordan advised. "I would

not underestimate him in the least. Just because he speaks in monosyllables does not mean he is short a sheet."

"That is possible, I suppose," Ariel replied.

They all turned at the sound of thundering hooves in the near distance. Jane hopped up on a bench to get a better look.

"There he goes—Mr. Dudley," Jane cried. "At least he can ride a horse. He's on the chestnut. And he appears to do well, too. He isn't a failure on horseback."

"Jane, dear!" her scandalized sister exclaimed.

"Well, I wanted to see if he knew how to ride well. I have seen worse," Jane explained.

"The afternoon is growing late. What about this evening?" Jordan asked.

"I could not find out what his interests are," Ariel replied, her frustration clear.

"Ah . . . I hesitate to suggest this, but perhaps if we all stayed for dinner . . ." Celia began.

Ariel immediately continued, "It would prevent Mr. Dudley from attempting anything underhanded."

"Yes," Jane inserted ghoulishly. "Like trying to compromise you. I can just see him trying to do something terrible, like kiss you in the library!"

"Jane, dear," her much tried sister exclaimed.

Jordan looked down at Ariel's sweet mouth that trembled a trifle and vowed that dastardly Dudley would not have his way with her if he had to stand guard at her door.

"It isn't a bad idea," Percy said, agreeing with Miss Townsend. "That is, if your cook won't throw a spasm at the notice of four guests of a sudden."

"The cook in my house had better not take dinner guests amiss," Ariel said, an air of hauteur setting oddly with the wistful tilt of her tender mouth.

"Does anyone need to go home first?" Jordan inquired. "Otherwise, I believe you now have four extra for dinner. I will instruct Cotman to deliver a message to your parents, Miss Townsend."

"Oh," Jane cried with obvious delight, "this is so exciting!"

"Jane, this is not exciting," corrected Celia. "This is our at-

tempt to foil Mr. Dudley in any plans to force marriage on
Ariel."

"Exciting," Jane insisted.

Percy and Celia exchanged wry looks; then the five strolled
into the house fully prepared to execute their new plan.

Ariel quickly informed Cummins what was intended. The
butler looked somewhat bemused, but nodded his full understanding of the change in arrangements before heading to the
kitchen.

"Come with me," Ariel whispered to the others. "I do not
fear my aunt . . . precisely. She never seems to oppose me, yet
contrives to get her way. This is one time when I shall have my
way—but a bit of support will not come amiss."

With Jordan tucking her snugly against his side, Celia and
Percy behind, and Jane trailing after, gawking at all the paint-
ings, they entered the library.

"Dear Aunt, you will be pleased to know that I managed to
convince my friends to remain for dinner with us," Ariel cried
with delight. "I thought it would make the occasion a little
more festive for Mr. Dudley. After all, I expect my company is
rather dull for a London gentleman. Two other Londoners
should make him far more comfortable."

Sir Henry turned a trifle purple.

Aunt Maitland did not look quite so sweet.

"They demurred, but I told them that you would never inter-
fere with my having friends to dinner in my own home."

Ariel's concluding shot hit home. Her aunt fell back against
the desk chair with an air of defeat.

"How nice," Miss Maitland said faintly.

Sir Henry, quickly recovering from the shock of being
thwarted, smiled genially. "Of course Lady Ariel must have
her friends join her of an evening if she desires. I think it is
vastly thoughtful of her to help entertain my young friend."

"Jordan, would you care to wash? Celia, Mr. Ponsonby?"
Ariel said, more for the effect of having her aunt hear Jordan's
name on her lips than an effort to be a polite hostess.

Lord Harcourt bestowed an amused look on her, full, did he
but know it, of tender regard. "Thoughtful of you, my dear. I
trust we are all fine."

"Fine, fine," Mr. Ponsonby agreed. He drew Celia Townsend and Jane with him toward the central hall, remarking as they went, "Did Lady Ariel not say something about a new billiards table?"

"Ariel," Aunt Maitland commanded, "I wish to speak with you."

In the past, Ariel would have yielded at once. With the support of Lord Harcourt behind her, she was able to stand firm. "Perhaps later? I would not wish to neglect my guests, nor do I feel you would like me to do that." Ariel curtsied politely, then placed her hand on Lord Harcourt's arm to exit the library.

Utter silence reigned behind her, and she wished she could see the expression on her aunt's face. It would likely make a thundercloud seem mild.

They crossed the central hall, then walked to the billiards room, where the others had congregated.

"Well done, Lady Ariel," Lord Harcourt said warmly approving.

She marched over to select a cue, then turned to face him with a look of surprise. "I actually did it. I would never be disrespectful of my aunt in a normal way, but when she wants to marry me to that toad, well!"

"We will use every means at our disposal to prevent that from happening. You know, I feel there is more to this than meets the eye," Lord Harcourt said.

"Well," Jane inserted, "will someone help me? I've not played billiards before. I need a lesson." She looked to Mr. Ponsonby, then to Lord Harcourt.

With the faintest of sighs Lord Harcourt took a cue from the case, then began his tutoring.

Ariel watched the patience he had with the impetuous Jane and smiled. While nothing would come of his championing her, it was comforting to know that he was such a fine man, one her father could admire.

"I wonder when your father will receive your last letter," Celia said with a cautioning glance at Jane.

"Indeed," Ariel replied.

Cummins appeared in the doorway with a look Ariel interpreted as wanting to speak with her. She hastily joined him.

"Your aunt says Cook's not to fuss. I doubt that is what you had in mind, my lady." He gave her a straight look, one that spoke volumes.

"Thank you for coming to me. Of course I want Cook to do her very best. With four London gentlemen, including Sir Henry, to dine, we ought to excel ourselves."

"Indeed, ma'am. I quite agree." The butler bowed, then marched off toward the kitchen—humming!

Ariel turned to find Lord Harcourt at her side.

"It would seem that your aunt is to be surprised this evening," he murmured in Ariel's ear, stirring tendrils of hair. She smelled of roses and violets, he realized—most appealing.

"That will take care of this evening. What of the morrow?" She was very aware of his proximity. He stirred more than a tendril of hair. She felt a trembling within her down to her toes. She did not understand what was happening to her in the slightest, but whatever it was, it brought delicious tremors, a flurry of nerves, and an aching such as she had never known before when she merely looked at him.

"I shall think of something, never fear."

Chapter Eight

"What does one do to entertain a person who is determined not to be amused?" Ariel asked Celia as they strolled from the billiards room. The dinner gong had sounded, and all planning had to be put off until later. Indeed, Ariel had set aside any thought of changing for dinner because she did not wish to make her friends uncomfortable.

"It is a trifle difficult," Celia said in sympathy.

Ariel mulled over the strange feelings that came over her when she was close to Lord Harcourt. Considerate man, he insisted upon setting aside his investigation of his cousin's death to help her. He was most noble in character and surpassed his late cousin by far.

Now she was embroiled in a scheme to avoid marriage to the disagreeable Mr. Dudley and with none other than Lord Harcourt, the man she now thought might be a most agreeable husband. *To someone.*

Darting a surreptitious glance at the baron, she couldn't help but see the vast difference between Mr. Dudley and the elegant Lord Harcourt. His lordship was far from being a dandy. Rather, he wore that cultivated air of a gentleman upon whom the distinction of his rank sat with a casual nonchalance, whereas Mr. Dudley tried to be elegant and instead was futile in his striving.

They all gathered in the library before crossing the hall to the dining room. Aunt obviously did not wish Lord Harcourt to escort Ariel, but with rank determining the precedence, there was no choice. The baron assuredly outranked a baronet to say nothing of a plain mister, even if he might be heir presumptive to a viscount. Jane had the dubious pleasure of being escorted into dinner on the arm of a peevish Mr. Dudley.

"I believe I have the solution for tomorrow," Lord Harcourt said quietly as he conducted Ariel to her place at the foot of the table.

"Indeed?" Ariel looked to where Aunt Maitland gave an arch look at Sir Henry as he held the chair for her at the opposite end of the table, where Papa usually sat. It occurred to Ariel that Aunt would have a difficult time yielding her position in this house when Papa came home. He would soon, if prayers were answered.

"May I suggest a day trip to Tunbridge Wells tomorrow?" Lord Harcourt asked those at the table once the soup had been served. "I have been wanting to visit there again, for it has been some time since I last went. It's a charming town, with many new shops and inns, I understand."

Ariel looked up from her mushroom soup. "What a delightful notion. Do say you approve, Aunt." Ariel strove to sound as though it made no difference to her one way or the other. She knew that if she truly wished something, it was better to pretend it was not important.

"What do you say, Dudley?" Sir Henry prodded. "Should be a pleasant outing. Tunbridge Wells is not quite the gay, scandalous spa it was some years ago, but there are still numerous attractions."

"It is not so far," Miss Maitland coaxed. "Why, there have been a great many houses improved so that the town has an air of freshness about it. You will not see prettier-fronted houses even in Brighton. And I fancy the shops have the latest things in them direct from London."

"We could use my landau and perhaps a gig from Stafford?" Lord Harcourt asked Miss Maitland, most correctly ignoring Ariel. "There will be six partaking of the treat. Your mother would have no objections were you and Miss Jane to go, would she, Miss Townsend?" Lord Harcourt inquired, turning to address Ariel's friend.

Jane sat silent, wide-eyed, and obviously awed at the thought of venturing to Tunbridge Wells with the older and so-sophisticated gentlemen along.

"I expect she will have a commission or two for me," Celia replied. "She always seems to think of something she requires when one of the family goes to town. I believe the excursion would be a lovely plan."

"Oh, good," Jane declared softly. "If you approve, Mama is bound to agree to the scheme."

Celia smiled at this outburst from her younger sister. "It ought to be a nice day tomorrow. This is a lovely time of year."

"You frown, Lady Ariel," Lord Harcourt said quietly under the cover of Sir Henry enumerating other sights to be seen in Tunbridge Wells. "Are you displeased with the plan?"

"What? Oh, no, my lord. I believe a jaunt to Tunbridge Wells would be vastly entertaining. It is to be hoped our visitor will enjoy it as well," she added with a peek at Mr. Dudley, who looked as though his soup had disagreed with him. "It is kind of you to include Celia and Jane. They are dear girls who deserve a treat."

"They have an attractive home on a most prosperous property. From what Mr. Shirley has said, Mr. Townsend is well situated." He allowed the footman to serve him a bit of the chicken with a heavenly aroma, followed by a helping of appealing sliced potatoes that had been baked in Cook's special cheese sauce, and green beans. There were other dishes as well, but apparently the baron believed in eating well, yet simply.

"Mr. Townsend was offered a baronetcy, but declined the honor," Ariel explained. "Said he didn't want the expense and bother. Indeed, they only want for an heir, although he dotes on his two girls. Since there is no entail involved with the property, the girls will share the inheritance, which will be substantial, I fancy."

"Percy has no need of such, but I have been told one can never have too much money," Lord Harcourt murmured, looking to see Percy eyeing Miss Townsend with a fond gaze.

"Ariel," Aunt Maitland demanded, "did you hear what Sir Henry said? There is to be a special assembly in Tunbridge Wells. He heard about it at the Rose and Crown."

"How nice," Ariel replied with caution. Was her aunt actually thinking about allowing her to attend? "When?"

"A week from Wednesday," Sir Henry replied. "You will

find Mr. Dudley an accomplished dancer, Lady Ariel. He quite shines there."

Ariel smiled and nodded, thanking her stars that she was in the act of chewing and thus spared the necessity of a reply. She would have been horridly tempted to say something to the effect that it was certain that he did not excel in conversation!

Talk ensued of the changes that had taken place since Lord Harcourt had last visited the town and the elegance of the Tunbridge Wells assemblies.

"Beau Nash set the standards, you know, as Master of Ceremonies," Miss Maitland observed with a nod. "He divided his time between Bath and Tunbridge Wells and thought the town quite charming. All the ladies were delighted that the winter Season in Bath did not clash with summer in Tunbridge Wells. You will find it is possible to exchange pleasantries with anyone you meet in Tunbridge Wells, thanks to him."

"Anyone in a public place can talk to anyone else, without the distinction of rank or gender," Celia added with a faint blush. "I understand Bath is much the same?"

Dinner continued with additional discussion of the merits of Bath versus the elegancies of Tunbridge Wells, totally ignoring that upstart town of Brighton, which, after all, had no more than an accidental advantage because of the patronage of the Prince Regent. The rivalry between the two towns had brought an awareness of the need for improvements in Tunbridge Wells—thus producing nicer shops, two bookstores, and a doctor in seasonal residence. Dr. John Mayo of London had a flourishing summer practice; his house on Mount Ephraim was much admired. Permanent residents were moving in, resulting in the remodeling of a great number of houses.

Following dinner, they retired to the drawing room, where Ariel was persuaded to play the piano so Mr. Dudley could teach Jane the latest dance performed in London.

Celia and Mr. Ponsonby joined them, and even Miss Maitland and Sir Henry condescended to learn the steps, it being a very simple longways dance. Lord Harcourt turned the pages of the music for Ariel, to her appreciation.

The company did not stay very late. Twilight lasted long that time of year, and there was a moon rising, but the

Townsend girls wished to have a good night's sleep for the excursion on the morrow.

"I have a letter for your mother, Miss Townsend," Miss Maitland said smiling, offering the missive she had penned earlier. "I trust she will permit a bit of fun for you girls. It is not often you have such a treat."

Celia and Jane curtsied politely and were gone, escorted by Mr. Ponsonby and Lord Harcourt, with the estimable Cotman driving.

"Dashed pretty girls, those two," Sir Henry said to Miss Maitland.

"Pretty is as pretty does," she said with a demure smile.

"Father well to grass, I suppose. Those gowns were not sewn by their maid, I'll wager?" he probed.

"Indeed not," Miss Maitland replied, rising nicely to his bait. She proceeded to relate much the same tale that Ariel had told Lord Harcourt at dinner, embellishing it so as to make the girls seem like great heiresses in her desire to impress Sir Henry with the quality of the neighborhood.

Ariel returned to the piano to play quietly for a time, thinking it too early to go to bed.

When Aunt Maitland signaled it was time to retire, Ariel went gladly. While she undressed, she wondered what tomorrow would bring after the excitement of today. As she slipped beneath her covers, her thoughts turned to Lord Harcourt. He joked about wearing shining armor, but in her mind he gleamed with true English gallantry. She had no doubt but that he would rescue her from danger if need be.

"Egads, why does that fool Dudley have to go with us?" Percy demanded as he and Jordan drove back to Harcourt Hall, seated comfortably in the landau.

"I thought it would help to entertain him if we could go someplace where there are a goodly number of people. It would also serve to keep Lady Ariel safe from his attentions. Isn't there a saying, safety in numbers?"

"Well," Percy said grumpily.

"For a man who is supposed to be courting Lady Ariel, he

has a strange way of doing it," Jordan mused as Cotman drew the landau to a halt before the front of the Hall.

"I suppose you would know how to court any better?" Percy scoffed, leaving the carriage for the pleasant warmth of the house. "And when did you acquire any practice at attracting a young lady? You are usually running in the opposite direction. You know you do!" They entered the library as he chortled with glee at the mere thought of Jordan pursuing any woman.

"Perhaps I shall make the attempt," Jordan said, his mind already made up. He poured out a glass of claret, then offered it to Percy before pouring one for himself.

"Tomorrow," Percy challenged, "I should like to see you take the Lady Ariel right away from under that nitwit's nose."

"I'll not make a wager on it, but I do accept the dare. After all, she was once engaged to my cousin—never mind how distant he was. I could always say that I agree with the estimable rector, Mr. Lytton. A toast to the challenge!"

The two men raised their glasses, then downed the fine wine. Upon that worthy action the pair engaged in a game of cards before retiring.

The excursion to Tunbridge Wells was favored with excellent weather. Again Cotman drove the landau while Mr. Dudley showed his skill with the ribbons to Jane, the only female likely to be impressed. She obligingly expressed admiration for ability that was but moderate, at best.

Once in the attractive, though smallish, town, they had Cotman let them down before the Church of King Charles the Martyr. The groom jumped down to take the reins of the gig from Mr. Dudley, then headed toward the nearest stables, followed by Cotman driving the fine landau.

The group set off in the direction of the Pantiles.

"This is where everyone meets in the morning," Lady Ariel explained to Jordan.

"Tell me about it," Jordan suggested, drawing her closer to his side. She seemed pleased to explain.

Happy to lead her away from the tiresome Mr. Dudley, Jordan took full advantage of his position. He set out to charm the girl who had sought his aid. He'd jested when he told Percy he could take Lady Ariel away from under Dudley's nose. Now he discovered it an inviting prospect. He did know that he intended to protect her from Dudley come what may. That chap didn't deserve her.

"Do you intend to sample the famous waters?" Lady Ariel asked with an impish smile as they neared the tiled area where the spring bubbled forth.

"Indeed. What was good enough for King Charles must be good enough for me," Jordan declared bravely. He suspected the mineral spring water was nasty-tasting. Mineral waters usually were. He was proven correct.

The water-dippers served Percy, Mr. Dudley, and Jordan each a glass of the foul-tasting water. None of the men wished to be thought cowards, so each drank the water, which tasted strongly of iron. Fortunately, the dipper had offered Jordan a glass that held but a slight amount of water in it. Perhaps the woman thought he was not in need of the noxious stuff.

Extending from the well was the Pantiles, a spacious avenue bordered by shady trees and lined with fine shops.

"Perhaps we can stroll along here and survey the goods on display," Lady Ariel suggested, her delight obvious.

"Now we can begin!" Jane declared after the glasses had been returned. She ignored the look of disdain from Mr. Dudley and guided him up the steps and along the shop fronts, pausing frequently to admire the various items for sale. She particularly admired a window displaying kites.

Lady Ariel bore a wistful expression when they paused before a hat shop that vied with a London establishment in elegance. While Jordan did not consider himself to be an expert, he judged the bonnets displayed in the window to be of the very latest design from Town.

"Does my lady wish for a new bonnet?" he inquired teasingly.

She smoothed her countenance to one of polite interest. "I should go into the library to take out a book instead. Wanting a new bonnet is wickedly naughty of me. I truly have no need of one." The wistful look returned, and Jordan found himself urging her into the shop, pointing out to the woman in charge the particular bonnet that had captured Ariel's eye and presumably her heart.

"You would have to loan me the sum," she whispered, looking embarrassed, while the woman was fetching a charming printed box to hold the hat after Lady Ariel had tried it on and found it irresistible.

"Of course." He hastily dug into his pocket to offer the right amount. Jordan knew better than to offer to pay for the article. It wasn't proper, no matter how much he wished to buy it for her. Her expression was his reward for helping her to obtain the treasured hat.

"I would like to have bought you the bonnet," he said as they left, gesturing to the pretty box that held the confection of straw, feathers, and riband, "but we know it is not done. Instead, I shall please myself by buying you a book. There can be no harm in that, surely!"

"I must explain," she insisted once outside the shop. "Normally, I would have had the shillings with me. Aunt seemed to be a trifle short, and I had no time to ask Mr. Greenwood. I rarely have need for money, you see."

Jordan was appalled. Every young lady needed pin money. What possible motive could Miss Maitland have for keeping her niece on such a tight rein? Well, he would do what he could to make the day a memorable one for her.

Nothing would do but that Jordan escort Ariel into Sprange's Library to select any volume that pleased her. The others soon joined them, with Mr. Dudley giving Jordan the blackest of looks.

"Sir Henry's guest seems a dour sort of fellow. I vow he has not smiled once," Jordan said in an aside to Lady Ariel as she clutched a book on flowers, a thing she had desired for an age.

"I cannot say, not knowing him well—nor desiring to, either—but I suspect your assessment of him is correct," she whispered. "At Stafford he always has the look of having bitten into a sour apple."

"I do believe he is jealous of me, for I bask in the sun of your company," Jordan said gallantly. He plucked the book on flowers from her, paid for it, then presented the nicely wrapped package to her with a flourish.

Ariel wondered at the twinkle in Lord Harcourt's eyes, yet she could not help but treasure his regard and his kind words. Never had she received the well-bred attentions from a gentleman of such London polish—nor the gift of a treasured book. Mr. Dudley would do well to study his lordship's manners and emulate them!

They strolled along the covered walkway, pausing before the bespoke perfumery shop, where Celia Townsend had an errand for her mother. It seemed a bottle of lavender scent was needed for a birthday gift. They all entered the charming little shop to look about with admiration at the various vials and bottles of many scents.

Ariel wished she might buy a bottle for herself.

"Ladies, I would have each of you to have a memento of our outing today," Lord Harcourt suddenly announced, to Jane's obvious delight. He turned to the shopkeeper and said, "A bottle of lavender scent for each of these three pretty ladies—a large size, mind you." Turning to Ariel he added, "It is perfectly acceptable for a gentleman to offer a gift of a book or a bottle of scent to a lady, particularly when it is to all ladies present."

Ariel felt the warmth of his smile all the way to her toes.

Not to be outdone, Percy declared that he desired them all to partake of tea at the smart little shop at the far end of the avenue next to Mr. Delves, the grocer.

Bottles of scent safely tucked into the various reticules, the party set off in the direction of Bath Square, where the grocer had a pretty place arranged for the serving of tea, with biscuits and scones offered as well for the enjoyment of shoppers.

A neat young woman with a clean yellow apron served them with quiet efficiency, accustomed to the flood of visitors in the summer months.

Mr. Dudley could have soured the milk merely by looking at it.

Others entered the little shop, and soon the place was overflowing with tea drinkers busy exchanging the latest gossip. Ariel happened to look out of the many-paned window only to see her aunt.

"Good gracious," she murmured to Lord Harcourt, "I do believe my aunt has come to town. Why, she never does go anywhere."

Celia turned around in her chair and gasped. "So it is. What can have brought her today?"

"Perhaps she also wished to partake of the delights to be found in Tunbridge Wells after urging us to enjoy them," Lord Harcourt said quietly.

Ariel hoped her aunt would not spoil her outing. Lord Harcourt seemed to sense her distress and momentarily placed his hand over hers. Even through her gloves she felt the strength and compassion he offered. "Should I make our presence known to her?" Ariel asked her friend and defender.

"I believe Mr. Dudley has just now done so." Lord Harcourt gestured to where Mr. Dudley stood by Sir Henry and Aunt Maitland, gesturing and doing more talking than he had done the entire day.

"How odd," Ariel murmured, not wanting the others to share her thoughts. "He can express himself when he wants."

"We shall soon find out what he has said, I'll wager," Lord Harcourt murmured back.

Miss Maitland led the way to the table where Jane, Celia, Mr. Ponsonby, Lord Harcourt, and a trembling Ariel sat.

Lord Harcourt rose to his feet, as did Mr. Ponsonby.

"Good day, Miss Maitland, Sir Henry," Percy said. "You decided that Tunbridge Wells was too appealing to resist, did you? I vow it was all your descriptions that brought it on; you could not stay at home. Such a fine day, as well. The weather has been kind to us all. Would you care to join us for tea?"

Whatever Aunt Maitland had been about to say was left unsaid at the genial flow of words from Mr. Ponsonby. She sputtered like a frustrated hen, then at Sir Henry's nudge sat on one of the dainty chairs Lord Harcourt had courteously drawn forward for her use.

Jane, looking like she might explode, stared at Aunt Maitland. Celia fidgeted with the reticule in her lap. Mr. Ponsonby merely looked uncomfortable.

Mr. Dudley looked vastly pleased with himself.

"I gather you have had a splendid day?" Aunt Maitland's

words sounded innocent, yet they had a faintly ominous tone to them.

"Indeed we have," Lord Harcourt replied while Ariel sat waiting for what might follow. "Your niece found a lovely bonnet that looks charming on her. We paid visits to the bookshop and the bespoke perfumery so Miss Townsend could fill a request for her mother."

Aunt slumped visibly. "Indeed," she said stiffly with a pained look at Lord Harcourt. She dug into her reticule, then handed a note and a few shillings to Ariel, looking as though it was a distressing exercise. "I suppose you had to borrow from someone."

"Thank you, Aunt," Ariel said, although she was certain the money had not been Aunt's. Her aunt never spent a penny of her own money and was tight as could be with Ariel's own funds. One would think it was her duty to prevent the spending of the earl's—and Ariel's—fortunes.

Mr. Dudley's smug expression faded.

The young woman brought more tea plus a tray with biscuits and scones and tiny fairy cakes, all of the first stare of quality.

"Please partake of the refreshment, Miss Maitland and Sir Henry," Mr. Ponsonby said with the grace and charm of a London gentleman of means.

"I had no idea that Tunbridge Wells possessed a pastry shop of *this* quality," the lady said reluctantly.

"Indeed, sir, this is a treat," Sir Henry declared with far more enthusiasm. "Bath couldn't do better."

Mr. Dudley sank upon his chair, deflated like a hot-air balloon that had come to ground.

"The day was so fine we could not remain at Stafford when the delights of Tunbridge Wells awaited us," Sir Henry continued expansively, after savoring the flavor of a delicate almond cake.

"People come here to gossip," Miss Maitland observed of the others in the pastry shop.

"Ah, but my dear lady, they also take walks, read, ride, and above all, shop. How nice you found a new bonnet, Lady Ariel," Sir Henry said with a darted look at Mr. Dudley, who said nothing. "It has been my observation that nothing like a new bonnet elevates the spirits of a young lady."

"I fancy that Miss Maitland would enjoy the same, even if she is not quite a young girl," Lord Harcourt replied kindly.

Miss Maitland appeared not to know quite how to respond to that remark. She seemed to thaw. "Your mama had a commission for you, Celia?"

"I was able to buy the bottle of scent she wished. It is a gift for Aunt Eulalia."

Jane eagerly leaned forward to add, "Lord Harcourt insisted upon buying the three of us each a bottle of lavender scent as a memento of our day, as though I would ever forget it."

Celia placed a hand over her sister's, silencing her without a word.

"It is most acceptable, dear Aunt. I vow that we have all behaved with utmost propriety," Ariel said, willing to defend Lord Harcourt with all her being.

"Hpmf," Miss Maitland murmured, but looked appeased when she washed down her seed cake with a cup of finest bohea tea.

"We must be on our way, I fear," Lord Harcourt said at last when it appeared there was to be no more conversation and Miss Maitland had consumed the last of the cakes.

A round of thanks was offered to the genial Mr. Ponsonby before they all departed the pastry shop.

Jordan was not unhappy to part from Miss Maitland. She had not been critical, yet cast a pall on the party.

"We shall see you later, then," Sir Henry said genially. He gave Mr. Dudley a significant look, and Jordan wondered what it meant.

"Could we take a stroll in the Park before we leave, perhaps?" Jane said with eagerness.

"I doubt we have the time," Celia admonished.

"It is better to be just us," Lady Ariel said candidly to Lord Harcourt. "I have noticed that oftentimes older people cast a damper on young spirits."

"How true," Jordan agreed. He tucked her hand in his arm, then strolled along the Pantiles until they reached the Assembly rooms, where all paused.

"We will be here a week from Wednesday," Jane said with rapturous delight.

The others smiled, then continued on until they spotted Cotman with the landau and the groom with the gig.

"I say," Mr. Dudley said of a sudden, "I should like to have Lady Ariel drive back to Stafford Court with me."

All were so astounded at this complete sentence coming forth from the most silent gentleman any had known that no one knew what to say at first.

Jordan thought back to the significant look from Sir Henry and decided to challenge this change in seating. "Why, sir, you would deprive Miss Jane of the opportunity to have a chance to observe a fine whip once more? She may never get another."

"Yes, Mr. Dudley," Lady Ariel seconded as she placed one hand on the door of the landau. "Miss Jane will be quite cast into a green melancholy."

Jordan took the opportunity to hurry Lady Ariel into the carriage while Percy rushed Miss Townsend in behind her. Percy plumped himself beside her, then Jordan stepped in, shutting the door firmly behind him.

Mr. Dudley gave Jane a look of utter loathing, but assisted her into the gig. There was no other way out.

The walk in the Park indeed had to be omitted, considering how the time had flown by.

"Jane will be desolate," Miss Townsend commented.

"Another time, perhaps?" Jordan said, then sat back to enjoy the drive back to Stafford Court and the Hall.

They had just passed the brick-making works on the way out of town when it happened.

A shot rang out.

Lady Ariel, Celia, and Percy looked on in horror as blood rapidly began to seep from the sleeve of the elegant coat Jordan wore.

Jordan felt a stinging pain in his right arm such as he had never known. *This couldn't be happening!*

Lady Ariel scrabbled to find something useful to stanch the bleeding, while Percy shouted to Cotman, "Turn us around. We must get him to Dr. Mayo at once!"

Jordan's last coherent thought was to wonder who wanted him out of the way.

Chapter Nine

Mr. Ponsonby leaped forward to come to his friend's aid, managing to crunch the hatbox in the process. Celia maintained a cool head and stayed on her side of the carriage, not screaming or succumbing to the vapors.

Ariel had sensibly taken a scarf from her neck to tie around Lord Harcourt's arm to stem the bleeding. He had been but inches away from her, and the thought crossed her mind that in a second she would have been the recipient of the shot. Guns were often inaccurate in aim, and the carriage was moving. Her feelings regarding the death of his cousin flashed in her mind. Could there be a connection? It seemed an odd coincidence that her late betrothed should die and now the gentleman who appeared to court her was shot, narrowly missing death.

Fortunately, Cotman had studied the map of Tunbridge Wells while they had spent the day rambling about the town. When Percy told him Dr. Mayo lived on Mount Ephraim Road, he knew precisely where to turn. In short order they drew up before the building about the same time that Lord Harcourt roused.

"Sorry, cannot think why I passed out," he murmured, sounding very groggy. Mr. Ponsonby leaped from the carriage to help his friend exit. With the groom on his other side, the gentlemen made their way to the door.

The girls sat in silence for a time, considering all that had happened in the last minutes.

Celia looked at the smashed hatbox and wryly shook her head. "I fear you are doomed to wear your old bonnet a trifle longer." She shifted to sit next to Ariel, enabling them to speak softly.

"Indeed. You realize that had Cotman chanced to urge the horses to increase their speed, I might have been the one shot, and perhaps not just in the arm."

Celia digested this and nodded. "Or, had the one shooting been a trifle quicker, it could have hit Lord Harcourt to do terminal damage."

Ariel grew faint at the mere thought of Lord Harcourt dead, and collapsed into Celia's lap.

A levelheaded girl, for want of a better restorative Celia hastily found the bottle of lavender scent in her reticule, unstopped it, then wafted it under Ariel's nose. The seconds seemed to drag, but it was not long before Ariel came to her senses, shaking her head.

"Forgive me. The realization that Lord Harcourt might die affected me strongly." Ariel adjusted her clothing as she sat up, avoiding the comprehension she knew she'd see in Celia's eyes.

"I believe you are coming to care for your shining knight. Will your aunt approve of him anymore than she did the previous Lord Harcourt? Is Mr. Dudley an effort to prevent you from—" Celia's words were cut off at a warning look from Ariel.

At that moment Jane and Mr. Dudley drove up beside the landau. "What happened?" Jane cried, seeing that the men had gone. "I looked behind, and we saw the carriage turn up this way. I insisted we follow." She shot an incensed look at Mr. Dudley.

Ariel found she could not speak, so it was Celia who replied. "Some insane person was out shooting, and poor Lord Harcourt happened to be in the way."

"Odd way to put it—in his way?" Mr. Dudley said.

"I should think you would have been terrified!" Jane cried, her face all curiosity.

"What makes you think we were not?" Ariel said, even now feeling more than a bit shaken. "They have been in that house for an age." She stared at the door as though it might magically open to bring forth her friends.

"Oh, I trust it was not a fatal wound," Jane cried with chilling fervor.

The door to the house opened, and Mr. Ponsonby came out to the carriage. "Dr. Mayo says it is a clean shot, and he will permit Harcourt to return home under strict condition he go straight to bed."

Celia and Ariel exchanged relieved looks.

"He will be out soon?" Ariel inquired, only to see Lord Harcourt leave the house on the arm of the groom.

There was a trifle more color in his face. He walked slowly, but did not look as though he would collapse. His coat was removed and draped over his shoulders; a black silk sling cradled his arm close to his chest to prevent additional harm. The very sight of him brought tears to Ariel's eyes, tears she instantly repressed.

Once he was in the carriage, Ariel insisted, "Here, put your head on my lap and rest for the trip to the Hall. We shall endeavor to make you as comfortable as possible."

"Hear now," Mr. Dudley objected, "not proper."

"And what have you to say to anything, Mr. Dudley?" Ariel asked, allowing her dislike of the man to surface momentarily.

He subsided, turning to Jane to suggest they begin the trip back to Stafford.

"I should rather follow the landau in the event something is needed where we might be of help," Jane said quietly, but most firmly.

Celia gave an approving nod. Mr. Dudley sat back in the gig with a sullen pout.

Once again Lord Harcourt was encouraged to pillow his head on Ariel's lap. The others arranged themselves as best as they could. At the signal from Mr. Ponsonby, Cotman brought the carriage into sedate motion, one that it was hoped would least jounce Lord Harcourt.

Jordan tried to ease into a more comfortable position. He felt like a fool, passing out because of a mere bullet wound in his arm—no more than a scratch. He reflected on the danger— to himself and to Lady Ariel. A moment either way and it would have been the end for one of them. That had frightened him more than the shot—especially the danger to Ariel. She was too precious to be lost to—all.

"I should like to know why anyone was shooting this close

to Tunbridge Wells and near a main road out of town," he said to Percy in a somewhat unsteady voice.

"We were right by the brick works when it happened. Perhaps there has been a spot of trouble there?" Percy queried.

"I doubt it," Celia Townsend said instantly. "There has been no trouble with workers anywhere around here. They are all too glad to get work to create trouble. Not a great deal of poaching going on, either."

"Poaching? In the middle of the day and so close to town?" Percy queried. "I doubt that."

"Why would anyone wish to put a period to Lord Harcourt's existence?" Lady Ariel exclaimed softly, giving voice to the thought that had lingered in all minds since the shooting occurred.

"Who can say?" Jordan speculated. "Thank goodness the carriage had moved just enough so the bullet went through my arm and not my shoulder."

"You will have to rest easy for a time, my lord," Lady Ariel said, brushing back his dark hair from his forehead with a gentle hand, lingering just a bit more than necessary.

Jordan snuggled more comfortably into her lap, occasionally allowing his gaze to stray to her face. Ariel's tender caress and the concern in her eyes brought warmth to his chilled heart, eased the ache in his arm. It would seem that she was very worried for him, and her caring deepened his regard for her.

It seemed to take forever to make the return trip to Harcourt Hall. Even though Jordan felt measurably better as time passed, he remained where he was, content to enjoy Ariel's comforting ministrations.

At the Hall Mrs. Longwood bustled forth to meet them. Once aware of her employer's injury, she took charge. She was never bossy, nor did she raise her voice, yet within moments the servants had matters to hand, assisting his lordship from the carriage and into the house.

"It would be most improper for me to remain here to nurse Lord Harcourt," Ariel said. It was clear she wished she might.

"Your aunt would have a prolonged case of the vapors, I

vow," Celia replied, the shadow of a smile crossing her pleasant face.

Percy returned from the house at that moment. "He would like to see you shortly. Wants to thank you for your care, I'm sure. Then I will see you home." He turned to where Celia sat silently to add, "If you will wait a moment, I will see you home and explain matters to your parents. Jane ought to be there by now, but she does not have all the facts."

"Indeed," Celia said with a sigh. She entered the house with Ariel while Cotman took the landau to the stables, intent upon arranging for the curricle to be harnessed for the short drive to Miss Townsend's home and then later to Stafford Court.

Leaving Celia in the drawing room, Ariel followed Mr. Ponsonby up the stairs until they reached the room where he indicated his friend rested.

Ariel paused outside the oak door, casting a concerned look at Mr. Ponsonby. "You will remain with me? I fear I shall burst into tears and utterly disgrace myself. Poor man, to be so injured while giving us a treat."

Once he assured her he would be at her side, Ariel opened the door to enter the room.

It was a distinct shock to see the vital Lord Harcourt flat on his back. He had yet to change to his nightshirt—a matter she surmised Barton would handle in a trice. His lordship reclined on the bed, his coat removed. A thick bandage covered his upper arm; the shirtsleeve had been cut away and his arm was otherwise bare, and quite still. A faint pink tinge stained the linen. The valet stood guard on the other side of the bed, ready to take charge at any time if need be.

"It isn't as bad as you might think. Within a day or two I shall be as right as a trivet," Lord Harcourt said, his voice still shaky but stronger than she had expected.

"I wish I might do something to help." She clasped her hands together, wishing she might be there to soothe his brow and offer comfort. That he wore a thin cambric shirt, his cravat tossed aside, and a goodly amount of skin was revealed she quite ignored. The significance of the stain she set aside to be worried over later.

The gentlemen exchanged looks.

Lord Harcourt spoke. "You were more than kind to help me on the way home. I thank you for that."

Mr. Ponsonby touched Ariel on her arm. "I believe it is time to go. He needs some sleep, I think."

Unable to prevent herself, Ariel reached out to gently touch Lord Harcourt's hand. "I trust you will be well as soon as possible."

"Indeed I shall. We have an assembly to attend if I make no mistake. You shall promise me two dances."

A ghost of a grin passed across his face, and she wanted to weep. Ariel could find no words to scold him at the moment. She merely shook her head, then left the room, thankful for Mr. Ponsonby's comforting presence beside her.

She wiped her eyes and blew her nose on the handkerchief Mr. Ponsonby proffered, then composed herself, stiffening her spine and forcing the tears to recede.

"There now," he said with an awkward pat on her shoulder. He ushered her to the drawing room, where Celia awaited them. "I suggest you wait here until I have taken Miss Townsend home and given the explanation. It may be possible for you to check on Harcourt again before you leave for home."

Celia gave Ariel a hug, promised to see her as soon as possible, then hurried along with Mr. Ponsonby to where the curricle awaited them.

Mrs. Longwood bustled into the drawing room, bearing a tray of tea and scones. "Sit you down, my lady. Nothing like a restoring cup of tea for frazzled nerves, I always say. My, I would have swooned, I would."

Taking pity on the housekeeper's curiosity, Ariel swallowed a comforting sip of tea, then said, "It was most frightening, I can tell you that. Celia remained calm, and I knew it was important to stay composed. I felt it was necessary to cushion Lord Harcourt's head and keep him still so I had to remain alert, did I not? Cotman did a splendid job of driving us home. Scarcely a jolt the entire way."

"Oh, my lady," Mrs. Longwood cried, instantly elevating Lady Ariel to sainthood.

Ariel sipped the strong tea and consumed a bite of scone, finding she was actually hungry and most thirsty. She felt a trifle guilty, yet perhaps it was the best thing to do. No point in fainting away now. "I should like to see Lord Harcourt again before I leave if possible—just to reassure myself he is doing well. I'd not talk."

The housekeeper nodded, leaving the room at once. Ariel could hear her walking up the stairs with quiet steps.

The tea proved welcome, and the scone actually soothed her nerves that she had thought quite numb. She absorbed the peace and tranquility of the house while she waited. It would take Percy some time to drive to the Townsend house, explain, then return. She leaned back in the chair and closed her eyes to rest. When she did, the memory of that awful moment returned to haunt her.

"Please," she prayed, "help him to survive and be fine once more." She ignored the tears that silently slipped down her cheeks.

She must have dozed ever so briefly, yet the sun had not changed position very much when she felt a touch on her shoulder. Flashing her eyes open, she found Barton standing there, silent and yet somehow approving.

"Mr. Ponsonby will be here before long. You wished to see Lord Harcourt before you leave?"

"Yes, please." She rose and followed the valet to the hall and up the stairs. They paused a moment before entering the bedroom where his lordship had been placed. Ariel appreciated that—it allowed her to gather the courage she knew she'd need.

Upon entering, Ariel was relieved to see Lord Harcourt resting comfortably with his arms on the counterpane and only the slight bulge of the bandage beneath the white nightshirt to indicate he had been wounded.

"Well, I should think you malingering did I not know you are not the sort of man given to such folly," she said with a hint of tartness to her voice. If she were to be sympathetic, she would burst into tears, and that would never do.

"I shall be out of this bed before you know it," he replied with a ghost of his familiar smile. "Can't have a little thing like this lay me low."

"The man could have intended to hit me, you know," she

said when she had not intended to voice an opinion one way or the other. "You *may* not have been his target."

"So you believe it to have been deliberate as well?" he queried. He glanced to Barton, then back to Ariel. "Barton would have it that there is someone who wants *me* out of the way."

"Perhaps that is so. I believe it would be best if I did not see you again, my lord," Ariel said bravely, knowing that more than anything in the world she wanted to be close to this man. "The previous Lord Harcourt was betrothed to me and he was killed. Now you have paid me particular attentions, and you have been shot. I fear it is more than a coincidence. I'll not have your death on my conscience."

He frowned—whether from pain or anger, she didn't know. "I believe it is my decision to make . . . and I would by far prefer to see you, my dear."

Jordan watched her face turn pale, then a blush creep over her delicate skin. He wondered if he had been too bold. But he would not be dictated to by anyone, least of all the one who meant the most to him in the entire world.

"I suppose I cannot dissuade you. My papa is the most stubborn man there could be. He would do the same—just as he pleases, I daresay." Lady Ariel exchanged a look with Barton, then stepped to the door. "I had best leave now. I have broken more rules of propriety than I can count today. It bothers me not in the least, however. All that matters is that you get well." With that daring statement she slipped around the door and disappeared.

When she had gone, Jordan sat up and exchanged a look with his valet. He was barely scratched, but it would serve his purpose to allow whoever had shot at him to believe him near death's door.

"The young lady is very courageous, milord," Barton commented. "I believe she truly cares for you, yet she would give you up rather than risk your life."

"Noble, indeed," Jordan replied, reluctant to discuss the matter with his valet, never mind that they had been as close as inkle-weavers all these many years.

Taking due caution, Jordan rose from the bed and went to

the window to watch Percy return to enter the house. It was not long when he left with Lady Ariel on his arm. She entered the curricle, and in short order they were gone.

"I suppose I had best remain in bed, no matter I could be sitting in a chair." He glanced at his bandaged arm, then at his valet.

"That is true, my lord," Barton agreed. "It would serve your charade were you to remain abed for the rest of this day. Servants may be loyal, but even the best might let something slip when least suspecting."

Much struck by this bit of wisdom, Jordan nodded. He ignored the banyan he'd hoped to don. It was a magnificent item in dark blue brocade embroidered in silver thread and most comfortable.

"Tell Percy to come in here if you see him before I do," Jordan instructed upon returning to his bed, its comfort surprisingly welcome. Perhaps he was weaker than he knew. The pillows he leaned against felt good, too.

"I shall bring up a tray of tea and scones, milord," Barton informed his master. "You need nourishment."

Jordan gave his man a wry smile and nodded. Perhaps it was just as well that he remain quietly in his room. The doctor indicated he might do as he pleased, but did caution against doing too much. Jordan was anxious to investigate the shooting. It might be a good idea to sneak back to Tunbridge Wells and have a look at the area where the gunman had been situated when the shot was fired. It might be possible a clue lingered behind.

Barton left, quickly returning with a tray of tea and scones. He poured tea, then offered it and a scone.

Jordan took a sip of tea, then a bite of scone while he considered who might benefit from his death. The list was not a long one, but it merited study.

The door opened and Percy stepped in, standing before Jordan with hands on hips.

"Well?"

"That poor woman is in tears and believes it all to be her fault," he stated with a shake of his head.

"By poor woman you undoubtedly mean Lady Ariel?" Jordan quizzed.

"Who else?" Percy shot back, drawing a chair close to the bed. "She doesn't realize you are not at death's door. I've not seen a doctor pour brandy over a wound before. Must have stung like the devil."

" 'Effective cleanser,' he said. He was out of basilicum powder." Jordan grimaced when he moved his arm slightly, then casually inquired, "What do you say to a return to Tunbridge Wells and the location of the shooting?"

"Clues? Allow me to drive the curricle, and I might agree," Percy insisted. "Even though your arm is merely grazed, the doctor suggested you take it easy."

"Would you?" Jordan challenged.

Percy gave his friend an abashed look and nodded. "Of course I wouldn't. I'd be out of here as fast as I could manage."

"Tomorrow will likely be soon enough. Whoever performed the deed will not expect anyone to come snooping about that area so soon, if at all." He thought a moment, then added, "Ask Cotman to dig out the ball from the carriage. There will be no clue in it, but I should like to see it all the same."

"Will do," Percy snapped back at once. He jumped to his feet and was gone in an instant.

The door had been left ajar, and very soon Prince edged around it, giving his master a mournful look.

"I know, old fellow, I've neglected you shamefully."

That was all the encouragement the bloodhound needed. He ambled across the room, then jumped on the bed to drape himself across Jordan's feet with a sorrowful sigh.

Jordan was staring at the ceiling when Percy returned, lead ball in hand. "Here 'tis. Cotman was about to toss it away, so it was a good thing I went immediately."

"The other one I found is in my top drawer over there. Be a good chap and get it for me." Jordan pointed to the dog reclining on his feet, a smile on his lips.

Percy did as requested and handed the small items to Jordan at once.

"All we can tell is that they are the same size and resemble every other ball made for a flintlock rifle in the past ten years." He put the two lead balls down on the table at his side.

"That means that Lady Ariel *could* be right. The same person who shot at your cousin might be the one who shot you." Aghast, he again sank down on the chair to absently pick up a scone. He took a bite, then said, "Who?"

"That is what I would like to know. It is all the more imperative I return to Tunbridge Wells. What reason can I offer?"

"Need you have one?" Percy said, looking up from the tray as he poured himself a cup of tea.

"I believe you stuck your foot in Lady Ariel's hat box. Perhaps I could go to town to replace it?"

"I should be doing that," Percy replied, looking embarrassed.

"I shall send a message to Lady Ariel to see if she wants the same bonnet," Jordan mused. He moved a bit only to receive a morose look from the dog.

"Good company for you," Percy said with enthusiasm. "You ought to take him along tomorrow. After all, he is a bloodhound. He might find something of interest."

Jordan smiled at Percy's hopeful expression. "If I take him, you will have to handle the ribbons while he sits on me."

"I said I would drive us. What makes you think Barton, Mrs. Longwood, and Cotman will let you go out? They are most protective of your hide, my friend."

"I shall tell them I wish to consult with Dr. Mayo again. He is quite an eminent physician. Indeed, I think I am fortunate to be able to see him at all since there is no surgeon in town. You may hint that it would be beneath the gentleman to come into the country, even for a baron."

Percy gave him a crooked grin. "Sad thing is that you are likely closer to the truth than either of us know. I heard that there is one doctor in London who took in over twenty thousand pounds last year."

"While I doubt it would be Dr. Mayo, he likely earns well over eight thousand."

"Pity," Percy mused. "He may be an agreeable chap, but he would never do in Society."

"There are some who desire money more than approval."

Percy recalled his friend's limited means before he inherited the title and estate, and nodded his agreement.

"And then, you have those who want the title *and* the estates *and* money as well!" Jordan said bitterly.

"We have both seen those, I fear," Percy said with equal tartness. "Write that message for Lady Ariel, and I'll take it over now."

"They might be dining," Jordan reminded. Country people were given to earlier meals than those in the city.

"Oh, bother," Percy said with a laugh while he found paper and quill for Jordan. Once settled with those, he brought the bottle of ink, then waited while his friend penned a few lines.

"Harcourt, what will you do first?"

"Improve rapidly, drive to Tunbridge Wells in the morning, and decide what next after that. We have an assembly coming up next week, and I intend to be there."

Percy picked up the folded paper, then looked closely at his friend. "That shot affected you more than you will admit. Rest while I'm gone, will you? We can talk about that assembly later."

Once Percy had left the room, Jordan did as suggested and settled on his pillow to nap a bit. A refreshed mind would think more clearly.

Percy tooled his way from Harcourt Hall to Stafford Court in no time at all.

Cummins welcomed him with surprising warmth. "They will go into dinner shortly, sir. I believe Lady Ariel would be pleased to receive you," he pronounced after Percy had revealed that he had a message for her ladyship from Lord Harcourt. He ushered Percy into the library with great courtesy.

Lady Ariel entered the room, looking as though she had hurried every step. "What is it? Has something happened?"

"Here, Harcourt sent this to you. Best read it at once, then I can take your answer back with me."

Giving him a curious look, she accepted the missive, read it over, then stared at Percy a moment before speaking. "He is going to Tunbridge Wells in the morning? By himself?"

"I shall go with him. He thought he could consult with Dr.

Mayo and pick up a replacement for your bonnet at the same time. I'm dashed sorry about stepping on it, you know. I shall be the one to pick up the bill, you may count on that."

"Indeed? I am sure you are sorry, Mr. Ponsonby. But I insist upon going with him. After all, I very much doubt there is another hat just like the one I selected. I would like to choose the replacement. If you please," she added politely, but with a firmness that bordered on stubborn.

"He intends to take the curricle. He cannot drive himself. I doubt you can handle the ribbons," Percy replied a trifle smugly.

"You have it outside? Now?" she queried sweetly.

Percy suddenly developed misgivings. "Yes."

"Allow me to set your mind at ease." She turned to where Cummins lurked by the door. "I will be back directly. Tell Aunt they had best begin dinner without me." She found a pair of gloves, then confidently led the way with Percy following reluctantly in her wake.

The sun shone through scattered clouds in the morning, promising a pleasant day, if not a warm one.

Percy had driven the curricle over to Stafford as early as he dared to find Lady Ariel dressed and waiting for him near the gate to the avenue. Her dark blue spencer topping a simple blue-and-white striped gown looked quite sensible for travel. A neat close bonnet of blue velvet framed a face taut with worry.

She climbed in, taking over the reins while explaining, "I did not want Aunt asking uncomfortable questions. I have never done anything like this before, but I hope to scrape by without too much grief."

Percy nodded, knowing what his mother was like with his sisters. When he and Ariel reached Harcourt Hall, they found Jordan leaving the house, Prince at his side.

Jordan looked at Ariel as Percy jumped down. She stared at him with a worried gaze, her heart in her eyes if she but knew it. It served to ease the aching a bit to know she cared that much for him.

Percy assisted him into the curricle, then stood back after

hoisting the dog up to sit on Harcourt's feet. "I believe I shall go over to the Townsend place. If I remain here, I will have to answer questions, and I do not know any answers. Do be careful, both of you."

Ariel nodded, then gave the horse the office to proceed. They soon left Harcourt Hall behind and were moving smoothly along the road to Tunbridge Wells, thankful they could avoid entering the village of Stafford.

"Percy was right. You are gifted in handling the reins," Jordan said after a time.

"Papa taught me when I was a little girl. I haven't had much practice of late, but I suspect it is something one does not forget."

"I want to stop where the gunman lurked yesterday."

"Very well. Percy explained that you heal rapidly, but I think you were not hurt as badly as we feared," she said, darting a glance at him before returning her steady gaze to the road ahead.

"You do?" Jordan inquired, but did not explain a thing. It was better that way.

"So I am not to know? So be it. But I demand to explore the area with you. Two heads are better than one, my nanny was wont to say."

"And we have Prince with us as well, thanks to Percy."

They quietly chatted about yesterday's excursion and what they contemplated for the coming assembly, an outing in which Jordan insisted he would still partake.

"You are very brave," Lady Ariel commented.

"Or stupid," he countered.

"Perhaps a closed carriage? I suspect the Townsend traveling coach would do very well. It would seat six, and you must know that Jane will not remain at home."

"How did you manage to shake Dudley?"

"He had not yet arrived at the house this morning. I could scarcely invite him to go with me anywhere when he might still be abed at the inn. Could I?" she demanded with a chuckle. "Cummins will inform him that I have gone calling."

"I believe Cummins has a soft spot for you," Jordan said with a smile.

"He has been at Stafford since I was born. I couldn't imagine the house without him."

"Ah, we are coming into Tunbridge Wells. Watch for the brick works on the right."

"I believe I see it ahead." She carefully guided the horse to the side of the road, then neatly drew to a halt.

"Nicely done, Lady Ariel."

She jumped down from the carriage and tied the reins to a nearby tree, then returned to encourage Prince to get down.

"Here is a lead for him. I do not expect it will be much good. Stubborn dog seems to have notions of his own." Jordan gingerly exited the curricle, then walked at Lady Ariel's side to the far side of the brick works.

The dog to began to sniff around, tugging Ariel along behind him as he explored the area. "Where do you think the man was when he fired his rifle?" Ariel inquired.

"So, you think it a rifle?"

"A mad guess, nothing more. What else would it be?"

"Let us explore," he said, putting his good arm about her, leading her toward a place where some shrubbery met the sloping roof of the works. "This looks like a likely spot."

"Prince, see what you can find," Ariel urged, ignoring the disbelieving look from Lord Harcourt. "You never know what that dog may uncover unless you try him."

Prince nosed about while Ariel enjoyed the closeness to his lordship. It was remarkable that he could even walk today, let alone assist her over rough grasses. Then she observed fine beads of sweat on his brow and knew that it was costing him more than he would admit.

The dog dug his nose into the grass, snuffling at something, and Ariel at once leaned down to poke about, coming up with a small powder flask of an unusual design. "How odd. My father has one just like this."

Chapter Ten

"**H**is powder flask is unusual in that it is made of silver with a silver-gilt spout," Lady Ariel pointed out. "Papa bought it in London. I suppose it's possible there is another just like it." She studied the powder flask before handing it to Jordan. "I have polished it any number of times for Papa as he does not like the servants to handle it. Not even Cummins. What can this mean!"

Prince sat up proudly, and if a dog could grin, he grinned.

"It looks to hold two and a half drams of powder to one ounce of shot," Jordan murmured, handling the flask with care. "And it means that either someone in Stafford Court was able to get access to it, or that another just like your father's powder flask exists. And I give leave to doubt that," he concluded with a meaningful look at Ariel.

"If Papa's is missing, I wonder who could have taken it? It should be in his library, in a special case. How frightening to contemplate," she said with a shiver that had nothing to do with the early morning air.

"Shall I keep this for the moment?" Jordan said before slipping the flask into a pocket of his coat after a nod from Lady Ariel indicated it was agreeable with her.

"Yes, do keep it safe for the present. I will be most interested to check Papa's case to discover if his flask is missing. Although I truly wonder that anyone would be so foolish as to steal such a thing. Will all be gone? The gun, everything?"

They began strolling to the carriage, Prince pacing at their sides like a guard of old.

"Fool thing for anyone to do—to take such a distinctive powder flask, much less a gun. It makes me believe that whoever is shooting is someone who does not do so as an occupation. An expert would have plain items."

"Oh," Lady Ariel gasped. "There are such people? Perhaps that is why both you and your cousin were not hit—that is, you were merely winged as it were," she mused as they returned to the curricle. "Your cousin was missed completely, and had his horse not been spooked he might be alive today." It seemed to Jordan that the possibility of his cousin still being around didn't seem to appeal to the lady at his side. At least, she made no sighs, nor did she wipe tears from her lovely gray eyes.

A man from the brick works came out at that moment to give them a curious look. Jordan paused, then said, "Go to the carriage and wait for me. I would ask a question or two of this man, and he might be hesitant to speak before a lady of quality."

"Very well." Lady Ariel obeyed instantly, Prince trotting at her side after a lingering look at Jordan. Jordan appreciated her lack of argument in this instance, and it was as well that the dog went with her as a sort of protection. Amazing that the dog had proven so worthwhile.

He approached the workman, hoping that his arm didn't do anything beyond its present ache, like resume bleeding, for instance. He supposed he ought to be home in bed instead of tearing about the country.

Ariel watched Lord Harcourt chat with the workman, nodding, gesturing to where they had found the flask, even showing the flask briefly. The man also gestured, shaking his head, but talking at some length before turning to leave. Lord Harcourt made short work of his return to the carriage.

He looked a trifle pale, and Ariel could see he was grateful to sit down on the carriage seat. Sweat beaded his forehead. She was glad that Prince had hopped into the carriage with no more than encouragement from her. Lord Harcourt was in no condition to be hauling a dog of that size up or down.

"I must know if you learned anything," she quietly demanded after setting the carriage forth to the center of Tunbridge Wells.

"Not much. The chap saw a young man around here about that time yesterday, but he did not pay him much heed. Apparently there was nothing out of the ordinary about whoever was here."

Ariel continued to drive into town, baffled at their dilemma. "How can we possibly deal with this when we cannot learn who is behind the shootings?"

"But we now have the powder flask," he reminded her.

"When I return to Stafford, I shall inspect Papa's case. Since we do not know *how* it was taken, anyone can be suspect. Correct?" She gave him a brave smile, hoping she did not appear as frightened as she was.

"Indeed, how very perceptive of you. I see we are approaching Bath Square. Since we are in town, we had best purchase that replacement bonnet for you. Percy was rather chagrinned to discover that he had completely ruined your new bonnet," Lord Harcourt said, thus changing the subject.

They left the carriage and horse close by, with Prince sitting a guard on the seat, lord of all he surveyed.

The same woman was in charge of the hat shop when Ariel and Lord Harcourt entered. She gave them a surprised look until his lordship explained what had happened.

"That is too bad, my lady," the woman said. "Sadly, I do not have another just like the one you bought. Perhaps we can find something else that will please?"

With Lord Harcourt seated on a somewhat dainty gilt chair, the search for another bonnet began.

It took perhaps half an hour to look through the selection of bonnets, then choose one that both Ariel and Lord Harcourt approved. The rich blue grosgrain was trimmed with cream bands of ribbon and a cluster of short feathers to one side. It was a jaunty cap style, a type Aunt Maitland had deplored as fast—which meant it was the latest thing from London and she was not about to accept it yet. Ariel found it utterly delightful.

As they left the shop, Ariel turned to Lord Harcourt. "It is kind of Mr. Ponsonby to replace that bonnet." She fiddled with the ties of the bonnet box a bit, strolling in the direction of the carriage as she spoke. "As tempting as it would be to linger in Tunbridge, I feel it would be best to return to Stafford at once. I will not rest easy until I have looked at that gun case." Besides, his lordship looked as though he was ready for a good rest.

"Some other time we will wander about at will," he promised, assisting her into the carriage with his good arm. He joined her, placing the bonnet box by his feet. Prince eyed the box with disfavor, then scrambled up on the seat between the two people, both of whom gave the animal a dismayed look. He made it a squeeze, for certain.

Within minutes they had left Tunbridge Wells behind them, passing the brick works with uneasy glances. Ariel guided their carriage through what little traffic there was with surprising skill, then gave the horse its head once the town was behind them.

"I know there is no one there now, and you have the powder flask, yet I could not help but be uneasy," Ariel said in a low voice.

"I confess I felt an apprehension, myself."

"You told the others you intended to see Dr. Mayo. Are you certain you did not wish to go there?"

"No, the man would think I am the malingerer you thought me yesterday. The wound is much improved today."

"Sir, this jaunt has taken a great deal out of you, and as soon as we are at Harcourt I beg you to take your ease. Solving the riddle of the shooting can wait another day. And in any event, you may be able to think while on your back in bed."

Jordan glanced at the lovely, innocent miss at his side. There were a lot of things he could think of to do while in bed. At this moment, mulling over the would-be killer was not one of them.

Lady Ariel was indeed a brave young woman. No vapors for her, no Byronic silliness, either. On the other hand, she might not find him in the least appealing, and that thought disturbed him for some odd reason. That he had come to have a regard for this charming woman he set aside for the moment. Of course, there was that look he'd caught in her eyes that told him she cared. How much was another thing.

A silence fell between them, one heavy with unspoken words and worries.

Ariel worried about Lord Harcourt. She hoped that few people knew of this expedition to town. Might someone suspect that they found something of vital interest while away? If the would-be assassin learned where they had gone and what they had found, he would not be pleased.

"Whoever shot at me—and I do *not* think he intended to hit you, my dear—may be under the authority of someone else. Had you considered that? It might even be an employee, either of Stafford or Harcourt, who bears a grudge or otherwise wants to rub me out for some reason."

She gave him a puzzled glance at the unfamiliar expression, then shrugged. If to "rub out" was akin to "do away with," it was clear what it meant. She shivered at the thought of eliminating someone so completely.

At that moment a carriage came tearing along from the opposite direction at a speed Ariel found alarming. She hastily guided their curricle to the side of the road as far as possible, slowing, watching to see what that other fool driver might do.

Prince gave a low growl, but remained fixed between them, alert and intent.

Jordan placed a warning hand over Ariel's, stilling any inclination upon her part to panic, although he didn't think that was likely to be her reaction.

He was proven right when she held firm, not allowing his horse to bolt or shy.

"How odd. Did you see who that was?" she said once the mad driver had passed.

"No one I recognized," Jordan replied.

"That was the young fellow who used to work at Stafford Court—the one who left to go to London. It would seem that either he has returned or never left the area. You don't suppose that he had something to do with all this? That someone hired him to dispose of you? He would be familiar with the layout of the house, for once or twice he brought messages to my aunt."

"And what is your conclusion?" Jordan asked quietly, wishing he had the strength to take over the reins. At this point he was doing well to merely sit at her side.

"I'd not be surprised if he is on the way to the brick works to find the powder flask he left behind. Why else would he be tearing along this road on the way to Tunbridge Wells?" She urged the horse to a trot, disregarding the gentle pace she had kept out of consideration for Lord Harcourt's wound. "We'd best get home as fast as we can."

Within minutes she had them settled at a fast clip. Considering the state of the road, it was as good a speed as Jordan would wish. "You are so sure?"

"Call it intuition, perhaps. I find it odd that he disappeared after your cousin was shot, and here he is again—right after you have been wounded."

Jordan lapsed into an uneasy silence the rest of the mad dash. When they reached the gate to Harcourt, he gave a relieved sigh. "Take the carriage around to the stables. Cotman can take you home. I imagine you are exhausted."

"It was a strain, yes. I've never driven like that in my life." She bestowed an exhilarated smile on him. Obviously, she was not a woman to panic easily. Her air of animation stirred him; he felt stimulated just to be with her in spite of his wound and needing rest.

She eased the tired horse into a gentle walk around to the stables. There was no one in sight, not even a face at a window. Prince leaped down from the carriage, obviously intent upon a cool corner of the stable.

Jordan didn't know where everyone was, but he decided to take advantage of it. He turned to the valiant young woman at his side, and reached out his good hand to touch her chin lightly before placing a gentle kiss on her tempting lips. They more than tempted him. He would have liked nothing better than to explore the matter more deeply when he reminded himself where they were.

"Oh," she whispered, drawing back to stare into his eyes, somewhat bewildered—yet he sensed an awakened awareness of him as a man. No words poured forth, the kiss apparently rendering her speechless.

Then the stable yard suddenly turned to bedlam. Cotman erupted from the stable interior; a young groom burst forth from the gate to the field. Mrs. Longwood came bustling from the house with a furrowed brow, looking ready to give a scold. At his side, Ariel sat as though carved in stone.

"I will not apologize for that—it was delightful. And it was by way of thanks—for the moment. You are not angry with me?" Jordan touched her lightly on her hand, offering consolation if need be.

"How could I be, sirrah? I have led you a merry chase when you should have been abed. I suspect that had Mr. Ponsonby have driven you, the situation would have been a bit better; you'd have nabbed that mad driver. No apology is required." She gazed into his eyes as though memorizing them, then turned aside to accept Cotman's help from the carriage, taking her hatbox with her. The groom assisted Jordan down, then led the exhausted horse away to be royally cosseted.

"My lord, I cannot believe my eyes. I thought you still in bed," Mrs. Longwood chided. "And here I kept everyone as mute as fish."

"I am going there at once," Jordan said, thinking that perhaps being flat on his back would be a good thing. "We had a small errand. Cotman, see that Lady Ariel gets home, will you?" He half turned toward the house to see Percy.

"I can do that, Harcourt," Percy said as he marched up to where they stood. He had driven into the stable yard while the others had clustered about the curricle. Now he stood by the carriage, giving Jordan a concerned look. "I trust you will have a tale to tell me when I return?"

"One you will find hard to believe," Jordan said, suddenly very weary. He turned to Lady Ariel, taking her hand in his regardless of the audience around them. "Again, I thank you for all you did. I know it was not a simple matter. Now, take care once you are at home. I do not think you need worry about . . . anything, but proceed with caution." He slipped the powder flask into her hand in the process and without a blink of an eye, she palmed it as neat as wax. No one could have noticed a thing.

"I promise," she said softly, gazing at Jordan with concern. "Off to bed, you hear?"

He chuckled at that. "I hear and obey."

"For once in your life, I'll wager," she said softly before turning to join Percy in the carriage he had taken when he went to call on Celia Townsend.

Percy whisked Ariel off to the main road and up to Stafford Court, asking questions every yard of the way.

"If Lord Harcourt is still awake when you return, you may learn something from him. I think it prudent for me not to say anything, particularly here." She gestured to the land lining the avenue leading to the main house. There were clusters of tall shrubs dotting the verge behind which anyone might hide and overhear what was said. "Perhaps I am being overly cautious?" Ariel said quietly with a hesitant smile.

"I doubt it. You appear to have a sound head on your shoulder—which is more than I can say for most young women I have met. Miss Townsend is another sensible woman. Fancy, beauty and sensibleness all in one nice package!"

"I am glad she pleases you. Lord Harcourt told me that you are a good judge of people, especially ladies. I think Celia Townsend is matchless, but I speak as a friend who has known her forever. How nice to have an elegant gentleman from London agree with my opinion."

Percy straightened and even preened a trifle as they reached the main house. Ariel immediately exited the carriage, hatbox in hand. "No, do not get down, there is no one about to help with the horse. I shall see you later, I expect. Lord Harcourt insists he wants to attend that assembly in Tunbridge Wells!"

"We shall see how he mends, Lady Ariel," Percy responded.

"Yes," she said, sobering. "That we shall see. Do let us know how he does." She watched as he wheeled about and took off down the avenue as though hounds chased him.

Taking her bonnet box in hand, she approached the house. The silver powder flask was safely in her reticule, slipped in when Mr. Ponsonby was occupied with his driving. Now all she had to do was transport it carefully to her room. Since Aunt Maitland rarely appeared there, she should have time in which to conceal it.

"Welcome, my lady," Cummins said in a barely audible rumble. "I trust you wish to take your new hat to your room at once?" he suggested after glancing at her box. "May I suggest you prepare for a quizzing when you come back down for nuncheon?"

"Why, thank you, Cummins. I left so early that I did not

wish to disturb my aunt. My bonnet was destroyed in that melee yesterday. Mr. Ponsonby kindly insisted he replace it for me." If she could convince Cummins, he would persuade the rest of the staff.

Once in her room, she set the bonnet box on her bed, then paused to consider the best place to hide the powder flask. Where could she put it that Merry, her curious maid, might not stumble on it? Or anyone else? Would someone dare to enter her room to prowl about, looking to see if the flask was in her possession?

While she doubted it, she did not wish to take chances. In the end she tucked it beneath the shawl she rarely used except at Christmas. She had no better idea for the nonce.

She was in the act of brushing out her curls when Merry entered in a rush.

"There you are, my lady. Cummins said as how you returned looking a bit windblown." There was more than a hint of question in her voice. Ariel elected to ignore it.

"Indeed, the wind does have that effect. I had best hurry down to Aunt Maitland. Cummins said she is in the breakfast room."

"Oh, yes, she is and waiting for you, unless I miss my guess," Merry replied, opening the bonnet box to remove the blue hat. "Oh, my lady, this is very pretty!"

She should have seen the one that was ruined, Ariel mused. "I think it most pleasing," she said blandly.

With that, she quit the room, skimming down the staircase to hurry along to the breakfast room, where her aunt liked to enjoy her nuncheon. She paused before entering the room, then, taking courage, stepped inside.

"Ariel, I understand you were out this morning," her aunt said pleasantly.

"That is true, Aunt," Ariel said dutifully as she slipped onto a chair at the far end of the table from her aunt. She welcomed a bowl of carrot soup with a crusty roll and hoped that Lord Harcourt was either having a light repast or asleep in his bed by now.

"May I ask where you went?" Aunt Maitland said with a thin smile. She turned to Sir Henry, who seemed to have more meals at Stafford Place than he did at the Rose and Crown. "The dear girl is so thoughtful; she would never wake me if she takes it into her head to go calling early in the morning or bother me while I am busy."

"I did wish to see that Celia suffered no ill effects from our ride to Tunbridge Wells yesterday," Ariel admitted without saying that she had actually gone there. Since no one at Stafford appeared to have seen her sneak from the house at an early hour, how could anyone refute what she said now?

"How thoughtful, my dear. I wonder how Lord Harcourt goes on?" Aunt Maitland lavishly buttered a piece of roll, then took a dainty nibble.

"I met Mr. Ponsonby and gather that his lordship is doing as well as can be expected." That was another statement that had an element of truth. Ariel knew she could not fabricate a tale out of whole cloth. It was best to stick to the truth as closely as possible. No one would know of the sweet, brief kiss Lord Harcourt had given her. Ariel knew she would treasure it always.

"It is a sad thing when one is not safe in a little town such as Tunbridge Wells, Sir Henry," Miss Maitland said with a sigh. "It is difficult for a woman alone, I can tell you."

"Now, now, Frederica. We must be thankful that Lady Ariel returned from her excursion unharmed. It's a pity that Harcourt was hit. Was it serious, do you know, Lady Ariel?" Sir Henry paused in his eating to give Ariel a searching look.

"I really could not say, Sir Henry," Ariel answered with perfect truth. She dare not reveal anything to anyone.

"Pity." He turned to concentrate on his food.

"Wherever is Mr. Dudley today? Did he perchance return to London?" Ariel hoped she did not sound overly eager for Mr. Dudley's departure, even though she wished the man to the other ends of the earth.

"I understand he rode into Tunbridge Wells to do a bit of shopping," Sir Henry replied.

"How nice," Ariel said cautiously. Well, she hadn't seen him there, and a good thing that was, too. Although, he wasn't likely to patronize a hat shop!

"I merely wondered if he planned to attend the assembly in Tunbridge Wells with us come next Wednesday."

The fork dropped from her aunt's hand, clattering on the table. Sir Henry gave Ariel a sober look of disapproval.

"What is it? Have I said something wrong?"

"I only wonder that you would consider returning to Tunbridge Wells after the accident yesterday," Miss Maitland said with an anxious look.

"I should think if we go in the traveling carriage it ought to be safe enough. We could always have a couple of the men as outriders. Surely, there are servants who know how to shoot a gun?" Ariel gave the pair what she hoped was an innocent look, before returning her gaze to her bowl.

"I do not know . . ." Miss Maitland murmured, dabbing her napkin on her mouth with a fluttering motion.

"Now, Frederica, you know we intended to make our announcement to one and all," Sir Henry coaxed.

"That is true, dear Sir Henry. Goodness knows that with Ariel taking her time about a decision on Mr. Dudley it makes it difficult for us. You are a man of great patience." She gave him what Ariel could only describe as a coy smile.

"It is not necessary for you to wait to be married. I feel certain there must be someone who could stay with me until Papa returns. And he will make arrangements for me to wed, so you need have no concern on that account." Ariel placed her spoon in the near-empty soup bowl and waited.

"Ariel!" her aunt gasped. "As though I would not do my duty by you. Your father will have no idea how to go about arranging a marriage for you, my girl."

Even Sir Henry gave Ariel a look of rebuke.

"There is no need for you to be angry, dear Aunt. I shall not marry until I have at least a fondness for the gentleman in question. I have not the slightest fondness for Mr. Dudley." Feeling as though she could not eat another bite, Ariel rose abruptly from the table. "Excuse me, please. I do not care for anything else."

Without waiting to see if her aunt protested her sudden departure, Ariel fled from the room. It was unthinkable for her to marry anyone but Lord Harcourt. And that gentleman had made it plain that he was not in the market for a wife. Besides which, until they solved the mystery of the gunman, she dare not jeopardize his life.

In her humble estimation there was a connection between her and the death and wounding of both Lord Harcourts. It was just to figure out what that might be.

Since Aunt and Sir Henry were still occupied in the breakfast room, Ariel thought she might be able to sneak into the library to investigate the gun case. She was about to go there when Cummins announced Miss Townsend and Miss Jane Townsend to see her.

Reluctantly setting aside the thought of investigating the case, Ariel greeted her friends warmly, drawing them into the library with the thought that if the girls were in the room, her aunt would not wish to join them. She always declared that their chattering gave her a headache. Though, to be true, the girls talked in soft voices, not wishing to be overheard.

"Have you any news of Lord Harcourt? Percy . . . that is Mr. Ponsonby could not tell us a thing," Celia said, her eyes worried and a frown on her delicate brow.

"You must note that Celia called him Percy. Mama scolded her, but I think Celia has a tendre for Mr. Ponsonby," Jane inserted.

"Yes, indeed, I agree. And I am of the opinion that he could not possibly find someone of a more agreeable disposition nor more suited to managing his home than our Celia," Ariel said with great fondness in her voice. She realized that as long as she remained in the library no one would be able to enter to hunt for the gun case—either to return something, or remove same.

Miss Maitland peered into the library with what appeared to be irritation, then announced that she and Sir Henry were taking a little drive.

The girls did not look sorry to see her go. Indeed, they enjoyed a comfortable coze until Ariel grew uneasy, wanting to check the gun case before her aunt returned. She faked a yawn, hating to keep anything from her dearest friends, but deciding the less they knew, the better off they were. "Oh dear, that morning ride affected me more than I thought. I am so sorry."

Jane jumped to her feet at once. "We are cruel to keep you from your nap."

Celia gave the woman she had known from infancy a shrewd look, then nodded while adding, "From what Mr. Ponsonby said, you must have had an early and busy morning ride."

"True," Ariel replied slowly. "When I am able, I shall delight in sharing everything with you."

"I understand," Celia said while rising to follow her younger sister to the door. "Do not let us stop you from whatever you intended to do before we came." She winked at Ariel, then whisked her sister from the house before she could ask embarrassing questions.

Ariel closed the door, turned the key in the lock, then went to the drawer in the desk where she knew the gun case was stored.

Quickly, she opened the drawer, then removed the case. Her fingers fumbled slightly as she hurried to open the exquisitely gold-embossed wrought leather case.

The powder flask was missing.

At the sound of her aunt's voice in the hallway, Ariel hastily replaced the case and shut the drawer. She dashed across the room to unlock the door before her aunt could try the knob. The last thing Ariel wished was to raise any suspicion regarding her activities.

When her aunt saw her coming along the hall, she beamed a broad smile and held out her hand.

"Dear girl, while Sir Henry and I were on our little drive we decided it would be best to announce your betrothal to Mr. Dudley the same evening as we publicly announce ours. Next Wednesday at the assembly in Tunbridge Wells, all will know."

How apt for her penny-pinching aunt to use a public assembly for her own purposes!

Chapter Eleven

"I beg your pardon!" Ariel exclaimed, thinking she simply could not have heard correctly. No matter that her aunt pinched pennies—this was the outside of enough!

"We, that is, I believe you have dawdled enough. Mr. Dudley, as heir presumptive to Viscount Stone, is quite suitable to be your husband."

Ariel gasped, thinking of the wondrous kiss she had received from Lord Harcourt. How could she begin to contemplate marrying the insipid Mr. Dudley when she had fallen in love with Lord Harcourt? It didn't bear considering. She was too wise to voice her thoughts to her aunt, although she did confess, "But I scarce know him."

"Enough! As your guardian I have the right to arrange your marriage since I believe your father is dead and will never return from India. My letters to him were returned. It would not do to see you wither away on the vine, so to speak." Aunt Maitland smiled, then trundled off to the rear of the house with Sir Henry in her wake.

Ariel felt as though the breath had been knocked from her. *Father? Dead?* It simply could not be! She would have been notified. She would know, feel intuitively that all was not well. Surely Aunt was saying this to get her own way about the marriage to Mr. Dudley?

"Celia. I must talk with someone who is rational," Ariel whispered, thinking her aunt must have become unhinged to believe Papa was dead. And to think her niece would willingly wed Mr. Dudley was preposterous.

It didn't take her long to go to her room and change into her gray habit. After slipping the powder flask inside her jacket, she ran lightly down the stairs and almost bumped into Cummins.

"I am going to see Miss Townsend, Cummins. If my aunt should inquire, tell her I expect to return in time for dinner."

"If I see her, I shall impart the information, Lady Ariel." The butler gave her a ghost of a smile, then held the door open for her.

Thinking that Cummins had undergone a number of odd changes, Ariel put the man out of her mind, hurrying to the stable block before her aunt could catch her to demand she remain home, most likely to allow her supposed betrothed to pay court to her. *Betrothed!* Well, he might be that, but never her husband if she had anything to say about it.

Weems brought forth a saddled Blossom even as she entered the stables. "Thought you might be goin' out," the elderly groom opined.

"Perhaps you heard my aunt and Sir Henry talking?" It was difficult to be distant with a man who had helped her learn to ride her first pony and watched her grow up.

"That I did, my lady. Sad day when your papa let that woman take charge of you."

About to mount Blossom, Ariel paused, staring at him intently. "May I ask why?"

"Not for me to cut up short, but she likes it here right fine and would not take kindly to having to leave, if you ask me." He stood close by, ready to assist Ariel to her saddle.

"I see," Ariel said slowly. "You believe that after my marriage my aunt intends to remain here? Mr. Dudley has no home so we would of necessity live here at Stafford."

He threw her up into her saddle, then stepped back. " 'Taint my place to say a thing, but that Sir Henry has been snufflin' about the stables and everywhere else, just like he intended to buy the place."

"Good heavens! Thank you, Weems. I shall not forget your loyalty, you may be sure." After giving him a tense smile, she spurred her mare forward and within seconds was galloping down the avenue to the main road.

Blossom enjoyed a good gallop and the distance to Celia's home was not great. It was well the horse knew the way, for

Ariel's eyes were blinded by tears. *Her beloved Papa dead? No!* The mare showed no signs of tiring when Ariel reined her in once she reached the front steps to the Townsends' lovely manor house. Ariel maintained a calm face in spite of her anguish.

After looping the reins about the post and wiping her eyes on her sleeve, Ariel ran to the front door that opened wide just as she lifted her hand to use the knocker.

"I happened to see you dashing up the drive to the house from my window. What on earth has happened?" Celia exclaimed. "You seem greatly distressed. Not long ago you were ready for a nap."

"Recall that Aunt and Sir Henry went for a drive earlier. When they returned my aunt announced she believes Papa dead, and then she—no, *they*—had decided that I had dawdled quite enough and that she intended to announce my betrothal to Mr. Dudley Wednesday night at the Tunbridge Wells assembly."

"Well, love, it would save her the cost of a party, and she does tend to lean toward the cheeseparing side of things." Celia drew Ariel to the back parlor, where Jane was working at some mending. "I have wondered if she actually would have that promised party."

"You are not the only one. I must find a way to prevent her announcement. Celia, I cannot believe Papa to be dead! Impossible! If that *were* true, I should have no hope of escaping this dreadful marriage. I have reason to believe Aunt and Sir Henry intend to move in with me—and Mr. Dudley." Ariel paced back and forth until Jane popped up.

"You are making me dizzy. I will fetch some lemonade and biscuits from the kitchen. Do not say anything fascinating until I get back!" Jane cried before she hurried from the room.

Once they were alone, Celia pulled Ariel to the small sofa near the stone fireplace. It was a cozy spot, a place where Celia and Ariel had often exchanged confidences.

"Do not give up, my dear," Celia said quietly. "I cannot believe your father is dead. And there must be some way out of this dilemma."

"Well, I suppose I could try to stall, demand an autumn

wedding and hope that Papa would return by then. I refuse to accept he has gone aloft!" Ariel said with an anguished sigh. "I am certain that Papa would not wish me to marry Mr. Dudley, even if he is heir presumptive to Viscount Stone. It is clear there is another reason my aunt desires this marriage, and I am beginning to see what it might be."

"What?" whispered a spellbound Celia, her eyes wide.

"Aunt is convinced that Papa will not return from India. In that event I shall be a countess in my own right, so I may stay here come what may. *She* wishes to remain at Stafford *and* wed Sir Henry. If I marry some nonentity, she will retain control, and she and Sir Henry can continue to live in luxury while I will be a virtual captive. They could spend my inheritance as they please!"

"Oh, my dear, surely not!" Celia objected.

"Can you imagine a less prepossessing man than Mr. Dudley? He scarce has a word to say for himself," Ariel said bitterly.

Jane reentered the room with a tray holding a pitcher of lemonade and a plate of fresh biscuits. "Well?" she demanded. "What will happen now?"

"Ariel must marry someone else, that is what," Celia declared softly.

"That is hardly amusing," Ariel said, quite on the verge of tears. Her insides performed odd little flutters as she thought of the one she would prefer to wed.

"But it *is* the answer. If you are committed to someone else, your aunt can scarcely insist you wed Mr. Dudley." Celia poured out three glasses of lemonade, passed them around, then offered crisp ginger biscuits. "Recall, Lord Harcourt suggested you become betrothed. He thought it might be necessary as a last resort. You could not marry two men!"

"My shining knight, you mean?" Ariel absently picked up a biscuit, not even thinking that they were favorites, while considering what Celia had suggested. "Aunt would not accept it is real—a betrothal, that is."

"He knows how odious Mr. Dudley is. He is bound to rescue you! Such a fine man, truly noble! He said he would, did he not?" Celia earnestly patted Ariel's hand.

Ariel felt the lump of the powder flask against her ribs, and paused, biscuit halfway to her mouth. "I do need to talk with him. How can I best get word to Lord Harcourt that I must see him, Celia? Could I send one of your grooms? It would be a good idea to speak to him where Aunt cannot know about the meeting."

Jane jumped to her feet, an eager look on her face. "I shall ask one of our men to go at once. Oh, this is so exciting, just like a Minerva novel." She rushed from the room, leaving Celia and Ariel alone.

"I am embarrassed to ask Lord Harcourt to pretend such a thing. I'd truly not wish to see him compelled to wed when he has no desire for a wife." Ariel glanced at Celia, then shook her head in denial of what had to be done.

"Consider his behavior that day at Stafford Court. I think your aunt may be convinced and unwilling to admit it," Celia said thoughtfully. "Or, perhaps she wishes to prevent it by claiming a prior engagement to Mr. Dudley?"

"Oh, dear!" Ariel exchanged a worried look with her dearest friend, then sipped her lemonade.

"We should make plans in any event," Celia suggested.

"True. What do you intend to wear?" Ariel inquired prosaically. "I might wear black!"

Celia frowned. "They would likely think your father had died."

"Which is precisely what my aunt would like everyone to believe," Ariel said carefully. "What a pity it takes so long for a letter to reach him."

"Lord Harcourt ought to be here shortly," Jane cried as she returned to join the two on the sofa.

"You will stay here with me, won't you?" Ariel asked, suddenly anxious when she considered what she intended to request of the baron. "I need advice, and men are more acquainted with laws and such than a secluded woman."

"If needful. Mr. Ponsonby will likely come with him, and perhaps I may learn something useful from him?" Celia said with a diffidence that did not fool Ariel in the least.

"I quite forgot for the moment that you find the gentleman most attractive. You must talk with him if the opportunity pre-

sents itself. And Jane"—Ariel turned to the younger girl—
"you must not tag along with your sister and Mr. Ponsonby
should they take a turn in the garden. I would deem it a favor
if you could disappear?" Ariel said hesitantly, not wishing to
hurt Jane's feelings, but knowing how difficult it might be for
Celia to encourage Mr. Ponsonby with a younger sister around.

Jane nodded seriously, then said, "Perhaps we had best talk
about what we will wear to the Assembly on Wednesday?
Mama has said I may have my hair put up and wear the dress
Celia had last year, the peach one."

"That's a lovely gown, and with some new white satin
ribands, perhaps a knot or two, and a few silk flowers at the
flounce, it will look fresh," Ariel said, trying to tear her mind
away from the awful promise of the future her aunt deemed
proper for her.

Celia offered a few comments on her gown, while Ariel
struggled to remember what she had planned to wear—likely
the blue silk she had intended for the party if it was ready in
time. Nothing seemed important at the moment other than
finding a way out of marriage to Mr. Dudley. That her aunt,
who had seemed so faithful and concerned for her niece declared Papa dead and was deeply involved in some scheme of
her own distressed Ariel as well.

A sound from the front of the house turned all eyes to the
doorway.

"What has happened?" Lord Harcourt asked as he entered
the sitting room. "I know you would not summon me here unless something serious was afoot."

Ariel rose to greet him. "How are you? Poor man, scarce a
chance to rest!" She nodded to Mr. Ponsonby, who had followed his friend. That he was smiling at Celia brought Ariel to
mind the earlier conversation. "Celia, perhaps you would like
to show Mr. Ponsonby the lilacs while I discuss my problem
with Lord Harcourt?"

"I must ask Mama about my gown for the assembly," Jane
said quietly. "I do believe those knots of white riband and the
silk flowers will be just the thing." She slipped from the room
with tactful grace.

Celia gave Ariel an amazed look, then accepted Mr. Ponsonby's arm. "The lilacs are unusually fine this year, sir," she said as they strolled out the door leading to the back gardens.

"I gather this has been discussed at some length before I reached here?" Jordan said with a nod at the departing figures. "It must indeed be serious."

"Celia is my best friend and is remarkably sensible . . . usually." Lady Ariel fiddled with the gloves she had removed to eat her biscuit, casting hesitant glances at him until he took one of her hands to lead her to the doorway.

"I suggest we walk the opposite direction from Percy and your friend. I would hear the worst that has happened and at once."

"Perhaps that is best." They left the house behind them as they strolled along the first path they came to, one that led away from Percy and Celia. Spring blooms peeped from the border, offering brilliant hues in a wide variety. Jordan paid them not the slightest attention, rather he concentrated on the lovely young woman at his side. That she would not have summoned him there unless the situation was dire was not lost on him. He could only hope to turn matters to his own advantage if possible.

"First of all," she began, "the powder flask *is* missing from my father's case. I have it here, and I would prefer you to keep it for me. In the event my father returns in time, I may have need of it as proof that something was not right. Just what—I am not certain at the moment, but there have been some developments."

She retrieved the powder flask from inside her neat gray jacket, giving it into his keeping. The silver and gilt gleamed brightly in the filtered light offered through the shade of a row of birch trees.

Jordan took the flask still warm from her body. He looked at it, then slipped it into his pocket. "I'd not expected to see it again. But you said first . . . What else has occurred?" Jordan felt her hand tensing on his arm and wondered what could be so terrible that she found it difficult to talk about now they were no longer strangers.

"I had just discovered the absence of the powder flask when I heard my aunt and Sir Henry return from a drive. I was in the library still. She came to the doorway to inform me that *they*, ostensibly she, had decided that I *must* marry Mr. Dudley! What Sir Henry has to say to my marriage is beyond me, but there he was—looking as though butter wouldn't melt in his mouth. Aunt Maitland is convinced my father will not return from India—she declared him dead, and believes that as my guardian she has the right to arrange this marriage. Needless to say, I am devastated."

"There must be something you can do. You wrote your father. Since no word has come to you regarding his death, you must believe he is still alive. When he discovers what is afoot, he is bound to return at once," Jordan said, hoping he sounded more encouraging than he felt.

"She means to announce the betrothal at the Wednesday assembly." Lady Ariel paused to look up at him, searching his face for something she wished to see. "I do not know when she plans the marriage, but I doubt if I can delay a wedding until autumn if she is determined."

"That puts an entirely different slant on it altogether," Jordan said slowly, continuing on the path. The sound of crunching gravel and a few birds was all that was heard for some moments.

"The most maddening thing about this is that Mr. Dudley is nowhere to be seen. I do not even merit the decency of a proposal, much less the opportunity to say no! Were it not so outrageous, it would be laughable." She sounded near to tears. Jordan drew her to a pretty little stone bench beneath a birch tree that waved delicate, pale green leaves in the slight breeze. He placed a comforting arm around her shoulders, pulling her against him and taking hope from the lack of any resistance.

"I told you that it might be necessary for me to step into the fray, as it were. Come Wednesday evening, *I* will bring an engagement ring with me to the assembly, and you and I will announce our engagement *before* your aunt can say a word. I'm certain I can bribe the master of ceremonies to allow me to be first. However, if my ring is on your finger, Dudley can scarcely place a second one there."

Jordan wasn't sure how he could convince the master of ceremonies that it would be proper for him to announce the betrothal rather than a member of the family. "I believe that *if* I point out how your father is absent that it would be proper for the gentleman involved to make the announcement he may agree."

"You would do this for me? It would be just until my father has returned. I promise."

She looked at him with an expression he found hard to interpret. However, if he could accustom her to having him at her side, perhaps, he thought, she might be willing to make it permanent? And that was most ironic, since he had declared while on his way to Kent that he had no need of a wife. *That* was before he met Ariel.

"I will do this for you and more if you but ask," Jordan began, then stopped at the odd look in her eyes. Had he gone too far?

Ariel studied the man at her side. She had dreamed of a romantic proposal, with the gentleman sweeping her off her feet, offering a promise of love and devotion. She certainly had never expected to bargain for a betrothal, especially with the man she would truly like to marry. He had revealed a compassionate nature and an excellent mind, not to mention other skills as well. He also had told Miss Vipont that he was not looking for a wife. Ariel hoped he had changed his mind; if not, she would work to that end.

"Then I accept your generous offer." She lifted her face, hoping he might bestow another kiss. He didn't fail her. And it proved far better than the hastily snatched kiss in the stable yard. Perhaps there was something about a stone bench beneath a gracefully arching birch tree? If so, she would request more birch trees to be planted at Stafford Court.

Jordan fought the desire to sweep Ariel into his arms and kiss her as he would prefer. A gentleman didn't do that with an innocent, not if he wanted to advance his cause. He reluctantly released her and was most pleased when she did not draw away from him, but remained in his embrace, close to his side.

"Be careful not to say anything that might give away our intent. We would not want to forewarn your aunt what we plan. Pretend you accept your fate. But I promise you that I will do everything in my power to protect you from whatever your aunt and Sir Henry have in mind. You do not think they will attempt to wed you against your will, using a special license?" he asked.

She pulled from his embrace, jumped to her feet, and began to pace back and forth, her steps crunching loudly on the gravel. "Mr. Lytton would never agree to such a thing, I am certain of that. He would be our ally."

"Perhaps I ought to tell the gentleman what we intend to do? Could he keep a secret? If we have made arrangements with Mr. Lytton, your aunt can scarcely command him to marry you to someone else. Particularly when he would see you wed to me." Jordan smiled at Ariel, his fellow conspirator.

"Isn't it odd how things work out?" she mused, glancing at him from the corners of her eyes. But she looked very cautious. He might have convincing to do.

"Indeed." He stood, wanting to enfold her in his embrace and ward off the dreaded marriage and whatever else was planned. He suspected that more was involved than the marriage. That was merely the beginning. Was it possible that the aunt, with Sir Henry at her side, intended to take control of Ariel's fortune? Dudley wouldn't stand a chance against a determined pair. He had as much fortitude as an overcooked spear of asparagus. Jordan turned at the sound of someone approaching, only to see Percy and Celia Townsend.

"Here you are," Celia said with delight. "We found you had left the sitting room and wondered what had happened." She turned to Ariel and asked, "Has he thought of a solution?"

"Lady Ariel has consented to make me the happiest of men; our engagement will be announced the night of the Wednesday assembly in Tunbridge Wells," Jordan said firmly with a significant look at Percy.

"Oh, my, you intend the proposal real?" Celia cried, groping for the stone bench as she sank down. "This will certainly put the cat among the pigeons. What about the man who shot at you?"

"I had almost forgotten that," Ariel wailed. "I cannot allow you to make that announcement. To do so would place you in great danger. Remember—the last Lord Harcourt was killed. I do not want you to die!" She placed her hands on his chest, offering a beseeching look.

Jordan smiled down at her, effortlessly enfolding her hands in his and quite ignoring the twinge of pain in his arm. He had not forgotten anything and would continue to pursue his investigation, but quietly on his own. "It will not happen, my dear girl."

"I am not so certain," she countered. "We do not know who was responsible for the shooting—either of you or your late cousin." She turned to Percy. "Please sir, make him see sense."

"The previous Lord Harcourt was not killed by being shot," Celia reminded them. "He was thrown from his horse and broke his neck."

"And we learned little from the recovered lead balls." Percy shook his head. "I hate to say this, my friend, but it would appear you are asking for trouble. Whoever shot at you before may not miss the next time."

"That does it," Ariel said with a firming of her lips. "You will not announce our betrothal come Wednesday."

"You go tamely to marry Mr. Dudley?" Jordan said in an innocuous manner that didn't deceive anyone, least of all Ariel.

"I will think of something else that will not place you in such jeopardy." She placed her fists on her hips, giving Jordan such a defiant glare it was all he could do not to snatch her into her arms and forget the world.

At that moment Jane came rushing along the path, looking anxious and not a little flustered.

"What is it, dear?" Celia queried. "What has happened to upset you?"

"Mr. Oswald Dudley is here—that is what happened. He is looking for Lady Ariel, to escort her home from her visit to Miss Townsend. Shh, I believe he intended to follow me," Jane whispered.

The crunch of gravel gave them a warning. Ariel immediately composed herself on the bench at Celia's side. Jane moved close to Ariel's other side, standing as though she might in some way defend her friend if necessary.

With a look at Percy, Jordan moved to stand opposite to Ariel and the other girls.

Mr. Dudley joined them in a few moments, coming around the row of birches with an air of bewilderment that looked quite natural to him. Then he caught sight of the group and halted in his steps. "I have come to take you home. Your aunt wishes you to change for dinner. There is to be a little party this evening." He looked at Jordan, then suddenly assumed a superior air. "I suppose Lady Ariel has shared her news with you? We are to be married."

Jordan refrained from hitting Dudley only because of the look from Ariel.

"How interesting, since I have not been asked, nor have I agreed to anything of the sort. I hereby give you notice that I will not marry you, Mr. Dudley, no matter what my aunt and Sir Henry have told you."

"But she said . . . he said . . . that is, it is all arranged." He floundered, appearing truly at sea.

"Precisely what is arranged?" Percy inquired.

"The wedding. Miss Maitland said it would be three weeks from Sunday." Mr. Dudley edged away from Jordan, apparently not liking his expression.

Ariel was thankful she was already seated, or she would have most likely collapsed in a dead faint. "There will be no wedding, Mr. Dudley. Mr. Lytton would never agree."

"I believe she said something about the bishop," Mr. Dudley replied, now a trifle unsure of himself with all the hostile faces aimed in his direction.

"My aunt has overstepped her authority. I will not wed without my father's consent to the marriage." Lady Ariel rose to confront Mr. Dudley. Jordan stepped behind her, while Celia and Jane ranked the other side and Percy joined his friend. All it wanted was Prince to make the scene complete, Ariel thought wildly.

Apparently Mr. Dudley found this front more than he cared to oppose. "You are wanted at home," he insisted, but without his earlier arrogance.

"Stafford Court is my home, not yours—not yet, not ever," Lady Ariel said with determination.

"I meant your aunt wishes you to return now," Mr. Dudley repeated, looking more and more flustered.

"Shall I go home to Stafford Court?" Lady Ariel asked Jordan urgently. "Dare I?"

"Would you wed Lady Ariel against her will? It would be illegal," Jordan said with a deadly calm.

"Of course not," Dudley stammered, taking a step back.

"May I suggest that we all gather tomorrow morning to spend the day in a . . . a . . . picnic," Celia Townsend suggested. "It would be a pleasant way to relax. You are welcome to join us, Mr. Dudley."

"Celia," Percy began only to be silenced with a look from her lovely eyes.

"I shall go home now and meet you first thing in the morning. But"—Ariel turned to Jordan—"please take great care of yourself."

He smiled down at her, again wishing he might crush her in his arms. With everyone looking on, all he could do was smile, place a kiss on her hand, and say, "Until tomorrow, my dear Lady Ariel."

The look from Dudley was almost comical. Almost.

Ariel turned from her friends and joined Mr. Dudley to walk to the carriage. They followed immediately behind the hapless pair.

A groom awaited them with Blossom. Ariel gave a triumphant smile and walked over to her horse. "I shall see you at Stafford, Mr. Dudley."

Jordan lifted Ariel to her saddle, then stepped back, unable to prevent a grin.

Ariel spurred her horse ever so slightly, and they set off down the avenue that led to the main road. This time she stayed not on the road, but took off across country. She would be at Stafford many minutes before her supposed suitor.

"We shall see you tomorrow, Dudley?" Jordan said politely as the other chap lifted the reins to signal his horse.

"Indeed, I'd not miss it," came his terse reply before the gig set off in the direction of Stafford Court.

Jordan, Percy, and Jane all turned to Celia, the collected frowns most daunting.

"Well, I thought if we knew where he was and kept him

away from Miss Maitland and Sir Henry there could be no more planning done. At least he wouldn't know about it."

"I cannot say if that is good or bad," Jordan mused. "Sometimes it is better to know what the enemy is planning."

"I shall tell Mama that we will need a picnic on the morrow." Jane turned to leave for the house to be stopped by Jordan's touch on her arm.

"Allow me to offer my cook's services," he said at once. "It is the least I can do. I feel as though I should have taken Dudley apart limb by limb, then the aunt and Sir Henry."

"Oh, what are we going to do?" Celia cried.

"We will think of something by morning." Jordan and Percy walked to where the groom now stood with the curricle.

"In the meanwhile, think of poor Dudley. He is supposed to marry a woman who refuses to have him, and he is at the mercy of Sir Henry and Miss Maitland. I think he may be very glad to be gone tomorrow—even if it allows them to plot in private."

"Plot!" cried Jane in dismay. "Oh, dear."

Chapter Twelve

Percy leaned back on his chair, resting his arms against the dining table. "Are you certain this picnic tomorrow will be safe?"

"As safe as anything else around here," Jordan replied, toying with his wineglass. The meal presented by Simnel had been outstanding as usual, but Jordan had little appetite for the excellent food.

"You growl at me, but you must know that whoever shot at you before may decide to strike again," Percy argued with perfect logic.

"And you believe that next time the aim may be more accurate? I still cannot fathom why anyone would want to rid the world of my hide." Jordan finished his wine and rose from the table, followed by Percy.

"Indeed, one wonders why," Percy mused as the two strolled down the hall to the drawing room. "My friend, I have to think this will be a perilous engagement you propose."

"What do we *know* at this point?" Jordan argued, mostly for his own benefit. "Only that the previous holder of my title fell off his horse and broke his neck—*perhaps* after someone shot a rifle in his direction. *If* that rifle was fired at the time he was there, and *if* the noise made his horse rear, and if . . . if . . . if! So, actually we know precious little for certain."

"True. But you did find the lead ball in the tree not far from where he fell," Percy said.

"Prince helped me find it," Jordan reminded him in all fairness to the dog.

"Perhaps it would be a good idea to bring him with you tomorrow?" Percy flung himself down on the most comfortable chair in the room, first nudging Prince out to do so. He smiled at the dog, patting him on the head, then scratching him behind the ears. Prince sighed blissfully, leaning against Percy to beg for more.

"I believe I will—and keep him near, even if it does prevent me from being as close to Lady Ariel as I might like." Jordan gave his friend a wry smile. "Although, I misdoubt you would take the slightest interest, as wrapped up in Miss Townsend as you are. Good thing we have Jane Townsend to divert Dudley."

"Precisely where does he fit into the picture now?" Percy wondered. "He obviously has not the slightest interest in Lady Ariel; he barely speaks to her much less woo her as a true suitor ought. He seems to do as Miss Maitland and Sir Henry say, like an obedient dog," he concluded with a look at Prince. "I expect him to sit up and beg at any moment. Dudley, that is, not the dog."

"I doubt he could mastermind anything beyond the most simple of matters, like tying his cravat or something. But that leaves Miss Maitland, and I refuse to accept that the woman could be the culprit. I suppose it does not pay to underestimate her, however. She is determined on the matter of that engagement to Dudley. I'll proceed with the proposed betrothal to Lady Ariel to scotch that. I'd say Sir Henry is a possibility, but as far as we know he was not around here when my cousin died." Jordan gave his friend a frustrated look.

"That leaves us with a disgruntled servant," Percy said, rising to pour himself a glass of claret. He glanced at Jordan, then poured him one as well.

"I cannot think why someone who was angry at my cousin would transfer that anger to me—unless he is is a revolutionary with a hatred for the peerage. Lady Ariel has a theory about that lad who used to work in the stables at Stafford. He was here when my cousin died, and we saw him on the way home from Tunbridge Wells the day after I was shot. Could there be a connection?"

"That is possible," Percy said consideringly.

"Lady Ariel fears I will be killed if we announce a betrothal," Jordan said after some hesitation. "What do you think? As far as I can see, it is the only way to stop this insane marriage to Dudley. Two people more unsuited for marriage I cannot think."

Percy snorted in derision. "Stupid, unsuitable marriages occur every day. Consider how many arranged marriages there are and how few are based in genuine liking between the parties, let alone love. That divorce is nearly impossible adds to the misery. Lady Ariel must either pretend to be your betrothed or flee her home."

"Where would she go?" Jordan paused in the act of sipping his wine, his interest stirred.

"India, for starters. That is where her father is living. He is the only one who can truly save her, and the dratted man is too far away to be of help."

"You must admit that would be a bit drastic, old man. Is there no other relative around? How about the Townsends? Would they risk sheltering her?"

"Who would risk harboring an heiress from her legally appointed guardian?" Percy countered.

"But is she? Is Miss Maitland the legally appointed guardian, that is? From my limited understanding of the law, I thought the guardian was usually a man. Who would be the man assigned the task when Lady Ariel's father is absent or dead?"

There was a moment of silence before Percy replied, "Just so. Who?"

"His solicitor?"

"There is to be a picnic on the morrow," Mr. Dudley humbly informed Sir Henry. "I suppose I must go?"

"We want Lady Ariel protected at all times," Sir Henry reminded him.

Ariel, standing just outside the library door wondered why she needed protecting. Lord Harcourt had insisted that he was the target, not her. Perhaps he was mistaken? She went around the door to enter the room. She dare not inquire; it would reveal she was eavesdropping.

"Ah, Lady Ariel," Sir Henry said genially. "Dudley was just

telling me about the picnic tomorrow. Where is this to take place, may I ask?"

Ariel gave him a thoughtful look. Why did he want to know the location? Was he merely curious? Or did he have a more sinister motive? "It is to be a surprise. I adore surprises—most of the time, that is. I did not appreciate being told I am to wed a stranger in a little over three weeks, however." She gave Mr. Dudley a hostile look before turning a narrowed gaze upon Sir Henry.

Sir Henry darted an annoyed look at Dudley, then said in an almost oily manner, "My dear girl, surely you must know that your aunt has your best interests at heart?"

"Does she, indeed? I give leave to doubt that, sir."

"At any rate, arrangements are under way," Sir Henry snapped. "She has written to the Bishop of London regarding the ceremony. You are aware that he is the provincial Bishop of Kent for the Archbishop of Canterbury?" Sir Henry asked in a superior manner.

Ariel gave him a dry look. "I know that, and I also suspect the Bishop of London has far more to do than come haring down here to perform a ceremony! If you intend to use banns, why not inform Mr. Lytton? Presuming that the marriage does proceed, that is?"

"Ah." Sir Henry hesitated a few moments before continuing. "Mr. Lytton indicated that he would not unite you to Mr. Dudley without written permission from either your father or your guardian." Sir Henry bit his lip as though he had inadvertently said something he ought not.

"My aunt is not my guardian," Ariel said, not questioning, although this was something that had been kept from her. Apparently her father had not considered it necessary to impart that information to her before he left.

"Well," Sir Henry said with a deprecating gesture of his hand, "a woman generally is omitted from legal processes. It takes someone with greater understanding," he concluded unctuously.

Cummins entered at that moment to announce dinner.

Ariel almost smiled to see how relieved Sir Henry was to avoid additional questioning. She resolved to say nothing more, thus dulling suspicion on their part. However, it was something she would investigate. And she would pray that the Bishop of London had stacks of letters and bishopric papers to read, not to mention duties to perform for the archbishop, and that the request to perform a ceremony to unite the only child of the Earl of Stafford to some insignificant twit would be at the very bottom!

The evening that followed dinner was boring to the extreme. Ariel found a book to peruse and thus was able to ignore the others. The men played a game of piquet while her aunt sat with her knitting.

Going to bed was the highlight of the evening for Ariel. The next day would be the picnic, certainly something to anticipate with delight.

Once in bed, Ariel curled up against her pillow to think of Lord Harcourt. *Jordan.* It was a strong name for a man with character, and a man she had come to care for too much. She was a danger to him.

Yet, from a practical standpoint it would be far more sensible for her to marry him. He owned the rich land that marched with hers, or what would eventually be hers. He possessed great wealth, as did she. Whereas Mr. Dudley had no title, no temporary style to give him any status; he also had no land, no money—only vague expectations. It was entirely possible the Viscount Stone might marry and produce an heir. So much for her aunt's aspirations.

So why was her aunt bent upon this marriage? Was it what they suspected? If it came down to the actual event, she would request a private interview with the Bishop of London. He was a powerful man, one who would be able to help her should it be needed. But . . . she would need proof that there was something havey-cavey about this marriage. And she would say no *if* she was asked if she would take Mr. Dudley to husband. Surely there was no manner in which they could force her.

Her thoughts did not make for easy sleeping, and in the morning she had delicate shadows beneath her eyes.

"My lady, what do you plan to wear this day?" Merry asked as she placed the tray with breakfast chocolate and a roll before Ariel.

"Ah, I have a picnic today. I shall want my new bonnet—the blue with the cream bands on it. And I think the blue gown trimmed in cream and rose. I have had it for an age, but it is a favorite."

The maid went about her duties, draping the simple blue gown over a chair, then locating proper slippers and the new bonnet as well as the hose and other necessary items. The last item set out was a blue-and-cream parasol with pretty fringe around the lower edge.

Ariel went down to the breakfast room with mixed feelings. Lord Harcourt had promised to call for her this morning. Would her aunt permit her to leave with him when he arrived? Surely Aunt would not make a scene! Nothing was said, and Ariel breathed a sigh of relief when the small meal ended.

When the time came, she was pleased to observe he was prompt. It said much for a man who paid attention to details like being on time.

Cummins sought her out where she waited in the sitting room. "They are here, my lady," he said with that odd smile again.

"They, Cummins?" she gently queried, wondering if Mr. Ponsonby and Celia had come as well. That would have meant some early fetching.

"The rector and Mrs. Lytton as well as Lord Harcourt."

"How curious," Ariel said with surprise. Why had Lord Harcourt invited the rector to join the young people on this picnic? she wondered. Did he have some purpose, perhaps? There was only one way to learn. She went out the open door to greet them.

"Lord Harcourt, what a lovely day for a picnic. Scarcely a cloud in the sky and a pleasant breeze," Ariel cried with delight as she walked down the steps.

"Lady Ariel, I am waiting," Mr. Dudley said with a trace of pomposity. He had brought Sir Henry's caned whiskey up from the Rose and Crown before breakfast even though she had informed him of her plans to go with Lord Harcourt. As usual, he'd paid no attention to her.

"I explained that I had made arrangement to go with Lord Harcourt. I gather you did not listen to me." She bestowed a coldly polite smile in his direction before turning to Lord Harcourt. The comparison between Lord Harcourt in his dark blue coat, biscuit breeches, with a dashing waistcoat, and Mr. Dudley, whose coat fit badly and whose cravat was tied any which way, was almost ludicrous.

Mrs. Lytton tittered. "Perhaps you could fetch Miss Jane Townsend, Mr. Dudley. I fancy she would welcome a drive in that lovely whiskey."

Mr. Dudley was not amused.

Ignoring any possible wrath from her aunt, Sir Henry, or Mr. Dudley, Ariel gladly stepped into the landau with the aid of Lord Harcourt's strong hand. "What a lovely surprise to see you are to join us today, Mr. and Mrs. Lytton."

"I'll explain later," Lord Harcourt murmured as he settled at her side. Raising his voice, he suggested Cotman proceed to the picnic site.

The country roads were such that it was difficult to converse. Ariel glanced back once to see Mr. Dudley far behind to avoid their dust.

"I did not realize that Dudley expected to escort you this morning," Lord Harcourt said with a frown.

"It would have been more sensible for him to stop by the Townsend's and pick up Jane," Ariel replied. "I imagine that my aunt suggested he come to Stafford this morning and he thought he could outsmart you. She did not bother to ask me if I had other plans."

They were first to arrive at the lovely wooded glen where an abundance of wildflowers scented the air, birds serenaded them from the treetops, and where there wasn't a cow in sight.

Servants had arrived beforehand to set up a table, carry baskets of provisions, and to assist in any way needful. Everything looked well in hand.

Ariel twirled her parasol, a delighted smile on her face, the worries of the night set aside. Wednesday seemed ages away, and she was not going to borrow trouble when the day promised so much enjoyment.

The Lyttons strolled across the grassy area to see the stream, murmuring happily regarding the unexpected treat as they went. Sunday's sermon would doubtlessly contain references to the many beauties bestowed on the world.

"So, tell me—how did you come to invite the Lyttons?" Ariel wondered in an undertone.

"He opposes the proposed marriage between you and Dudley. What better person to have present? Besides, I thought it might be a good time to ask if he knows anything regarding your true guardian. I suspect it is not your aunt. It's possible he may know."

"I asked my aunt about that as well and received no answer. At one point she insisted she acted as my guardian. Acting and being are not quite the same, are they?" Ariel said quietly. "Sir Henry as good as admitted my guardian is a man."

"We must find out who it is!" Jordan might have said more, but the arrival of Percy and Celia, with Dudley and Jane immediately behind them prevented it. "Excuse me. Our guests have arrived."

Ariel stood where he left her for a moment. Had he realized what he had said? *Our guests?* Giving a twirl of her parasol, Ariel followed him to greet *their* guests as well. Lord Harcourt gave her hope that he would uncover the identity of her temporary guardian, for such was his air of confidence.

"A lovely day, is it not?" Celia said, her eyes sparkling with pleasure.

"Since Lord Harcourt has come to Stafford, life has become far more interesting," Ariel murmured.

"Particularly for you," Celia said with a grin.

"I say," Jane muttered as she joined them, "I think Mr. Dudley is a grump. He said not one word the entire time we drove here, merely followed Mr. Ponsonby and Celia. I hope I do not have to return with him." She gave her sister an eloquent look.

"Adjust your parasol, dear," Celia instructed in a way guaranteed to annoy Jane.

The younger girl sniffed and went off to explore the creek with the Lyttons.

"How did things go when you returned to Stafford Court? I confess I worried about you."

Ariel managed a smile, then said quietly, "My aunt dared to write the Bishop of London if you please. She wishes him to jaunt down to Stafford to marry me to Mr. Dudley. Can you not see the important Bishop of London setting aside matters of consequence to perform a mere wedding? Not very likely, I should say. You know that Mr. Lytton refuses."

"I find that curious and rather hopeful. If only your letter to your father could have been sped to him."

"I read somewhere that during the war some pigeons were used to carry messages. It sounds lovely, if impractical. Can you not see pretty birds winging across the water and mountains, not to mention over cities and plains to reach Papa? I could not be so lucky."

"I am surprised they let you attend the picnic, to tell the truth," Celia said as they walked across to join the Lyttons.

"They could scarcely refuse. Aunt is not my legal guardian as she pretends. It is some man!"

"Lord Harcourt will discover him for you, I vow," the loyal Celia whispered. "Let us join the others."

There ensued a lighthearted game of battledore and shuttlecock, with Percy and Celia the winners.

Afterward, Ariel strolled toward the stream with Lord Harcourt her escort.

"I perceive your arm still troubles you, Lord Harcourt," Ariel said when she observed the presence of a bandage beneath the fine cambric of his shirt. His coat had been tossed aside for the game, and Ariel envied him the cool freedom. That is, until she saw the bandage.

"Mrs. Longwood insists I must keep it for a time longer," Lord Harcourt admitted.

"There is no danger of infection?" Ariel asked worriedly. "Lead balls have been known to kill even when they did not lodge in the body."

"Dr. Mayo cleaned it out well." He strolled at her side until they were a short distance from the others. "Come, I mean to ask Mr. Lytton about your guardian. It is possible he knows something of the matter."

"Mr. Greenwood might as well, come to think on it. Oh, what am I to do?" Ariel asked suddenly. "It seems so frustratingly hopeless. Since Aunt has written the Bishop of London I can only pray the good man is far too busy to drive here to do a wedding ceremony."

"He would wonder why the local rector would not do the job. Perhaps I should ask Mr. Lytton if he would consent to sending a missive explaining why."

Ariel drew closer to stare into his handsome face. "What an utterly brilliant idea. That ought to put a wrinkle in their plans!"

Jordan smiled at the precious face so close to his. It took every ounce of his willpower not to enfold her in his arms. "I shall attend to it as soon as the opportunity presents itself."

"I am most fortunate to have you as a . . . friend."

Jordan watched her walk over to join Miss Townsend and wondered what she had been about to say. *Lover? Future husband?* He hoped to marry her and wished her father would return from India. He was the one to solve their dilemma. If only he would return before it was too late. He bent over to collect his coat, only to find Mr. Dudley facing him when he straightened up.

"Pleasant day for a picnic, is it not?" Jordan inquired with civility.

"I do not know what you are about, Lord Harcourt, but I would strongly advise caution on your part. One never knows what is around the corner."

"True. Perhaps you have a special knowledge?" Jordan inquired lazily, motioning the other man to join him while they crossed to join the others. He drew Lady Ariel to his other side. He intended to keep her as far away from Dudley as possible today and forever, if he could. Should determination be the deciding factor, Jordan knew he'd win.

"Not I," the other denied, with a smirk at Lady Ariel that Jordan found offensive.

Ignoring the urge to rearrange Dudley's uninspiring face, Jordan instead invited his guests to sample the picnic foods. There were cold salads and meats, pastries, and strawberries from his protected kitchen gardens.

Rugs dotted the grass, so all could sit in clean, dry comfort. Jordan took advantage of the confusion while they selected their meal to appropriate Lady Ariel. Prince came loping up to join them.

"You brought the dog?" Lady Ariel said, surprise clear in her voice.

"I sent him with the servants, not knowing how he would like the Lyttons. Percy seems to think I'm in some sort of danger today," Jordan admitted.

"I was afraid of that." She turned her head to scan the distance. "I see no one, but that does not mean there isn't someone lurking there, ready to fire a rifle in your direction. I do wish you would be more careful."

"It would seem that you care." With tender amusement he noted the pretty blush that crept into her cheeks.

She seemed to gather her courage, then smiled that delicious smile that made him long to hold her. "I do."

"This is a lovely and wholly unexpected pleasure, my Lord Harcourt," Mr. Lytton said in his sonorous manner from off to one side. "As I said to Miss Vipont, we are most fortunate you now occupy the Hall. Your grandmother in her later years scarcely went about. Your late cousin had, er, other interests."

"I'm pleased you are enjoying the picnic. I hope to discuss a small matter with you sometime during the day," Jordan said, rising out of respect for the older man, a courtesy much appreciated by the rector.

Mr. Lytton glanced to where Jane spoke with Mr. Dudley and seated himself on the rug where Lady Ariel and Jordan had relaxed with their food. "Do explain. I am most curious."

Jordan complied at once, returning to his place beside Lady Ariel. "It seems that Miss Maitland has written to the Bishop of London requesting that he journey to Stafford to perform the ceremony uniting Lady Ariel and Mr. Dudley—the very marriage you refused to execute. Lady Ariel chanced to learn of it by accident. It slipped out when Sir Henry spoke with her about the wedding."

"How very interesting. It begs understanding as to how she believes a busy man like the bishop will jaunt down to Kent for a mere wedding. Even for you," he added with a half bow to Lady Ariel.

"The Earl of Stafford is a long established earldom, highly

respected as well," Lady Ariel volunteered. "I would think it important that the earl be present at the marriage of his only child. Would you not agree, Mr. Lytton? Besides, I would prefer to be married by you in the Stafford church!"

Mr. Lytton swelled with pride, then frowned. "The bishop must be made aware of all that is at stake here. You refuse to wed Mr. Dudley, is that correct?"

"Indeed, sir. I cannot think why my aunt pursues the matter."

"Enough said. I shall write the bishop this very day. If I may say so, my missive will take precedence over Miss Maitland's letter. I will point out that while your father is absent your aunt, who is not your guardian, is trying to compel a marriage against your will to the young man who is heir presumptive to Viscount Stone. And we all know how young he is."

"Accidents seem to happen, however," Jordan murmured. "Tell me, do you know who *is* Lady Ariel's guardian?"

"Bless my soul," the rector said in distress. Then he brightened. "I believe it is his solicitor. Yes, indeed, I recall the earl mentioning it once, some years ago. I doubt he has thought to alter that arrangement since then. Lady Ariel, we have become so accustomed to your aunt having charge of you that it is easy to forget she cares for you but is not your guardian."

"Yes," Lady Ariel said quietly. "At times Papa seems to forget I exist."

"Surely not, my dear lady. But he is a busy and most important gentleman." The rector smiled in a benign way at Lady Ariel, much like a father might.

Bless his gossipy heart, Jordan thought. He might not be the best rector around, but underneath he seemed a fine man, one who truly cared for his parish.

Prince growled just then, drawing their attention.

Jordan met Lady Ariel's concerned gaze.

"What is it, Prince? Go, dog. Find him." The bloodhound needed no further encouragement. He tore off through the long grasses, leaped the creek, then dashed up the distant hill.

"I think there is a man up there, behind that first tree," Lady Ariel whispered. "Can you not see his shoulder? Could he have a rifle?" She reached over to push Jordan to the ground, then threw herself beside him. The rector, alarmed at this strange behavior of his esteemed parishioners, looked on in amazement.

A shot rang out at the same moment—just seconds after Lady Ariel had pushed Jordan to the rug.

"I say," cried Percy, "it is happening again."

"At least we know that Mr. Dudley is not the culprit," Lady Ariel murmured with true British fortitude to Jordan as he slowly assisted her to sit once again. She searched the hillside, hunting for the elusive gunman.

"That shot just missed you," the horrified rector declared in ringing tones. "Look, there is the ball imbedded in that rug just behind you."

"Oh, Jordan," Lady Ariel whispered, "it could have so easily been you."

"Equally possible the chap aimed for you, my lady," the rector said while he pried the lead ball from the thick nap of the oriental carpet. "Pity it had to be damaged," he murmured. "Excellent rug, this."

"Indeed, sir. A great pity," Jordan said softly.

"It is better that the rug be damaged than Lord Harcourt be shot, possibly killed!" Lady Ariel cried at the same moment. She exchanged a look with Jordan.

The rector turned a deep shade of red. "Do apologize, I fear my wits have gone begging."

"Gunshots tend to have that effect," Jordan said wryly.

"He could reload and shoot again, this time determined not to miss you," Ariel pointed out while rising from the rug where she had enjoyed a pleasant meal with the man she cared for so much. How horrible it would be if this came about. She knew a pang of loss at the very notion he might be taken from her, that she might never know his love, that he might not achieve the fullness of his life.

"I believe it would be prudent to search the area," the rector declared. He turned to the servants, who had stood in astounded and frozen silence while all this was going on. "I suggest we fan out across the hill to see if we can learn anything of the man who tried to shoot Lord Harcourt."

Percy jumped to his feet and set off across the long grass, following the same path Prince had taken.

"Oh, dear," Celia moaned. "What if something happens to him!"

"I rather think that the villain has a different target in mind," Ariel murmured dryly.

The male servants swarmed up the hill after Percy, spreading out in every direction. It was not long before Percy came dashing back down the hill, Prince with him.

"Look what I have!" he exclaimed as he neared the trio, who stood in fascinated consternation.

Lord Harcourt took a step forward as Percy joined them.

"Here—a piece of fabric torn from the miscreant who shot the rifle. Prince took a good hold of the fellow's, um, backside. Chap took off, leaving the fabric behind."

"Now all we have to do is find a pair of breeches minus a piece of fabric in the, ah, back," Lord Harcourt said. "Simple."

"You were shot at before?" the rector gravely inquired, exchanging a concerned look with his frightened wife, who had sidled up to him.

"We were shot at while in Tunbridge Wells some days ago," Ariel said. "Goodness, it seems like ages rather than days. And now this."

"What could be next?" the rector inquired, his dignity now much on display.

"This coming Wednesday—the assembly." Ariel looked at Lord Harcourt, exchanging a look full of meaning. It also conveyed something of her true feelings for him.

Mr. Dudley watched all this with narrowed eyes.

Chapter Thirteen

"The fat's in the fire now," Mr. Dudley snarled at the older gentleman seated so comfortably in the Stafford library.

"I think you worry too much," Sir Henry protested.

Both men turned to face the library door at the sound of footsteps marching in their direction. Mr. Dudley assumed a sullen mien when he saw who it was.

"Well, Mr. Dudley, and how did you find our picnic?" Ariel inquired. "You could scarcely call it dull. Why, I fancy few London picnics have such a dramatic ending."

Aunt Maitland followed Ariel into the room, her face full of concern. "My dear girl, if I had thought you would be in such grave danger, I would not have permitted you on an outing of that nature. Whoever would have thought that an innocent picnic could be dangerous?" She spread her hands in a gesture of appeal, looking first to Sir Henry, then to Mr. Dudley.

"And you, kind sir," Aunt Maitland continued, addressing Mr. Dudley, "to be subjected to peril while visiting our village. Well, I am greatly sorry, and I do hope that this has not made you want to leave?"

Mr. Dudley gave her a scornful look.

"Dear Aunt, I believe Mr. Dudley was far from the scene of the shooting—the other side of the glen, to be precise—too far to be of help." Ariel gave him a contemptuous glance, then turned away.

"I do not know why you want me to wed this chit when she throws herself at Lord Harcourt. I saw." He cast a baleful look at Ariel before stalking over to the window, where he could survey the expanse of grounds that flowed away from the house.

"I did *not* throw myself at his lordship. True, I pushed him over when I glimpsed that figure at the top of the hill. I feared whoever skulked there was up to no good—and I was right. And I do wish you *would* go away," Ariel said firmly, ignoring her aunt's gasp of outrage at so rude a remark. "I have no intention of marrying you." But she did take note again that Mr. Dudley was capable of clarity when he wished. She had understood every word he said, and wished he had either mumbled or remained silent. She would rather her aunt and Sir Henry be unaware of her feelings toward Lord Harcourt. Better to let them be surprised at the Wednesday assembly.

Mr. Dudley's back remained toward her, but it gave the look of a determined man. Could nothing she say force him to leave Stafford?

"If you think I shall marry Lady Ariel, then she must be kept away from Lord Harcourt," Mr. Dudley said at last, turning around to look at Miss Maitland, then at Sir Henry.

"Niece, what do you say to this?" Miss Maitland demanded in a scandalized voice.

Ariel clasped her hands tightly before her lest she succumb to the temptation to slap Mr. Dudley's face. "Lord Harcourt is a kind neighbor, and if you recall, dear Aunt, I refused to wed him when Mr. Lytton insisted that my betrothal to the previous Lord Harcourt should be permitted to stand with the new baron."

"Mr. Lytton is a fool," Miss Maitland snapped, her usually serene countenance furrowed by a scowl.

"He is also our rector, and as such merits our respect," Ariel said, her voice tinged with ice.

"The situation is such that you are betrothed to Mr. Dudley and not to Lord Harcourt," Sir Henry asserted.

"And that has my guardian's approval?" Ariel asked innocently.

A silence fell over the room.

"I am your guardian, child," Miss Maitland said, her hands fluttering before her.

"According to what I have learned, you are *not* my guardian. I am reliably informed that it is Papa's solicitor. I insist that you obtain his written permission—with his stamp of approval—before anything like banns are read. Besides, since Mr. Lytton refuses to perform the cermony, *he* will scarcely read the banns."

"A special license," Sir Henry said softly. "Ought to have thought of that." He turned to Mr. Dudley and snapped, "See to it at once."

Mr. Dudley's sullen expression changed not a whit, nor did he move even one pace toward the desk.

"Well?" Sir Henry intoned.

"I doubt I'd know the proper form, sir," Mr. Dudley said, at least that was what it sounded like to Ariel. He had reverted to his mumbled drawl again. "And I suspect you want it a deal more than I do. I'm in no hurry to wed a reluctant bride."

"Well, there is no doubt that I am reluctant," Ariel declared firmly.

"This is most unseemly, child," Aunt Maitland said, clearly distressed over Ariel's willfulness. "A young lady accepts what her elders deem wise for her."

"Then I must suppose I am not a proper young lady," Ariel cried, unable to control her anger. She glared at the others, who now clustered near the far end of the room, staring at Ariel as though she were a recalcitrant child in need of a reprimand.

How could her aunt betray her so? Ariel wondered. Did all these years together mean nothing to her? Why was she so willing to force a repugnant marriage upon her niece, a niece whom she professed to love?

Unable to tolerate the three another moment, Ariel turned and fled from the library. She ran down the hall to the rear entrance, then out to the stable yard, where Weems was walking Blossom.

"She is saddled!" Ariel said coming to an abrupt halt, and giving the head groom a puzzled look.

"I had a premonition you might be wantin' a short ride, my lady, seeing as how those others are at you again, beggin' your pardon." Weems gave her a quiet look, but one full of meaning.

Ariel didn't know how he learned what transpired in the house, but she was not about to argue at the moment. Even without a habit, she could ride Blossom, and she desperately needed to get away from the house to think in peace.

The groom assisted her onto the saddle, then stood back. "If someone asks, I've not seen ye, my lady."

"Thank you, Weems. You are a true friend."

He said nothing more, merely watched as Ariel kicked her mare into a trot.

She rounded the back corner of the stable, then set off to the woods. She was so confused; life seemed to be closing in on her. Why didn't her dearest papa return? She refused to accept he might be dead. She wondered if Mr. Lytton and Lord Harcourt would be able to do anything to help her from her dilemma.

She soon found herself at the far end of the woods. The gardens at Stafford covered eleven acres, a part of that land in various fruit trees. Looking back, she could make out the pergola covered with cascades of wisteria. Beyond grew a viburnum brought from the colonies for her grandfather many years ago. Now the creamy white blooms of the tall shrub could be glimpsed between other, less spectacular greenery. Come autumn, the leaves would be a rich, deep russet. She wanted to be here to see them, and she began to wonder if she wouldn't rather be here alone.

Mr. Greenwood ought to know the address of the solicitor to whom her father had entrusted his daughter. She would seek him out. Since women had nothing to say about their money or their future, she had not been told who this man was. She supposedly didn't need to know. Ariel sat atop Blossom, as she so frequently had done in the past, surveying her grounds while she debated what had to be done. In this instance, her future, her very life was at stake. Regardless of whether or not a marriage to Lord Harcourt came about, she'd not wed Dudley, and somehow she would banish Aunt Maitland if at all possible.

She turned at the snap of a branch behind her. "Lord Harcourt. I am surprised to see you here." Joy filled her heart, and a smile banished her fears for the moment.

Prince eagerly trotted forward, but sat quietly, obedient to his master's order.

"I trust I do not intrude?" He paused, then replied to her remark. "You mean because someone apparently took aim at me earlier? I am not such a paltry fellow as all that." The baron rode over to join her. He gestured to the view obtained from the slight rise of land. "It is a fine sight from here."

"It is mine, and I refuse to share it with Mr. Dudley. They spoke of sending for a special license." Ariel thought a moment, then added, "Perhaps you could get word to Mr. Lytton regarding that? If he does indeed write to the Bishop of London regarding my aunt's request, he might caution the gentleman as to what is plotted on my behalf."

"Your aunt cannot have any control over the estate. I doubt your father would countenance such an arrangement. It continues to puzzle me why she insists upon a marriage. It would seem more likely that she would *prevent* a marriage at all costs." Lord Harcourt dismounted, fastened his reins to a sturdy young tree, and then walked to stand beside Ariel. He gave her a questioning look, and she nodded.

"I would get down, sir. If you would be so kind?"

He smiled, that bewitching smile that had tugged at her heart the first time it was directed at her. She found herself sailing through the air, held in his arms, his gaze intent upon hers.

Ariel, breathless and greatly affected by his touch, gave a nervous laugh as he set her upon her feet but did not release her. She did not retreat. Continuing to gaze into his remarkable dark eyes, she wished for his kiss. She thought she needed it to sustain her through whatever was to befall her. Shocking thought, but pleasant.

He did not fail her. He never did, it seemed. Ariel melted against him, taking comfort, strength, love, so much from his embrace and the kiss she had wanted ever since the last one. "Thank you," she whispered when he drew back. "I am glad to see you."

"And I you. Next Wednesday—will we proceed with our original plan?"

"Your plan to announce our betrothal? Aunt will be exceedingly angry with me . . . and with you. You still feel it to be the wisest course?" She leaned against him, placing her cheek most comfortably against that firm chest. The irrelevant thought that Mr. Dudley was more likely to be a soft cushion than a dependable oak flitted through her mind, and she smiled.

"You do not find me objectionable?" He pulled away so he might look down into her face.

Ariel continued to smile, shaking her head. "No, I find you most agreeable, sir. It is a good thing we neither of us want to marry. No hearts shall be broken once this is concluded," she fibbed. "I only know that I will not be compelled to wed Mr. Dudley. Like you, it puzzles me as to why my aunt insists on this marriage."

Prince wandered over to sit beside his master. He watched, alert for anything unusual. Ariel took note of the dog, approving this small protection for the man she loved.

"You love your home," Lord Harcourt observed. "I suspect your aunt is fond of it as well, quite thinks of it as her own, I daresay?"

"Indeed, she often remarks how much she enjoys living at Stafford." Ariel gave him a puzzled frown. "Why do you ask? Is there a reason why she would be unhappy here?"

"On the contrary. I suspect she fears you will marry and she will have to leave this paradise."

"But," Ariel protested, "she has agreed to marry Sir Henry. The baronet will have a home of his own."

"I seem to recall he said he sold it following his wife's death. Stafford Court would be a most comfortable place for a displaced baronet and his wife to live. Goodness knows that they could take over an apartment in one wing without your being aware they are around. Your funds would be at her disposal. That is why this proposed marriage does not make sense."

"Perhaps, but I do not see how we can get rid of Mr. Dudley," Ariel said, her mind in a whirl. She reluctantly stepped away from Lord Harcourt. He must think her a forward woman to be so bold as to welcome his kisses and depend upon his help as she did. Yet she instinctively knew that he would never harm her, nor would he impose his will upon her as others seemed intent upon doing. "I do not understand Aunt at all."

Jordan looked down at the lovely young woman who now

paced back and forth at his side. She had felt so right in his arms—and she thought they would go their separate ways once this predicament was solved? Not if he could help it! She needed wooing, coaxing, and most careful care.

"Someone is coming. You had best disappear. It would appear we have had a tryst. We don't want to reveal our intent before Wednesday," Lady Ariel said with an anxious expression.

However, when Weems came into view, she stayed Jordan with a touch of her hand. "No worry, I trust this man."

"My lady," the groom said while ignoring Jordan's presence, "your aunt be wantin' you at once. Thought I'd best find you before Mr. Dudley did." Then the groom's eyes met Jordan's, offering a silent explanation.

"Indeed, you had best return," Jordan agreed. "It was very good to see you, know that you do well after this rather harrowing afternoon we shared. I had expected a picnic to be tranquil. Instead, you saved my life by your quick thinking. I doubt if I can ever repay you for that, my lady," Jordan said quietly, yet knowing the groom heard every word.

She nodded shyly, then said, "I had best go. Church is tomorrow. I shall see you then?"

"Indeed. Mr. Ponsonby as well."

"And then shall come Wednesday and the assembly."

"All will be in readiness, Lady Ariel."

Her intrepid gaze met his for a moment, then she allowed him to help her onto her saddle. His hands lingered at her trim waist a moment longer than required. He found it extremely difficult to keep his hands off her. With Prince standing guard at his side, he watched her leave, her groom following faithfully behind.

His notions were beginning to fall into place. Now, if he could obtain the name and direction of that solicitor in London, he could proceed. He turned toward the Hall with that very purpose at the top of his list of things to do.

Once home, Jordan found it was not necessary to search out the name and direction of the Stafford solicitor. Upon his return, Mr. Lytton awaited him with information.

"It crossed my mind you might find need for the name and

address of Lord Stafford's solicitor. Ought to have offered it before, but I did not think of it until my wife reminded me it might be needed. Should have thought of it, and I'm sorry if it caused you any problems, my lord." He handed Jordan a slip of paper upon which was a name and a London address.

"If you will give me the letter for the Bishop of London, I can frank it for you. It has been my observance that the letter with a frank is always opened first," Jordan said with a certain amount of cynicism.

The rector beamed a look of gratitude on his ally. "It really is most fortuitous that you have taken a liking to Lady Ariel. I have worried over her future for some years. Her aunt refusing a London Season was quite sufficiently grave, but to encourage a marriage with this Mr. Dudley is above all things unwelcome."

"Well, as to that, you had best not put too much faith in any connection between Lady Ariel and me. She says we are friends." He thought of how she had tilted her face up to not so subtly ask for a kiss, and smiled. Unless he was greatly wrong, it should not be too far from friendship to love. There might be a few obstacles between the two, but he was confident he could overcome all barriers.

The rector took a chair near the window of the library. Jordan reflected that he never would have expected to become friends with the loquacious gentleman. But a gentleman he was, which was more than Jordan could say for either Sir Henry or Mr. Dudley.

"You plan to attend the assembly Wednesday evening?" the rector inquired after a sip of some fine claret.

"Yes. I suggested to Lady Ariel that a good way to prevent her aunt from announcing the engagement to Mr. Dudley was for me to proclaim a betrothal with her first." He waited to see what the proper rector would have to say to such deception.

"It would be a true betrothal?" Mr. Lytton asked, focusing his gaze on his glass but listening intently.

"As far as I am concerned it would be. It is possible I might have to persuade Lady Ariel. As well, there is the matter of the solicitor or her father to handle. However, since Miss Maitland does not have the approval of either, I feel I have a fair chance of obtaining what I want."

"I approve," the rector declared. "I shall be there that evening. I wouldn't miss the fireworks for anything. Miss Maitland will not like this."

"I suspect you have the right of it there, sir."

Sunday brought rain, but all attended services to hear Mr. Lytton expound on God's many blessings.

All Monday Jordan was kept busy with one thing and another. First, he composed a letter to the Stafford solicitor. He showed it to Percy for a reaction.

Percy, upon reading the epistle, proclaimed it first-rate. "Fine letter," he said, his enthusiasm most encouraging to Jordan. "Shouldn't have a spot of trouble from the chap once he reads that. Excellent notion to mention that the rector approves the match. Probably carries more weight than if you told him Lady Ariel seeks the marriage because she has fallen in love with you."

"What makes you think she had done such a thing?" Jordan asked cautiously.

"Her preference for you is marked, but more than that, I cannot imagine just any young woman pushing you over to save your life as she did."

"I can hope, I suppose," Jordan murmured.

The letter was sent off as an express, for although it was an outrageous expense, Jordan wanted it to reach London as quickly as possible and before any communication from Miss Maitland might. Considering that they were not far from London, the express rider might well reach the offices of the solicitor before he left his office for the day. A reply might be had by late Thursday—or even before.

The day proceeded with reports from Mr. Shirley, an outstanding nuncheon from Simnel, and Barton commenting that he expected his lordship's latest coat to quite outshine anything else worn.

"It is the cut and restrained color, my lord. Nothing so identifies a gentleman like the cut of his coat."

So, come Wednesday when Jordan appeared in his new dark -

corbeau coat and cream breeches, his cravat discreetly tied in a mathematical, and his chapeau bras in hand, Percy whistled his approval.

"Come on, let us be on our way and hope that Lady Ariel has not met with any obstacles."

"You mean like Dudley insisting she wear his ring before they leave Stafford Court?" Percy asked as they strode from the house for Jordan to take the reins of the curricle.

Jordan patted his pocket, and then relaxed when he found his grandmother's betrothal ring neatly stowed. "It is possible. I can only hope that Lady Ariel will be as inventive as she has been to date."

Ariel turned from the image in the looking glass, thinking that this had been the dullest day she had ever spent. To avoid being opportuned by Mr. Dudley or Sir Henry, or even Aunt Maitland, she had remained in her room, claiming a headache. It was nothing serious that a nap wouldn't set right, she had insisted.

"Beggin' your pardon, my lady," Merry said respectfully, "all you need is your hat and gloves and you are ready to leave."

Ariel nodded, wondering what the evening really held for her. Would Aunt prevail? Or could Lord Harcourt persuade the master of ceremonies to allow him to be first? She would place her money on Lord Harcourt. Aunt tended to put too high a value on her claim to attention because she came from Stafford Court. That set Ariel to thinking about her aunt in ways she'd not considered before.

Ariel allowed Merry to set the little evening hat in place. Clever little white feathers curled over the narrow brim of the minuscule white satin hat. Her gown of blue taffeta became her, she thought. It would have been nice to have her aunt's approval, but that lady was so incensed that Ariel had eaten her meals in her room that it was doubtful if she would speak to Ariel.

Upon checking the clock, she left her room to march bravely down the steps until she reached the entry. Cummins gave her a faint nod of approval—something she'd not had from him before. Perhaps he knew how annoyed her aunt was?

"The others are in the sitting room, my lady," he said with great dignity.

"Thank you, Cummins. Are they ready to depart for the Tunbridge Assembly?"

"I believe they await you with impatience, my lady," the butler stated, looking into the middle distance with a gaze of impersonal disinterest.

"Then we shall leave at once. Is the carriage ready?"

Upon learning that it waited without, Ariel hurried to the sitting room, where she paused in the door. "Time to leave." And those were the last words she spoke until they reached Tunbridge Wells.

The Pantiles was alive with activity. Carriages were discharging beautifully gowned ladies and polished gentlemen. Ariel unobtrusively searched the area to see if Lord Harcourt had reached there first. He was nowhere in sight, but that meant little considering how many people thronged the tiled walk before the assembly rooms. She listened as her aunt spoke to Sir Henry in an undertone likely not meant to reach her niece's ears.

"I will try to persuade the master of ceremonies to allow me to make the announcement at the end of the evening. I think it will have more of an impact than if I do it before supper—such as it is."

Ariel pretended she had not heard a thing, giving one and all a bland smile as they made their way into the assembly rooms.

"I shall find us seats," Sir Henry declared loudly. "I feel certain you will not wish to dance with strangers, Lady Ariel."

He forged his way through the crowd, leaving Mr. Dudley, Ariel, and Miss Maitland to follow in his wake.

When Ariel spotted Lord Harcourt, she relaxed a trifle. Then Celia bustled up with Mr. Ponsonby at her side, beaming a smile at Ariel and her party.

"It is a lovely evening with no rain or wind and the mildest of temperatures. I trust you had a pleasant drive to town? Mr. Ponsonby said their curricle went like the wind. I imagine Lord Harcourt wished to be here on time."

"His lordship is here?" Aunt Maitland said, casting a wary gaze about the room.

"Here he is now," Celia said, offering his lordship a bright smile as he joined them.

They all chatted for a time—polite and distant as people behave when they are obliged to talk with people they do not particularly like. Then Lord Harcourt turned to Ariel.

"I trust you have saved two dances for me? The first minuet and perhaps a country dance?" No waltzes or cotillions were performed in the countryside.

"Indeed, sir, I shall make note of it." She took the little page she had been handed when she entered to write his name by the first and fourth dances that were listed.

"And I claim the last of the evening," Mr. Dudley drawled.

At least that was what Ariel thought he said. "Indeed, sir." She wondered what would happen between now and then and if all would have changed.

The two men exchanged cold looks, then Lord Harcourt by right of his superior rank took Ariel's hand in his. "Why do we not circle the room, Lady Ariel? I believe I see the rector on the far side, and I know he would wish to greet you."

With the admiration of those ladies to either side of her most obvious, there was little Aunt Maitland could say other than agree. To have an elegant, handsome lord strolling about the room with her niece at his side could only be desirable in the eyes of the local ladies.

Once they were sufficiently distant from Aunt Maitland and Sir Henry, his lordship leaned over to murmur, "It is all arranged. I am going to make our happy announcement just before supper."

"Good," she said softly in reply. "Aunt told Sir Henry that she would declare the Dudley engagement before the final dance."

"Which explains why Dudley wanted that one," Lord Harcourt said with a smile. "Come, look amused, gay, possibly a little in love if you can. We are being observed by a large number of people, you know."

"That is to be expected considering I am the heiress from Stafford Court and you are the new baron at Harcourt Hall. We

are the topic of conversation for those who have nothing else
of interest to talk about."

He placed her hand on his arm, patting it twice before he
gave her a smile guaranteed to melt her to her toes.

"Oh, my. You are putting the cat among the pigeons, as
Celia said before. What fun." She concealed a grin behind a
hastily raised fan.

His brows rose at that. "Should we consider ourselves per-
formers, then?"

"I think so," Ariel said, then added with daring, "and I believe we ought to do ourselves proud."

As they greeted Mr. Lytton, the musicians tuned their instru-
ments, and the master of ceremonies announced the first
dance.

"I find it difficult to leave your side, Lady Ariel," Jordan
said, bending over her hand in the pattern of the dance.

She flashed him a demure smile. She'd be proper, but she
would also make it clear that she favored the gentleman above
all others. Not that she'd had much chance to learn such a
skill, when Aunt was so reluctant to allow her heiress niece to
public assemblies. If it had not been for Celia and Mrs.
Townsend, she never would have gone at all.

The fourth dance was a rather staid country dance. The
dances performed in London took ages to reach the provincial
towns, no matter that they wished to seem up to date otherwise. Jordan suspected the master of ceremonies had a lot to
do with it. Beau Nash might be dead, but his spirit appeared to
linger on.

Once they had completed that dance, another young chap
sought Lady Ariel's hand. She was in a whirl—albeit a proper
Tunbridge Wells whirl—until it was time to stop for the light
supper laid on for the dancers.

Lord Harcourt sought her out in the crowd, then drew her
with him until they reached the master of ceremonies. "Sir, if
you would be so kind?" Jordan said politely.

The gentleman tilted his head to study Lady Ariel, who was
beaming up at Jordan as she promised. His glance to where
Miss Maitland sat revealed nothing, as Mrs. Townsend had en-

gaged her in a chat. Celia stood close to them, blocking the view of the assembly room front and the master of ceremonies.

He cleared his throat with all the pomposity one might wish. "My Lord Harcourt has an announcement he wishes to make." With no music, the room fell silent at once. Heads turned; a few whispers scratched the air.

"I would like to share my happiness with you all. Lady Ariel Brandon has done me the great honor of consenting to be my wife. We trust you will join us in celebrating our happiness and coming marriage." From his pocket Jordan removed the betrothal ring he had found in his grandmother's safe. Taking Ariel's hand, he slipped the ring on her finger before Miss Maitland realized what was occurring.

An immediate buzz of chatter broke out, and then Celia crossed the room to join them with Percy immediately behind her.

"I believe that went extremely well," Celia said with a glance at Percy.

"Indeed, old chap, one would think you were an old hand at making announcements. Jolly good show."

"What?" There was a stir on the far side of the room where Aunt Maitland was seated.

"I believe someone has congratulated her on her niece's good fortune. That your properties are side by side and the families have been close for years makes this a marriage most desirable," Celia said with a chuckle.

"Come with me for supper," Jordan said to Ariel and the others. "It may be well to be together."

They had found a table and settled with their small plates of food when Aunt Maitland discovered them.

"Deceitful girl! How dare you?" she said in a low, angry voice, mindful of the throng of curious people milling about the room.

"Wish me happy, Aunt." Ariel bestowed a calm, defiant look on her relative that dared retaliation.

Towed along in Aunt Maitland's wake, Sir Henry and Mr. Dudley looked utterly furious.

"How could your aunt wish you well when you have deliberately flouted her wishes?" Sir Henry demanded in a chilling voice. "Unnatural niece! To go against the desires of the woman who has been like a mother to you."

"I brought a ring," Mr. Dudley said mournfully, holding out a simple band that Ariel recognized at once as one that was now too small for her aunt's pudgy hand.

"Mr. Lytton will not dare call the banns for you," Miss Maitland said triumphantly.

"On the contrary, I should be pleased to call the banns and perform this wedding," the rector said from behind her, a twinkle in his eyes. "Just name the date."

Chapter Fourteen

They had nearly reached the Court when it happened. Ariel had been dreaming about Lord Harcourt, recalling his fine appearance and how gallant he had been the entire evening when the world seemed to erupt into noise and fright.

"Halt!" A shot was fired in the air with great effect. The order was obeyed at once.

"Highwaymen?" Ariel whispered. How incredible to be attacked so near to home. *Could it be?* She glanced at her aunt and Sir Henry, both of whom sat frozen in place. The dim glow from the carriage lamps scarcely offered any light at all. Weems drove that road mostly from memory.

The carriage jolted to a stop, and Ariel peered from the window to make out the dim brass on a pistol in the hand of the masked man closest to her side. She thought she could see dim outlines of others but wasn't sure.

"What can they want?" she whispered to Sir Henry.

"Jewels and money, most likely," he whispered in return.

She pulled off her gloves and removed her precious betrothal ring to stuff it deep into her bodice, safe under her stays. They could have her pearls, for those could be replaced. Not so the ring. Then she pulled her little wrap tightly about her shoulders, restored her gloves, and wondered what would come next. Fear tightened her nerves.

The door flew open, and a gruff voice demanded, "Out wie you, milady." He grabbed Ariel, ignoring the others for the moment while Ariel tried to fight him.

Aunt Maitland screeched to wake the dead while Sir Henry made ineffectual noises. He made no effort to prevent the ruffians from pulling Ariel out of the carriage and down to the ground, nor did he say a word of protest. She screamed for help once, then a hand clamped over her mouth and she was dragged away from the carriage.

There wasn't a soul to hear or help what with pistols aimed at Weems and the grooms. She doubted if Sir Henry was about to be heroic, and her aunt would shriek but do nothing. Seeing that she might as well save her breath, she subsided, thinking that perhaps she might slip away, dark as it was.

However, she couldn't do a thing. Instead, someone bound her hands and tied a cloth over her mouth. Then she was roughly thrown over the back of a horse like a sack of oats. A man mounted behind her, riding the saddleless horse with no difficulty. He smelled of damp wool and sweat, ale and greasy food.

In seconds they were off and away, leaving her aunt and Sir Henry behind in the carriage, Aunt's screams echoing through the night. Ariel wondered if her aunt had been forced to part with her jewels and Sir Henry with that fine stickpin of which he seemed so proud. They had not touched her own pearls, nor searched her for valuables. *Perhaps that came later?* She wasn't acquainted with the etiquette of robbery. Her terror tore at her.

She struggled, kicking at the leg of the person who rode so close to her. With the blood rushing to her head, from her position, how long would it be before she lost consciousness? Her oaths and threats meant little when cried through fabric. It seemed that something must have penetrated his brains, for at last she was hauled upright and was dizzy with relief, her fears unabated, however.

"Sit still and I'll let ye be," her captor said, his voice rough. Not a local dialect, she decided.

Trying to keep her wits about her, she took notice that there was not much underbrush on the path they trod, for seldom did anything graze against her legs. That they were in a forest, she sensed, for she could smell moldy leaves and damp earth.

There was nothing to be seen in the pitch-dark night. Off and on she caught a glimmer of light to the fore of the group in which she traveled. It would be brief, as though someone sought to check the path by one of those lanthorns that had shutters. It was of little help to her, for one tree looked much like another when viewed in dimmest light.

When it seemed as though they had ridden along the rough track for ages, they came to a halt. She heard voices, low and some distance from her. She couldn't make out the words, worse luck. Nor could she tell just how many persons were involved with her abduction. She thought there were three, but it was impossible to be certain.

Her removal from the horse was swift. The man hauled her off with little worry for her or her garments. Her body protested the harsh treatment, yet she remained silent, calculating her cries would not merit gentler care.

With that faint light still some distance away, the man bundled her into a crude building. As they went in, the wood she was shoved against was rough and felt unpainted. Someone jerked the cloth from her mouth. "No help fer you here. You can shout all you please," the same voice she had heard before said. And he laughed. He left her then, slamming the door behind him, affixing some manner of lock to fall into place. She heard the click with horror.

All was blackness. She could see nothing, yet she couldn't remain where she was. It was like walking into an ebony hole. She stumbled twice before coming to a wall. She leaned against it, thankful for something solid in this world of darkness and nothingness.

The man had tied her wrists together with barely enough ease to keep them from going numb. She was alone in the dark, virtually helpless, and she could not imagine how anyone could possibly find her.

Well, perhaps not alone. She could hear rustlings of mice, creaks of the old building as it settled into further decay. An owl hooted, then was silent.

With no food or water she would not last long. Perhaps they might return? Surely, no one wished her dead? She slid down along the wall until she reached the floor and then stared off into the darkness, willing the mice away and any other creatures who took refuge in here.

Eventually, she fell asleep, exhausted from her attempts to free herself and a few calls for help. Deciding that there was no one to hear and that all she accomplished in trying to free herself was to make her bonds tighter, she gave up for the nonce.

Morning brought aching muscles and a dry throat. A cup of tea would be most welcome about now, she thought wistfully. Visions of the Stafford sideboard groaning with the weight of a morning meal danced in her head. Tea and food, even a crust of bread, would be appreciated.

Light filtered in through a narrow window high above the floor and over the lone shelf in the shed. The crudeness of the shed was even more evident by daylight. It was a wonder it still stood.

Ariel examined with care the little wood building in which she had been dumped. Early morning light enabled her to see there was little she might employ to help herself. The shelf on the opposite wall was bare. There were cobwebs aplenty, dust and dirt in abundance, but not a thing that she might use to free herself. In spite of the wood being rough, not even a splinter of a size to help saw the bindings could be found. The place was empty.

Her pretty blue gown was now crumpled and soiled, her favorite evening hat gone, her slippers scarcely useable. She was grateful she had the small wrap on since the night had been chilly. The assembly seemed like something that had happened in another world. She doubted Lord Harcourt, her knight, would find her here. He was a stranger to these parts, and she was deep in some wooded area, remote and uninhabited.

Why was she here? Who had brought her? They had not taken her pearls, although she'd expected it. At first she had feared assault. Instead, she had been handled like a sack of flour, dumped on the filthy floor. And she had been left utterly alone. *Why?*

"Well, you certainly did put the cat among the pigeons last evening, just as Celia said you would," Percy announced with a wicked gleam in his eyes. He took a last bite of toast, washing it down with a swallow of coffee.

"So I did," Jordan said. He grinned at his friend briefly until he recalled what Lady Ariel had said before they left the assembly ball later on.

"Miss Maitland was more than furious with you," Percy continued.

"Lady Ariel cautioned me that whoever had wanted her previous betrothed dead could still attack me. I cannot think why. I'm an amiable fellow, pay my taxes, I don't beat my servants, and treat my family well—what there is of us." His mother and younger sister lived in Hampshire, occupying a pleasant house left them by his father's will. He seldom visited them, but they did stay in touch.

"I would wager you will have a difficult time keeping that ring on Lady Ariel's finger," Percy said.

"It belonged to my grandmother, and I can think of no place more appropriate," Jordan replied with annoyance.

"Indeed," Percy agreed. "I merely voiced the opinion that you would have a devil of a time keeping it there. Her aunt does not look to be one who will be easily thwarted in spite of her seeming amiability."

"What can she possibly do now? The ring was most publicly bestowed, and the rector was there to add his approval to the match. The only thing lacking was her father."

"Or her real guardian. I wonder what sort of reply you will have from him? Do you think that the express will come from him today?" Percy drained his cup of coffee, then leaned back in his breakfast room chair, toying with an unused spoon. "You did ask for an immediate reply?"

A footman replenished the coffee, then left them alone at a signal from Jordan.

"Yes, I indicated I would foot the bill for such a speedy answer since time is of the essence here. Why all of a sudden Miss Maitland should take it in her head to rush her niece into an unwelcome marriage is beyond me. Am I missing something? I feel there must be a reason, but I'm dashed if I can see what it is for certain. And why should *that* chap be a better prospect than I am?"

"True," Percy said with a grin slashing his pleasant face. "He's a bit of a nodcock."

"He does not seem terribly bright, does he?" Jordan said thoughtfully.

"Bright enough to know that marrying an heiress with a substantial property is a good thing. Sir Henry seems to pull the puppet strings there. The few times we have been together, it seems he directs the younger chap."

"With Miss Maitland providing dialogue," Jordan concluded. Percy met Jordan's gaze, both nodding in shared agreement.

"Do you really intend to go through with the marriage? Have you actually asked her to wed you?" Percy dared to query his best friend.

"You know, I am not certain I did ask her—I believe we agreed that it was an excellent way to counter the forced marriage to Dudley," Jordan admitted with dismay. "But she agreed," he felt obliged to point out. "And to answer your first question, yes, I intend to marry her one way or another." The firmness of his answer offered little doubt as to his sincerity.

Mr. Shirley entered with a crisp missive in hand. "The express from the London solicitor, Harcourt. I felt certain you would want it immediately." He handed the piece of vellum to Jordan, then poured himself a cup of coffee before joining the men at the table.

"Couldn't be better news. It would seem there has been some communication regarding the Dudley matter before my letter arrived in London, as the solicitor was prepared with all documentation to hand. Miss Maitland will not be pleased when I tell her of these contents." He shared the letter with Percy and Mr. Shirley while enjoying another cup of coffee.

At this moment the sound of a scuffle in the hall caught their ears. Jordan gave Percy a perplexed look, then rose from the table to stride out of the room. Percy immediately followed.

"I demand to see Lord Harcourt!" an imperious and unmistakable voice declared.

"Excuse me. I shall see why Miss Maitland wishes to speak with me." Jordan strode down the hall to the entry, where the young footman did his duty. He looked most uncomfortable, and rightly so. Miss Maitland was not a lady to take lightly.

"What may I do for you, madam?" Jordan said with distant politeness. He kept his distance, assuming a haughty posture he hoped would intimidate her.

"You are harboring my niece. It was you who hired those ruffians last eve. I demand she be returned to me at once before her reputation is damaged beyond repair." She sniffed and folded her arms across her ample bosom.

Jordan wondered if she would also tap her foot while waiting. She did.

"What do you mean, harboring your niece? Is she not at home with you? I have not seen Lady Ariel since last evening. The last I observed she was with you and Sir Henry when you left Tunbridge Wells. Did you somehow misplace her?" Jordan asked with as proud a mien as he could muster in the light of the dragon who now faced him.

"She was taken from our carriage not far from the road leading to Harcourt Hall. I believe you abducted her, sirrah. Return her at once."

"I told you I've not seen her," Jordan repeated. He felt chilled, with growing uneasiness. Surely, Miss Maitland was not serious!

"You deny you hired ruffians to spirit her away from me? Sir Henry and I shall never recover from the shock."

"Ruffians, madam? I would have no need to resort to such skullduggery to bring Ariel here. I suspect you have something to do with ruffians if truth be known," he stated with icy civility. He placed his hands behind him lest he yield to the urge to throttle the lady. His fears increased as she spoke.

"I insist you know where she is," Miss Maitland accused. "The very idea that she would defy me, her dearest aunt, to agree to marry you is not like her in the least. You have taken her so that I will have no chance to persuade her to see reason. You have exercised seductive powers over an innocent girl!"

"Perhaps you should have given her a Season in Town. She might have met a duke there instead of a neighbor who is no more than a baron. I've never heard why you denied her that pleasure," he added with a narrow look at the angry woman who faced him, arms akimbo and mouth prim.

"Her father entrusted her to my care, and I see fit to marry her to Mr. Dudley, not you, my lord," Miss Maitland said. Her usual bland smile was missing.

"But according to the letter I just now received from the earl's solicitor in London, you do *not* have the authority to arrange her marriage. I am pleased to inform you that he agrees that a marriage between the future Countess of Stafford and Baron Harcourt is most acceptable. Lady Ariel will become my wife. And you may as well begin hunting for a new place to live, for you are to be replaced as soon as possible! The solicitor took a dim view of your attempt to marry her off without permission—and to a nobody at that. You, Miss Maitland are out!" He rocked back on his heels, hoping to appear nonchalant when he wanted to choke the truth from the harridan, who seemed to be revealing her real colors.

"But she will be the countess!" Miss Maitland protested angrily. "She deserves better!"

"Miss Maitland, a viscount ranks only a notch above me in precedence. I have far more to offer Lady Ariel, and you know it."

"You are a wicked man, Lord Harcourt," she cried, looking frustrated. "I demand my niece!"

"She is not here, and I rather think you are the evil one, Miss Maitland. I have no proof, but I cannot believe you innocent. Know this, *I* shall find Lady Ariel! Now I bid you good day." He took two steps back, bowing slightly.

The new footman, very conscious of his advanced position and elegant livery, walked in stately decorum to open the front door. He stood holding it, waiting for the unwanted caller to depart. He fixed his gaze somewhere on the ceiling, and Jordan couldn't help but feel that he had the makings of a very superior butler.

"You will regret this, Lord Harcourt." The menace in her voice made Jordan shiver. "I have a certain amount of influence around these parts and I shall not hesitate to use it. You have not heard the last of me!" Miss Maitland glared at him, then flounced from the house.

After exchanging a look with the impassive footman, Jordan rejoined the gentlemen at the table. "Miss Maitland demands her niece, says I hired ruffians who spirited Ariel from the carriage. She claimed her niece is here and that I used seduction to take her away. If it wasn't such utter rubbish, I'd laugh." Jordan remained standing. He'd decided to investigate Miss Maitland's wild accusations.

"You have all the authority you need for a marriage in this letter, my lord," Mr. Shirley pronounced after a very careful perusal of the document.

"All I need is my bride," Jordan said without humor. He looked to Percy. "I will go see what I can learn. There *must* be someone somewhere who knows something and is willing to talk for a price." Jordan turned to Mr. Shirley. "Is there ready money to hand?"

"Indeed, milord. I'll fetch you some directly."

"While he does that, I intend to get my mount and a bit of food and drink to take along. I have no idea where this search may take me," Jordan informed Percy. "I shall try to mouse around Stafford first."

"I'll join you," Percy said as he rose from the table and walked with Jordan toward the rear of the house.

They met the steward on their way. Jordan pocketed the sum of money, then said, "I'll go to the Court first, then return here for the food and water. See that something is ready for me." He charged from the house in the direction of the stables.

Jordan explained to Peachum and Cotman what had happened, at least what little he knew, while his horse was saddled.

"Somethin' havey-cavey afoot," Peachum declared as he led Fire King from the stables. "Mark my word, that woman has a hand in it."

"You think Miss Maitland has some part in her niece's disappearance?" Jordan exchanged a glance with Percy, then vaulted onto his steed before looking back to the groom.

"Never trust a mealymouthed woman, my lord," was all Peachum said in reply.

Percy mounted his horse as quickly as Jordan had, and the two headed to the upper pasture, then across the secluded and remote path he had taken to meet Ariel. As they approached the Stafford stable block, both men remained silent, keeping a wary eye on all around them.

Fortunately, between the size of the stable block, the brew house, and trees, they were able to remain unseen by anyone in the house. Little sound could be heard from the stable block.

With a look at Percy, Jordan softly said, "How about if I leave Fire King with you, then slip inside to see what is going on here, if anything? I'd rather not give them a warning that someone is coming."

A row of spreading trees offered shade and reduced visibility. Percy nodded, remaining silent.

It took but a few minutes to slip around the corner of the stable block and into the dim light of the interior. Weems was not to be seen. The place was unusually quiet, and it was with difficulty that he found an undergroom.

"Weems here?" Jordan asked in a casual voice and manner.

"No. Not seen him this morn." The answer was reluctantly given as though the man was afraid to talk.

"He brought the carriage home last evening?"

"Aye." The young chap's eyes were evasive, and Jordan suspected something was being concealed. But what?

"Trouble around?" Jordan asked indifferently. "Heard anything about highwaymen in these parts?" He glanced about him to note that the other groom was keeping his distance. Most likely he did not want to be questioned. If no one spoke to him, he didn't have to lie. Jordan's suspicions deepened by the moment.

"Nothin'," came the sullen reply.

Jordan noted Lady Ariel's mount, Blossom. "Her ladyship ridden this morning?"

"No, milord." The young groom backed away, obviously wanting to be elsewhere. But he knew who Jordan was, and he wasn't going to tell him anything.

Deciding his quest was fruitless, Jordan merely nodded and returned to where Percy awaited him.

"Weems is nowhere to be seen, and the groom I managed to catch wouldn't tell me a thing. Ariel's horse is still in its stall and hasn't been ridden. So where is she?"

"What do you suppose is going on? Was she truly kidnapped?"

"I don't know, but I'm becoming increasingly uneasy."

He mounted, and the two men turned to retrace their route. They had reached the edge of Stafford Court land when from a stand of firs a figure on horseback emerged.

"My lord, a word?" The second groom shifted uneasily on the back of his borrowed mare.

"Of course," Jordan replied, hoping that he might actually learn something of worth.

"The carriage came in late last night. That baronet fellow was drivin', and Weems was nowhere in sight. I pretended I didn't see nothin' and came around only when Sir Henry was standin' on the ground, waitin' for a groom. He didn't give no reason for Weems not bein' there. Just left. When I went over the carriage, I found this." The groom pulled forth a small object from under his coat.

Jordan eyed the elegant little white hat he had last seen on Ariel's head. "This belongs to Lady Ariel."

"One of the maids says she ain't in the house nowhere. She never came home last night." The young fellow anxiously eyed Jordan, looking worried and hopeful he had done the right thing to approach his lordship.

Jordan darted a glance at Percy, then turned again to the groom. "I appreciate your taking the risk to tell me about this." Digging in his pocket, he found a sovereign and gave it to the lad. The information wasn't much, but it did prove that Ariel never reached her home the night before. Tucking the little hat inside his coat, he continued the route back to the Hall.

"Just where do you suppose she has gone?" Percy wondered aloud. "Could she have sought refuge with Miss Townsend, perhaps? How much stock can you place in this tale of ruffians who abducted her?"

"Anything is possible. She couldn't stay with the Townsends for long, though, if she did flee there."

"Maybe I could ride over to talk with Miss Townsend? She may have some ideas for us."

"By all means, go. I have no idea where I am going or how long it will take me. I will not return without Ariel." Jordan gave his friend a firm nod.

"I shall be at the Townsends' for the time being." Percy

saluted, then headed toward the main road. Within a brief time he had disappeared down the avenue at a goodly gallop.

Jordan saw him leave, then turned to Peachum.

"Learn anything, milord?" the groom inquired, looking most concerned.

"It appears Lady Ariel has vanished along with Weems. Neither of them reached Stafford Court last night at any rate," Jordan said wearily. It might be early morning, but he felt as though he had been on the go for a week.

Peachum digested his bit of news in silence.

Jordan took the parcel of food and a bottle of wine from Mr. Shirley and prepared to follow Percy.

He was about to take his leave when a carriage rolled up the avenue. Jordan waited courteously for whoever it was to exit the unmarked vehicle once it had stopped before the house.

A plump, short man left the coach to stare at Jordan with an assessing eye. "I would imagine you are Lord Harcourt?"

"I am," Jordan said, suddenly uneasy. Who was this man who dared study him so boldly? he pondered.

"Miss Maitland from over at Stafford Court has accused you of doing away with her niece, my lord. I would have a word with you, if I may."

Chapter Fifteen

"Indeed, why do we not step into the house to discuss the matter?" Jordan said in what he hoped was a reasonable manner. "Miss Maitland came here this morning to make a rather wild accusation that I had ruffians abscond with her niece. I find it most curious that she now charges me with doing away with Lady Ariel—the young woman who is to be my wife and for whom I care deeply."

"Is that so?" the gentleman said, pausing before the door of his carriage. "To tell the truth, Miss Maitland struck me as a trifle rash in her claims, but Lady Ariel is an important person around this area, and no one could take lightly an allegation that she has been abducted, not to mention being done away with."

"Come . . . ?" Jordan urged. "Let us delve into the matter a bit more deeply."

"Sir William Fuller at your service. Perhaps we should, my lord." Sir William slammed the door on his carriage shut, nodded to his groom to take the rig around to the stables, then walked up the front steps with Jordan in seeming amiability.

Mr. Shirley was in the hallway when Jordan and Sir William entered the house.

"I thought you left?" Mr. Shirley inquired with a raised brow at the sight of Jordan with the justice of the peace.

"Sir William Fuller, here, says Miss Maitland thinks I have done away with Lady Ariel."

"How in the name of wonder could anyone think such a thing! Of you, in particular!" Mr. Shirley demanded, looking stunned. "Egads!"

"I suggested we might discuss this quietly—in the library,

perhaps?" Jordan ushered Sir William into the room, signaling Mr. Shirley to follow. He did at once, looking more than a little curious. Jordan was excessively frustrated at being kept from his search for Ariel and concealed it with difficulty.

He poured a glass of claret for each gentleman, then leaned against his desk, mulling over the predicament before him while eyeing Sir William with an assessing gaze.

"Indeed, sir, such spirited defense by a friend cannot help but impress." Sir William nodded at Mr. Shirley with approval.

Jordan recalled his manners. "Perhaps you know of Mr. Shirley, my esteemed steward and a member of the Shirley family of Derbyshire." Jordan looked to where Mr. Shirley leaned against the back of a chair, frowning at the unwelcome guest. "And I assume that you, Sir William, are the local justice of the peace for this region."

"I am indeed, and a thankless job it is, my lord," Sir William acknowledged. He rubbed his chin after sipping from his glass. "I must say I find it difficult to reconcile Miss Maitland's accusation with what I find here. I do know Mr. Shirley, and his opinion carries weight with me, you may be sure."

"Allow me to give an account of my time. If you wish, I can send for my friend, Mr. Ponsonby, who was with me most of last evening," Jordan offered politely, wanting to keep the gentleman well disposed. "He has gone to the Townsends to see if they know anything of Lady Ariel."

"Mr. Ponsonby can vouch for your whereabouts?" Sir William gave Jordan a shrewd look.

"Indeed, I have no qualms about having you ask him any questions, or anyone else who was present last evening. The rector, Mr. Lytton, can witness for the evening up until the time we left Tunbridge Wells. By the by, he is in favor of the marriage," Jordan replied, taking care to make it evident that he was unafraid of anything anyone else might say—other than the biased Miss Maitland and Sir Henry.

Then Jordan recounted the events of the previous evening with meticulous detail, leaving out not a thing as far as he could remember. He even showed the letter from the solicitor in London, the contents of which had the justice thoughtfully stroking his chin.

"And you say you and Mr. Ponsonby sat in this room to visit a bit before retiring?" Sir William asked, probing and watching Jordan with care.

"Actually, we had a glass of brandy and sat chatting about the coming marriages—mine with Lady Ariel, and, if all goes well, Percy's marriage to Miss Townsend. He has yet to put it to the touch," Jordan concluded with a wry grimace.

Mr. Shirley coughed slightly and looked amused.

"When Miss Maitland came bursting into the house, claiming that I must have kidnapped her niece, I was utterly astounded. She said nothing about a possible murder at that time. I believe she would have liked to inspect the premises. She certainly did not wish to accept my word."

"You did not permit her to search the house?" Sir William inquired, his voice very quiet.

"I confess the woman irritates me beyond belief. Had she been a more amiable person, I would have suggested she look the place over," Jordan admitted.

"You would have no objection to my searching the house, I take it?" Sir William asked.

"No, but I will tell you now it would be a waste of time. I should hope I know better than to bring a respectable lady, my future wife, to my home without a chaperon." Jordan exchanged a look with Sir William that said much.

"Then the question is now—where is Lady Ariel?" Sir William stated. "If you have not seen her and Miss Maitland claims she is not at Stafford Court, and she is not dead, ergo, she must be someplace else." Sir William studied Jordan with a concerned gaze.

"I intend to search for her with my bloodhound," Jordan said firmly. "My plan is to hunt around the area where Miss Maitland claims they were attacked, possibly get some manner of lead there. It should be not far from here on the Stafford road."

"When Miss Maitland appeared here, she said Lady Ariel had been abducted, but she made no accusation regarding any murder," Mr. Shirley reminded them. "Sometime between then and now she changed her mind."

"Or someone persuaded her to change her mind," Jordan

added. "Miss Maitland accused me of concealing Lady Ariel so I could marry her in spite of Miss Maitland's strong opposition. May I point out that Lady Ariel's guardian fully approves of the marriage between Lady Ariel and me? He would scarce do such a thing if he had any reservations about my character."

"I suggest that Lord Harcourt conduct his search," Sir William said after deliberating for a few moments, his eyes first on the solicitor's letter, then on Jordan. "If needs be, we could arrange for a Bow Street man to assist us. Goodness knows there is no one capable around here. I've not had many murders to deal with in my time, but usually it is pretty straightforward—and there is always a corpse—you will forgive the expression."

"No indication of a murder at all in this instance," Mr. Shirley murmured.

"I give you my word as a gentleman I had nothing to do with her disappearance," Jordan said with a level look at Sir William, who nodded. "If there is no objection, I shall be off. Prince," he called as he moved to the door.

The dog, who had crept into the house when the door was open, peered up from where he sprawled close to Jordan when he heard his name. He gave a couple of hopeful thumps of his tail and eyed Jordan to see what was wanted.

"A bloodhound usually has a pretty good nose, my lord," Sir William said while looking at Prince.

Jordan nodded. He snapped his fingers, at which Prince jumped up, ready and delighted to leave with his master.

Sir William heaved himself to his feet, placed the empty glass on the table, then held out his hand to Jordan. "I wish you luck, my lord. I expect I shall see you later when we shall conclude this matter?"

"I trust it will be a pleasant circumstance, Sir William," Jordan said. As anxious as he was to leave, it was difficult to exercise the polite courtesy due to the justice of the peace.

"As do I. Go on," Sir William said with a wave of his hand. "Your steward and I may exchange a few words. I know you are wishing me to Jericho and want to be off."

Jordan nodded. "I'll report to you whatever I find." His gaze met Mr. Shirley's briefly, then he was out of the house and mounting Fire King. Prince ran after him, rightly understanding he was to be allowed to go along.

The horse was ready for a run and cantered down the avenue at a goodly pace. At the intersection with the main road, Jordan turned to the left toward Stafford Court. He slowed the horse to a walk, inspecting the verge and beyond for signs of any disturbance. He would find his Ariel and soon, and pray God she would be alive!

Ariel woke again and attempted to stretch her aching muscles. True, only her hands were bound together, but that prevented little freedom, what with the door locked and no window close by.

Her thoughts winged to her dearest Lord Harcourt. Had he learned of her capture? Was he even now searching for her? She recalled the thrill of his arm around her at the assembly, the gentle touch of his hand when he took hers to place the lovely old ring on her finger. It had been such a happy moment, one of the happiest in her life. Surely, a man as caring as he would hunt for her. But as a stranger to the area, could he find her?

Light filtered in through the slit of a window, a dim light that did little to illuminate the gloom of the shack. The rustling she heard must come from leaves dancing in the wind—leaves on trees that hid a shack deep in a wood, for they had ridden many minutes. She considered the matter for a time, and decided the only place she could imagine that would contain such a site would be Stafford Woods.

They often passed the woods on the way from Stafford to Tunbridge Wells. It was dense, which would account for the smell of moldering leaves and the lack of sunshine.

No one ever went to Stafford Woods. There were few rabbits, no other game, and slim pickings for poachers. Even if she were to call out all day, she doubted if a soul would hear her.

So when would the kidnappers return? she pondered. And what did they want from her? She had feared ravishment last evening, fully expecting it after she had been dragged from the horse and pulled into the rough shack. Yet, in spite of some mutterings from one of the men, the man who had ridden with her had merely checked the strips of cloth that bound her hands, then left her—alone.

She hadn't been able to get comfortable during the night. Once she made up her mind to sit on the floor and lean against the wall, she hoped she could sleep. The scampering of the mice had made it difficult. And now? She gave a tired shake of her head.

Her mouth was parched. Her stomach rumbled with hunger. How long would she be left in this forsaken hut?

Only time would tell when those men would return. And then she would learn what it was they wanted with her. If not for ravishment, it must be money. She hoped her penny-pinching aunt would hand over what they demanded. She was heartily tired of it all! Her other fear she kept at bay, refusing to allow it to panic her.

Jordan walked his horse along the narrow road, studying the grassy verge with care. All at once he spotted an area where the grass had obviously been trampled by several horses. He dismounted, holding the reins while he gazed about the stretch of ground.

It also seemed to Jordan that the grass was trampled off into the woods. Mr. Shirley, when explaining about the estate boundaries, had pointed out a section called Stafford Wood on the map. It was densely wooded with underbrush here and there, and while not impenetrable, unwelcoming, to say the least.

He took Ariel's dainty hat from inside his coat and held it out for the dog to sniff. Prince seemed to know what was expected of him. He gave a bark and headed toward the deep and dark woods.

Remounting Fire King, with a whistle to Prince, who had been nosing about the trampled brush leading into the woods, Jordan set off. It was not a simple matter, to head through these woods. The trees grew close together, and it took time and skill to weave a path through them, even if the dog could wind his way at will.

Low branches whipped Jordan's face; the trampled path was

not easy to follow. At times it was clear. At other times he could not make out which direction to take. He took wrong turns, frustrating and time consuming. With poor light and knowing even that would fade before long, he urged his horse and Prince to hurry, not that it did other than comfort a desperate man. More than once Prince's bark led him in the right direction. Although the days were long now, the delay had cost him much time; the afternoon was near over, and before too long light would soon be fading completely.

He wanted to hurry to Ariel, for the farther they went into the woods, the more convinced he was that she was here. It was a good thing there was no one to question him, for he couldn't have explained it. A hunch? Intuition? Or the affinity that he had felt for Ariel for some time now? It was as though she called to him.

Prince gave a low woof, pausing, then trotting ahead.

In the distance was a small weathered shack. Lichen coated the roof, a thick green fur on the wooden boards. Weather-beaten wood that looked ready to collapse formed the walls. He could see but one window, a slit near the eave. Old, dirty, remote, it was an ideal place in which to conceal a person . . . or a body.

Spurring horse and dog forward, he soon reached the hut. He fairly leaped from the horse and hurried to the door. It was locked, but a latch in such poor condition was easily broken. He crashed open the door, sending splinters of wood flying.

"Ariel?" he shouted into the dim light. Then he saw her, huddled against the far wall. *Alive!*

"Jordan, how glad I am to see you," she cried, her voice hoarse, cracking. She struggled to her feet and took a halting step toward him.

He was at her side at once, tearing at the strip of cloth to release her from the bonds. Within minutes she was free and safely in his arms. "Oh, my Ariel," he whispered into her dark curls.

"I thought I would ever leave here," she murmured.

"Don't talk at the moment. Has anyone seen to you today? Brought food or water?"

Ariel shook her head, and Jordan held her close for a moment, relishing the precious feel of her against him. "I do not know who might have done this, but whoever it was, I shall make them pay." He carried her outside into the fading light and fresh air. Propping her against a slender ash, he chaffed her wrists, then offered her the food and drink he had thought to bring along.

She grasped the bottle with trembling hands, casting him a grateful look as she took her first swallow.

"Sip slowly and nibble small bites of the bread and cheese. There is more for you later."

"We must go," she whispered when she had eaten a little and sipped the tepid wine.

"True," he said quickly, looking about them to assure they remained alone. It had been so good just to have her in his arms that the rest of the world had simply faded from thought. Many hours had passed since he had left Harcourt Hall. Dusk was upon them and night not far away. And he had to remember that the men might return. Time was of the essence.

Slender as a willow wand, she proved no problem to carry. Once he had put her on the horse, he mounted behind her to offer support for her, as weak as she must be. With Prince tearing along before them, always returning to make certain they followed his lead, they plowed through the brush and dodged saplings, taking a course parallel to the way he had entered the wood. Not knowing his way and with no sun to guide them, he was reluctant to hare off in another direction lest they become totally lost.

"We are close to the way I came, but some distance away in case we should meet those men who kidnapped you. It is possible they mean to check on you or bring you water. I'd not risk anything more happening to you. Although I would enjoy getting my hands on their hides," Jordan muttered fiercely.

She clung to Jordan, and he prayed they could get some distance from the hut soon. He had no idea when those men might return. Unless they didn't mean to return? That made him shiver with the thought of what could have happened had he not found her. Jordan, she had called him, and she had smiled at him with luminous intensity.

Prince halted of a sudden. Jordan, curious as to why, stopped Fire King as well.

"There is someone out there," Ariel whispered.

They waited, silent, peering through the trees and thick brush, while two men rode along the path that Jordan had taken on the way into the woods. The men were in no hurry, talking quietly as they went in the direction of the hut.

Jordan gave the dog a warning look. The dog merely gave what Ariel thought to be an affronted stare. Had the predicament not been so dire, she would have laughed.

They couldn't hear what the men said, but Ariel knew they would reach the hut before long and find her gone. "We *must* hurry."

Her voice was raspy, and every muscle in her body must ache, yet he dare not cosset her now. "Right. They will find you gone and come hunting for you. We must be far gone by the time that happens." Jordan couldn't recall when he had ridden with a person leaning against him. It was not impossible, just difficult. In a time of danger, one forgets all that.

Ariel clung to him, her arms wrapped tightly around him. She buried her face against his chest as he began a mad race through the woods. Branches slapped them, brush hindered Fire King, yet the courageous horse kept going, led on by the dog.

Dusk crept over the sky; the woods grew darker, more threatening. Jordan wondered if Ariel could continue to cling, given her weakened state. It seemed the woods would never end, that they would remain in the green gloom of the forest forever. With the fading light, it was more and more difficult to make out where they were headed. He slowed Fire King to a walk, unable to continue their pace and figuring the kidnappers must be some distance behind them in spite of the path the horse had carved.

And then he saw it, the edge of the wood. "Do you know where we are?"

"Not far from the village," she replied, her voice still hoarse.

Prince gave a joyous bark and led the way.

"The rector is about to have company. I want to have someone with impeccable credentials to witness your condition. I will not take you to Stafford Court just yet," he concluded as he made their way into the darkening village.

Fortunately, the rector and Mrs. Lytton were at home.

"Dear Lord Harcourt and Lady Ariel! What has happened?" Mrs. Lytton exclaimed in horror at the sight of Jordan at the door with a battered Ariel in his arms. Prince stole inside as well, taking a position near the door, where he looked ready to guard all.

After settling Ariel on the sofa, Jordan said, "Some tea for her ladyship, and I shall explain everything to you." The rector wisely remained silent, watching.

"Indeed, my lord." The good rector's wife hurried away to return within minutes, bearing a tray that held a pot of tea and a pretty cup as well as some lemon biscuits. That it was their finest china and freshest baking Jordan had no doubt.

He saw to Ariel's needs first, coaxing her to drink slowly and nibble a biscuit between sips. Then he told the story as simply as he might. He concluded, "I am not certain who instigated the kidnapping or why it was done. Would you care for Lady Ariel tonight? I would not wish her to go another yard as tired as she is now."

"Tired and hungry, I'll be bound," the rector declared. "'Tis a sad day when one is not safe so close to home. They took nothing?" he added with a significant look at Jordan.

"Nothing," Jordan replied, understanding what the rector implied. "If I might carry Lady Ariel to a bedroom so she could sleep, I would go on to Stafford Court to inform her aunt of her safety. I am sure there is much worry there." If there was a touch of irony in his voice, it missed the good rector and his wife.

"Of course, how remiss of me. Dear Lady Ariel, what a dreadful thing to happen to you. Come, my lord, and follow me. We always keep a room ready for guests. We never know when a stranger will turn up at our door, needing help." Mrs. Lytton bustled into the hall and waited while Jordan scooped Ariel into his arms.

The stairs were narrow and steep. Jordan had to be extra careful not to jar Ariel as he carried her to the next floor and along to the room to which Mrs. Lytton ushered them. He low-

ered his love to the bed as though she were made of spun gold
and fragile lace.

"I'll return for you in the morning. I trust you will sleep
well this night." He searched her eyes for some sign of what
she truly wanted.

She nodded, reassuring him that she agreed with his intentions. "I shall see you come morning."

Leaving Ariel to the tender and sympathetic ministrations of
Mrs. Lytton and her maid, Jordan returned to the drawing
room.

"I shall be off to Stafford at once before returning home. I
intend to pick up Mr. Ponsonby at the Townsends' on my
way."

With the rector's blessing and good wishes, Jordan and
Prince returned to Fire King to find the rector's groom had
cared for the horse.

"All that remains is to get Ponsonby and see Miss Maitland,
then I can retire to my own hearth and decide what to do
next," he muttered to the horse as they trotted along the familiar road to Stafford Place.

Once out of the village, the road was visible by the starlight
and a faint sliver of moon. Setting Fire King to a pace as fast
as he dared, given the light, Jordan faced the prospect of con-
fronting Miss Maitland with mixed emotions. Pausing at the
Townsends' he learned Percy had returned to Harcourt Hall.
After a hasty explanation, he continued on his way.

At Stafford, he handed his horse and the dog into the care of
the second groom. At Jordan's inquiry he said, "Weems is
abed. His head aches somethin' fierce after the knock he took.
Small wonder he suffered hours before makin' it back."

Reflecting that whoever had done this had much to answer
for, Jordan walked to the front of the house.

Cummins opened the door to usher Jordan into the house.
He looked more grave than usual and took the liberty of re-
marking in an undertone, "It is a sad day indeed that our Lady
Ariel is taken from us."

"She isn't," Jordan replied bluntly. "I just left her exhausted
and hungry at the rector's house in the village."

The staid butler actually smiled as he conducted Jordan up

the stairs to the drawing room. When he announced the caller, Miss Maitland cried out in dismay.

"You! You dare to show your face here! Why are you not in gaol?" She took refuge behind her chair, clearly believing Jordan would wreak havoc on her, the house, or perhaps Sir Henry.

"After a chat with Sir William, our esteemed justice of the peace, I went in search for Ariel. I found her in Stafford Wood."

"You found her? But . . ." she sputtered.

"How can this be?" Sir Henry inquired. His glance at Miss Maitland had the effect of silencing her completely.

"When I inspected the area where you told me the abduction had occurred, I found evidence of several horses. I merely followed their trail until I found a crude hut deep in the woods. Do you have any idea who would wish to conceal her for a time?" Jordan asked with menacing quiet.

"No!" Miss Maitland's face turned the hue of undercooked oatmeal. "None at all."

"What makes you think we would?" Sir Henry asked, his eyes narrowed, bristling in obvious anger.

"Why did you not bring her home?" Miss Maitland demanded at once, as though to change the subject.

"Indeed, the village is not that far from here," Sir Henry said in an accusing tone and manner.

Jordan had prepared himself for this question and smoothly said, "When we came out of Stafford Wood, we were close to the village. She was in such a weakened condition I thought it best to take her to the closest safe place. What house would be safer than the rector's? The men who hunted us could have waited for us on the Stafford Road. I dared not take that chance."

Miss Maitland exchanged a wordless look with Sir Henry.

"Now, if you will excuse me, I need to return to my home," Jordan said, turning from where he had stood by the door. Without waiting for a parting remark, he headed for the stairs.

For people who had been so anxious about a missing niece, they were acting rather curiously. They had not invited him to sit, nor offered him refreshment of any kind. They had not even given thanks for the rescue of the heiress. *Dashed peculiar behavior, indeed.*

"You are to bring her home come morning," Miss Maitland demanded from the top of the stairs just as Jordan had attained the bottom step.

He turned to stare at her. "Madam, I was under the impression that I would be the last person you would desire to be with your esteemed niece. However, it will be my delight to fetch her in my carriage come morning. I shall arm my grooms, you may be certain, so there will not be a chance for another abduction." He gave her a hard look, then marched from the house.

Fire King and Prince patiently awaited him. As he headed back to Harcourt Hall, Jordan mulled over all that had happened. Ideas were crystallizing in his mind, but he needed more proof before he could act.

Peachum took his mount when he entered the stable yard. A strange vehicle awaited inside the carriage house, and Jordan looked to Peachum for a clue.

"You got company, my lord. Dunno who it might be."

Jordan nodded, striding to the house with impatient steps. This was all he needed, company when he had a great deal to occupy his mind.

Mrs. Longwood met him at the door, fluttering about and murmuring nonsense. "Had I but known! He awaits you in the library, my lord." She tottered off toward the rear of the house, muttering, "Oh dear, what next?"

Giving the suddenly addlepated housekeeper an exasperated look, Jordan walked to his library and opened the door.

A tall, very fit and tanned gentleman of some forty-odd years rose from a chair near the fireplace. He set down his glass of brandy and crossed the room to confront Jordan. Jordan studied the man, deciding he had never seen him before in his life, yet there was something oddly familiar about him.

"I have awaited your return with great impatience. All is well?"

"I fear you have me at an advantage, sir. I am certain we have not met," Jordan said firmly, yet with the politeness he sensed was due the stranger. He exuded an aura of command

and position. While there was no blustering or posturing, Jordan felt this man was a man with whom he must reckon.

"Forgive this intrusion, but your steward thought it best if I await you here. I wish to know all that has happened. You found Ariel safe and sound?"

At Jordan's sudden intake of breath, the man's expression softened.

"I am Stafford, her father."

Chapter Sixteen

Stunned, Jordan moved forward to greet his guest, extending his hand in greeting.

"How is it that you are here and not at Stafford Court? I just came from there and had no indication they knew you were here, much less alive."

"What do you mean—alive, Harcourt? Explain, please," Lord Stafford exclaimed.

Gesturing to the armchair where the earl had been seated before Jordan returned home, he said, "Miss Maitland claimed her last few letters to you had been returned and she is convinced you are dead."

"Interesting, seeing as how I truly have not received any mail from her. Ariel has written faithfully, but I fear the press of affairs and the constant moving I did prevented me from replying as often as I might have wished. I gather the letter informing her I was returning to England did not reach her?"

"Not as yet," Jordan said with a faint frown, wondering if the letter had been withheld.

"I sense there is more to this, and I would hear it now," Stafford said, leaning forward to study Jordan with a very astute gaze.

"Are you aware that Miss Maitland has assumed the role of guardian and arranged a marriage between Ariel and a Mr. Oswald Dudley?" Jordan queried.

"My solicitor told me that he had information of something of the sort. He also told me that he'd intended to replace Miss Maitland." The earl leaned back in the chair, thoughtfully rubbing his chin as he studied Jordan.

"Lady Ariel has refused the alliance, for some reason preferring our betrothal," Jordan said, keeping a sharp eye on his guest for any reaction—especially negative.

"My solicitor said that he had approved your suit, already being aware of your background and prospects. I believe you have a letter to that effect. I deputized a local resident to keep my solicitor informed of events. Mr. Lytton has been most diligent in his correspondence."

"May I ask why you came here first?" Jordan begged to know, still reeling from all he had heard.

"I paused at Lytton's home—I had a gift for him—and learned that Ariel was asleep upstairs. Mr. Lytton could tell me but the barest details and I would know more. Not wishing to waken her, I decided that this odd situation called for devious measures. I would hear all. Now."

Jordan leaned back against his chair, frowning as he collected his thoughts. Then he summarized the events of the time since the arrival of Sir Henry Banks, when Ariel's present woes began. Jordan sought to be concise, yet offer sufficient details to satisfy a concerned father.

"She was not greatly harmed?" his lordship inquired when Jordan concluded his tale with the seizure and rescue.

Suspecting he wished to know if the kidnappers had ravished Ariel, Jordan shook his head. "As far as I could tell she was hungry, tired, aching from being bound, but nothing beyond that. She said they tied her and left. I saw no evidence to the contrary."

"Thank God. But who paid these men to abduct her?"

"I have no proof one way or the other, sir. I might have a few ideas, but nothing concrete upon which to base them. One could scarcely make accusations on hunches. I am curious why your daughter did not have a London Season. Miss Maitland implied it was your decision."

"On the contrary. I received bills for gowns and my solicitor rented a town house. He wrote that Miss Maitland became ill and they were forced to cancel."

"Not quite true from what Miss Maitland has told hereabouts. She insists that a Season was not necessary, and now claims that Dudley is the ideal husband. He might be heir presumptive to Viscount Stone, but that gentleman is younger than you are and in excellent health. Barring a mishap, he should live a long time, may yet have an heir."

"During which Dudley would reside at Stafford with my daughter? He has no home?"

"Gambled everything away from what I've learned. He has been on best behavior whilst here, although I heard a rumor that he had played cards at the Rose and Crown with a group of cronies who just happened to pass through the village. It would seem he is not the best of card players if what the lass at the Rose and Crown said is true. My head groom had a pint at the inn and heard the tale there."

"And?" his lordship asked as though he knew Jordan had more to say about Dudley and hesitated.

"Dudley is a milksop, a man who wouldn't say boo to a goose. I cannot believe he is the sort of man a loving aunt would wish her dear niece to marry. I find it curious that Dudley was brought here by Sir Henry."

"Hmm, I see what you mean. Well, the hour is late, and I can see you are near asleep on your feet. I wonder . . . Could I impose on your hospitality to remain here for the night? I want to arrive at Stafford Court in the daytime, unexpected, and able to see firsthand what is afoot."

"It would be a privilege, my lord. I trust a bedroom will be ready in a trice."

Jordan rose to give the bellpull a tug. Shortly, Mrs. Longwood paused at the doorway, a questioning look on her kind face. "My lord?"

"My guest will remain here tonight. Be so good as to prepare a room for him. As well, we would both like a small meal as soon as Simnel can have it ready."

"Indeed, my lord," Mrs. Longwood said.

The chef prided himself on his ability to create a meal on a moment's notice. It would be interesting so see what issued forth from the kitchen at this hour.

Once they were alone again, the earl sat back in his chair for a time, staring at the fire while he considered all Jordan had told him. The silence was companionable until Jordan at last broke it.

"I should have a conference with Mr. Greenwood were I

you, my lord," Jordan said respectfully. "From little things Ariel has said, it would appear the books could stand an examining. Recently Ariel has mentioned the amount of time her aunt spends poring over the books when it is Mr. Greenwood's place to keep them, do ordering, and so forth. I always thought women of a certain age were more interested in needlework and gossip than in the affairs of an estate that is not theirs."

"How very perceptive of you. I begin to see why Lytton approves of you." The earl smiled, but made no further comment on his own feelings.

Mrs. Longwood interrupted at that point with the information that a meal was ready. She informed Jordan that Percy had eaten some hours earlier and retired to his bed.

Jordan rose, gestured to Lord Stafford to join him and they repaired to the dining room.

Little was discussed over the excellent supper, what with servants around. When finished, Jordan caught Mrs. Longwood's eye and at her nod, turned to his guest. "I suspect you have had a long and tiring day. I know I have. What say you to bed with more discussion in the morning?"

"Admirable notion."

The earl followed the housekeeper to a most presentable room, where he found his valet waiting for him, nightclothes warming before the small fire that took any chill from the room, and a bed awaiting his rest.

Meanwhile, Jordan wandered to his own suite, where Barton awaited him with barely concealed curiosity.

"I gather you want to know why the earl stays with us instead of at his own home not far away from here. The element of surprise, Barton."

With that remark Jordan yawned, thinking back to when he'd held Ariel in his arms. Thankful she was safe again, he submitted to Barton's care and was soon soundly asleep.

When Ariel came down for breakfast the following morning, having insisted she was feeling more the thing and not the slightest ill, she was astounded and happy to find Jordan awaiting her in the small drawing room. She wore a simple rose muslin belonging to the rector's wife.

His smile drew her to him at once. If she had thought to snatch a kiss, she was disappointed. He looked as though he wanted to kiss her, but dared not.

"Ariel, I have a surprise for you. Someone you have been longing to see is here." He turned to another.

With that, a figure stepped from the shadows near the door where she could not possibly have noticed him when Jordan was right before her. "Papa!" she cried, overjoyed her prayers had been answered.

"How good it is to be home again," Lord Stafford murmured with his only child held close in his arms.

"How did you meet Jordan, that is, Lord Harcourt?" Ariel asked with a guilty flush on her cheeks. She had been a trifle improper in using Jordan's Christian name, but as her betrothed she felt it reasonable.

"I awaited him in his library when he returned after rescuing you and making his report to your aunt at the house. I stayed at the Hall last night."

"What did Aunt say when you appeared at Stafford?" Ariel inquired with a frown, turning back to look at Jordan. "Surely she wondered at my whereabouts."

"She was not best pleased to see me, and demanded to know why I'd not brought you home. Never a word about your condition nor concern for your health—a matter I found disturbing."

Jordan noted the earl's angry expression.

"It would seem Miss Maitland is no longer fit to be entrusted with your charge. You need someone better." Her father frowned rather fiercely.

Ariel blushed, casting a shy look at Jordan. "She refused to allow me a Season in London, and had it not been for Celia and Jane Townsend, I would have felt like a princess in a tower with no friends or fun."

"You mentioned the previous Lord Harcourt in a letter." The earl remained close to his daughter as though to make up for his absence in some part.

"His horse threw him, and he broke his neck. Aunt did not want me to marry him, in spite of his being heir to Harcourt—not that I wanted it, mind you. And there was something havey-cavey about his death that has never been solved. Jordan was investigating it until the threat of my marriage to that odious toad, Mr. Oswald Dudley, arose."

"You will not have to marry an odious toad, my love," the earl said with a smile that rapidly sobered.

"This ring Jordan gave me was once his grandmother's. It is very lovely, and I should like to keep wearing it, Papa." She displayed the lovely heirloom retrieved from her place of safe-keeping.

"And so you shall, my dear. But first we have a few things to rectify. Have your breakfast while Harcourt and I pay a call at the Rose and Crown. We will see you before long, I trust."

Ariel looked troubled, but nodded agreement.

"It must be difficult for her to see you go when you have been away for so long a time," Jordan remarked as they returned to the earl's carriage.

"I had hoped my late wife's sister would have shown some common sense. It seems I was wrong." The earl gestured to Jordan to enter the carriage, then followed him after giving an order to his coachman.

Sir Henry was at his breakfast when the earl and Jordan entered the Rose and Crown. The gentleman murmured something to Dudley on the far side of the table, then rose to greet them. He glanced at the earl, frowning as though he ought to know him, yet knowing they had never met.

"Good morning, Sir Henry," Jordan began, then turned to the earl. "This is Miss Maitland's betrothed, Sir Henry Banks. The man with him is Mr. Oswald Dudley."

"I had not realized that my sister-in-law had found a husband. Good luck to you, sir." The earl bowed slightly.

The baronet turned ashen as he realized the identity of the man facing him. "Lord Stafford! From what Frederica said, I thought you dead."

"As you can see, I am not. When you are ready, we will proceed to the house." The earl swept Dudley with a disdainful glance. "You, Mr. Dudley, need not join us. I feel certain you wish to be elsewhere."

Mr. Dudley stood, gave the earl a bitter look, then turned his resentment on Sir Henry. "You said—" he began, only to be interrupted.

"Never mind what I said. It is all up now. Be gone—as the earl says." Sir Henry abandoned his meal, stepping from the table to join Jordan and Lord Stafford. "I am ready now." It had the sound of one who expects his doom at any moment.

"Good. Good." Ignoring the sullen figure still standing by the table, the earl swept from the inn, closely followed by Jordan and Sir Henry.

The ride to Stafford was silent, with the earl studying Sir Henry in a most disconcerting manner. Jordan was thankful he had been accepted, for he would not wish to be subjected to such a penetrating stare.

"I understand my sister-in-law has been most concerned with the estate books," the earl said just as they drew up before the house.

"Perhaps she has," Sir Henry admitted.

"Curious—I thought Greenwood most capable."

The earl left the carriage first, striding to the front door with the agility of a much younger man.

Cummins nearly fainted when he opened the door to discover his master on the other side. "Welcome home, my lord," he uttered in heartfelt tones that earned him a second look.

"Instruct Greenwood to meet me in the library. Inform Miss Maitland I wish to see her there as well."

The somber butler actually smiled, albeit a restrained smile. "Very good, my lord."

"It is nice to see that someone here welcomes me home," the earl murmured as he strode into the library. He found one of the estate ledgers open on his desk and began to peruse it.

"Come here, Harcourt. You look to have a good head on your shoulders. What do you make of this?" The earl pointed to a number of entries.

"Falsifying entries?" Jordan murmured in reply after scanning the opened pages. "One wonders why she bothered."

"It would seem that Frederica has a bit of explaining to do," the earl said in an undertone that could not reach Sir Henry.

The baronet stood near the windows, first gazing uneasily

out at the parkland, then back at the two men by the desk where Miss Maitland had devoted a portion of her recent days.

Miss Maitland burst into the room, a flurry of flounces and frills ill becoming a lady of her plump proportions. "Sir Henry, you wished to see me at this hour? 'Tis monstrous early."

He didn't reply, merely gestured to the desk.

Miss Maitland took a good look, gasped, and fainted dead away.

Cummins, prepared for this eventuality, entered the room with a bottle of vinaigrette in hand.

Restored to an awareness of her surroundings, Miss Maitland took another look at her brother-in-law and appeared about to pass out once again.

"Here, Frederica, stiffen your backbone," the earl commanded, his tone most bracing. "I should like to talk with you, for it seems a great deal has been happening while I have been away. Fortunately, my time in India is over, and I can now devote my energies to my daughter . . . as well as to my estate. I trust nothing is amiss? I see the latest account book is open on my desk. Is there a reason for this?" There was no mistaking the dangerous tone in his voice.

Before Miss Maitland could reply, Mr. Greenwood entered the room, looking harassed and frustrated. When he saw who stood behind the desk, he positively beamed with delight and what appeared to be relief.

"My lord, I *am* glad to see you!" he said with a heartfelt manner much like Cummins. "Welcome home, my lord. I hope this brings you to us for some time?"

"I am home to stay," the earl said while watching the pasty face of his sister-in-law.

"I . . . I thought you had business in India," she sputtered.

"Odd, I was under the impression you believed me to be dead, Frederica. Why? To my knowledge no one from the government sent you any post to that effect, nor has my solicitor communicated with you for any reason. He sent approval of Ariel's betrothal to Lord Harcourt. But you were obviously busy scheming to hastily marry her to a Mr. Dudley. Why?" he snapped.

Jordan smiled at the way the earl pronounced Dudley's name, as though it were a vile disease.

A disturbance in the hall brought all eyes to the doorway.

"Papa, Celia and Mr. Ponsonby brought me home. I'd not miss another moment of your company," Ariel cried from the library entrance. Behind her, Celia Townsend and Percy stood, looking concerned and a trifle perplexed.

Ariel immediately crossed the room to stand between her father and Jordan. She linked her arm with Jordan's, giving her aunt a triumphant smile.

"I see you are unharmed," Miss Maitland said after a moment.

"Indeed, although why you should have thought I was murdered, I cannot guess. Perhaps you wished ill to Lord Harcourt?" Ariel chided.

"Wish him ill? Never. Why should I? True, he has made a micefeet of my plans for you. I feel certain your father would prefer you married to a viscount rather than a mere baron," she protested. She gave the earl a superior smile. "And I feel my dear departed sister would wish that as well. She begged me to see to it that her precious daughter married well. I have devoted many years to training Ariel to be the proper wife to such a one as he."

"I rather doubt she was able to say that much on her deathbed, Frederica," the earl said dryly. "At least not when I was there."

Miss Maitland sniffed, then turned to Sir Henry. "I have everything prepared. We can leave at any time."

"What's this? You are thinking of leaving Stafford Court all at once? Why so?"

"I believe I can explain, my lord," Mr. Greenwood said with a narrow look at the spinster. "It is cleverly done, I'll grant her that, but she has been of late changing the entries and removing funds from the safe." Miss Maitland gave an outraged gasp of indignation.

"That is a serious charge, Greenwood," the earl said quietly. "Please continue."

"I sent a letter to your solicitor yesterday, once I'd collected my facts." Greenwood went on to detail what he had found when he recovered the books Miss Maitland had removed from his office with the excuse that she wanted to see where the money went on an estate of this size.

"And so I wished to learn," she asserted into the silence of the room.

"And now you intend to leave. And precisely what do you plan to take with you?" the earl asked casually as he strolled around the desk to confront his late wife's sister.

They had all ignored a retreating Sir Henry for the moment, concentrating their attention on Miss Maitland. So it was a shock when Sir Henry spoke from near the doorway. He held a pistol in his hand and had it aimed at Ariel.

"Fetch your things, my dear Frederica. But first, fetch that bag of jewels you collected. They will come in handy once we use up the money you squirreled away. We had hoped to remain here, but Harcourt upset those plans by announcing an engagement to Ariel. We intended her to be safely wed to Dudley. He is such a malleable sort of chap, you know. We could have lived quite well here. Now all those plans are for naught."

Jordan took a step forward, effectively concealing Ariel. "What you intended was to control this estate while Dudley took the position of husband to Ariel. Being of a meek nature, he wouldn't give you any trouble, would he? Whereas my cousin likely would have, and so I believe you plotted his death. Mine, as well."

"But I would have objected," Ariel declared, peeking around Jordan.

"You were merely a tool, my dearest. Miss Maitland and Sir Henry sought to live the life of a countess and earl through you. It was a most despicable plan, I vow," Jordan declared.

"And what do you plan now?" the earl inquired in a detached manner, quite as though it wasn't his money and his jewels that were being purloined.

"We shall leave here and take up life on the Continent," Sir Henry replied jauntily. "We shall do quite nicely, I believe. I should hate to be required to kill anyone, but I will if need be."

Celia gasped and drew back against Percy, who placed a protective arm about her.

Miss Maitland, who had opened the safe to remove a small velvet pouch, hurried from the room. Within a brief time she returned with two small cases.

"Ready, my dear lady? The carriage should await us by now. We will be on our way." Sir Henry edged to the door, never taking his eyes from the trio behind the desk.

"See here, Sir Henry, you will never make it out of the country," Percy pointed out.

Jordan stepped forward, ready to attack. "I'll put a stop to this. Justice should be done!"

"I would rather they went, actually," the earl drawled. "It would save me the bother of trying my sister-in-law for embezzlement and murder. I expect the ambitious Miss Maitland planned Ariel's kidnapping, then accused you, Harcourt," the earl added in a deadly quiet voice. "She wanted time, as I see it. She needed time to force the wedding of Ariel to Dudley. Is that not correct?"

"You horrible woman," Ariel cried. "I can now forgive myself for not loving you. You plotted to do *such* a thing!"

Miss Maitland said nothing in reply. She murmured something to Sir Henry, and they left the room, the velvet pouch and two bags in hand.

"You really are going to let them get away, Papa?"

"I'll not risk any life for a bit of money and a few jewels. Your mother's are safely in London for you, Ariel. These were nothing much and dispensable." The earl put a restraining hand on Jordan's arm, then added, "I am a great believer in poetic justice, Harcourt. Somewhere along the way they will reap it. I feel it in my bones."

There was no sight of Cummins in the entryway. Sir Henry took the chance to run and dashed out of the open door to join Miss Maitland in the carriage she had summoned. It was the simple gig, but would serve their purpose until they reached a posting inn.

"We are off," those in the library heard as the pair left Stafford for good.

"I cannot believe you let her go, Papa," Ariel said. "She ought to be punished! Think of all she did!"

Jordan took Ariel's hand in his to comfort her, but felt the same. "I agree, sir."

"Let them go. As I said, they will reap punishment. While in India, I learned much of their philosophy. What they have sown they will reap."

"That is what Mr. Lytton preaches in church as well, Papa," Ariel pointed out.

"Forget them. There must be a more joyous prospect than taking a woman to court and dragging the family name through the mud." He cocked an eyebrow at the pair before him.

Jordan longed to punish Miss Maitland for all she had done to Ariel, but he could see the earl's point.

Mr. Greenwood came to the desk and picked up the ledger. "I will present you an accounting of what I believe has been taken. She had been at the books for but a few days. She abandoned those when her scheme failed. She took funds from the safe, plus those jewels."

"I do not blame you, Greenwood. She was your superior and charged with the care of my daughter." He gave a dismissing wave, then strolled to the window to look out on the same scene Sir Henry had viewed shortly before.

Ariel begged to be excused, taking Jordan with her until they were on the terrace, alone and most private. She held out her hand, the dainty ring gleaming in the morning sun. She searched his face for a clue to his feelings.

"I meant our betrothal, Ariel," Jordan said, his voice husky with emotion. "Unless you wish otherwise, I want more than anything in this world to marry you. I love you, my precious one. I never want to let you go. No man could have suffered more than I did while searching for you, worrying that you were safe, hoping I'd find you soon."

"And I love you as well, dear heart." She held up her face for a kiss.

Jordan complied, murmuring over and over his love for her, his joy that their marriage would take place, and soon if he had his way.

Ariel took his face between her hands. "We shall be married. I cannot believe my father would deny me my happiness. We shall be husband and wife quite soon."

At those words, Jordan required a tender embrace.

It was some time before they returned triumphantly to the library hand in hand, their love shining from happy faces. They came to stand beside Lord Stafford. Celia and Percy smiled approval.

"Papa, may I wed Lord Harcourt? As you pointed out earlier, I need someone to care for me."

"I would not let you go to just anyone, my dear." He seemed austere, very much the earl.

"We are neighbors, my lord, and bound to see each other most days," Jordan pointed out.

"True, and I do love him dearly, Papa," Ariel coaxed.

"I will not be losing a daughter, I shall be gaining a son, is that it?" the earl said with a fond look at Ariel.

They settled down in the drawing room to discuss plans. Mr. Lytton would gladly perform both weddings, for the Townsends, upon the advice of Celia's Aunt Susan, had agreed to the marriage of their eldest daughter to Percival Ponsonby. At this most civilized scene, it was difficult for Jordan to believe that not so long ago the ambitious Sir Henry had held them at gunpoint.

Cummins brought in a substantial tea, and the earl said, "Now I know I am home."

The day proceeded with much planning and conversation about the earl's life in India, with Ariel asking a thousand questions.

Patience personified, the earl answered them all.

Jordan admired his precious Ariel, recalling with awe that it had not been so very long ago that he had traveled to Kent and Harcourt Hall with Percy, declaring that he was in no hurry to wed. And then he met his love.

Much later in the afternoon, Ariel at last ceased her questions. She suggested a turn in the garden with Jordan. They were about to take a stroll in the topiary garden when Cummins ushered in a breathless Mr. Lytton.

"My lord," the rector cried, "such a thing has happened. It is utterly dreadful!"

The earl raised his brows. "Tell us," he invited.

"Your sister-in-law and Sir Henry were killed in a carriage accident! He tried to pass a mail coach on the Dover Road, and his wheel caught in that of the coach. I understand it was quite shocking. The coachman has taken charge of their belongings and will send them on to you."

"Poetic justice," the earl said with satisfaction.

"Papa, you may tell Mr. Lytton our plans. Jordan and I have much to discuss," Ariel said quietly.

When alone in the topiary garden, Ariel said, "I cannot grieve for my aunt. Is that frightful? To think she arranged for me to be abducted destroyed all affection I might have had for her."

"Think of the future, my love—our future." He caressed her arm, slowing his steps.

Ariel halted and turned her face to him. Jordan knew what she wished and obliged. The kiss was all either Jordan or Ariel could have wished.

When Percy peered around the corner of a tall shrub, he smiled and drew back to be close to his Patience Celia. "Now for us," he said with a smile. "Lady Ariel and Harcourt have matters well in hand."

Close to the peacock topiary Ariel was swept into Jordan's arms for a wondrous kiss. When he released her, he murmured, "We can thank your aunt for bringing us together. That first day we met she piqued my interest by making it plain I was not suitable for you. From then on, the idea of marriage to the loveliest girl in the world took hold of my mind."

"I was certain you would be a Town fribble. How wrong I was. You are my shining knight, coming to my rescue in time-honored fashion." Ariel toyed with his cravat before gazing up to his eyes. "I believe you will always be my knight. My very own knight. I doubt it is possible to be happier than I am at this moment."

"I wonder how soon we can manage that wedding?" was Jordan's only reply before he sought her willing lips once again.

Nearby, Prince barked in seeming agreement.